Accidental Christian

A Novel of Forgiveness

SHARON LEE FOLEY

WESTBOW
PRESS®
A DIVISION OF THOMAS NELSON
& ZONDERVAN

Scripture quotations are from the ESV® Bible (The Holy Bible, English Standard Version®), copyright © 2001 by Crossway, a publishing ministry of Good News Publishers. Used by permission. All rights reserved.

WestBow Press books may be ordered through booksellers or by contacting:

WestBow Press
A Division of Thomas Nelson & Zondervan
1663 Liberty Drive
Bloomington, IN 47403
www.westbowpress.com
1 (866) 928-1240

Because of the dynamic nature of the Internet, any web addresses or links contained in this book may have changed since publication and may no longer be valid. The views expressed in this work are solely those of the author and do not necessarily reflect the views of the publisher, and the publisher hereby disclaims any responsibility for them.

Any people depicted in stock imagery provided by Getty Images are models, and such images are being used for illustrative purposes only.
Certain stock imagery © Getty Images.

ISBN: 978-1-9736-2175-1 (sc)
ISBN: 978-1-9736-2174-4 (hc)
ISBN: 978-1-9736-2176-8 (e)

Library of Congress Control Number: 2018902675

Print information available on the last page.

WestBow Press rev. date: 03/22/2018

Amber Grace Barton heard a light knock on her door. Amber closed the book on mystics that Rachel had insisted she read and sat up on the bed. Although Amber had shared her friend's curiosity and harmless dabbling in the subjects of fortune telling and clairvoyance, no premonition warned her that this was going to be a conversation that would change her life.

The door eased open and Amber's grandmother came into the bedroom. Gram stopped for a moment and just stood looking at her. Amber's grandmother was a gentle woman, even subservient one could say, and… and Gram was the only mother Amber had ever known.

"What is it?" Amber asked, putting her book aside and standing up.

Gram just walked toward Amber and wrapped her arms around Amber's thin body. They stood silently holding each other for several minutes before Amber pushed back a little and looked into her grandmother's soft troubled face.

"Please, just tell me," Amber said.

Gram nodded. "Yes. Yes. Let's sit." So, they sat beside each other on the bed. "It's your mother, dear," Gram said. "She's coming home."

Amber stiffened. "What? Home? She's coming home? Like you mean here home?"

Gram nodded again.

"When?" Amber asked, and then it suddenly occurred to her that she first needed to ask the real question. "Why?"

"Miriam said she would be here tomorrow," Gram said.

"But why? Why is she coming? Why now? I mean if she is coming back for my graduation then please tell her I don't want that. I don't need her to come for that. I don't need her for anything."

"No, it's not that," Gram said, her words a bare whisper. "Miriam told me she is coming home…to… to die."

"What? Die? What does that mean?"

Gram's face crumbled and she stifled her whimper with her hand.

"Die? That doesn't even make any sense," Amber continued. "She's only...what? Thirty-six."

A tear escaped and streaked down Gram's cheek. "Cancer doesn't care," Gram whispered.

"No," Amber protested. "This does not make any sense."

"I know," Gram said. "I have feared all these years that Miriam may already be dead. I tried not to think about the things that could have happened to her out there alone, in all kinds of dangerous places. Who knew what kind of bad people a girl alone could get mixed up with?" Gram sighed heavily at the years and years of worry. "But when Miriam left home...she just left. She never called. Never wrote. Just handed you to me and drove off. And now, eighteen years later I finally hear from her and she wants to come home. She finally wants to come home and now it seems it's just... just too late."

"Tomorrow?" Amber said, and then repeated. "Tomorrow? Really? Without any warning she just called out of the blue that she is dying, and she wants to come back into our lives tomorrow? Unbelievable! She has no right to do this to us."

"She is my daughter, dear. She always has a right to come home."

Amber stood up. Yes. Yes of course. Of course, her grandmother would need to see her daughter no matter what Miriam had done to them all. That's how Gram was. But Amber was not Gram.

"I understand, Gram. I do." Amber finally relented. "But you can't expect me to stay and be a part of this. I don't know her. I don't have any memories of her. And, of course, I know that you do. I know there must have been some good times for the two of you before she left but, to be honest, I do not have the strength or will to be as generous and forgiving as she would need me to be right now. I'm sorry she has cancer. I'm sorry anyone has cancer. But she can't come back and put that in our laps, in my lap, and expect me to know what to do with it. Because I don't. I don't know what to do with it."

"What are you saying?"

"I'm saying that I'll just take some of my stuff and find another place to stay while she is here."

"Oh, Amber, no. That isn't right. This is your home and I, well, I don't want you to make a decision right now that you will regret later."

"Gram, the guilt and regrets have never been mine to carry."

"You say that, and you are right, of course, but life doesn't work that way. You will, over time, look back and regret that you missed this one small window to meet your mother."

"Then when that happens, I will just have to remind myself that it never bothered her that she may have missed some small window of opportunity to know me. Not even a birthday card, Gram. Not even one word in eighteen years!"

Gram stood up and came to put her arms around Amber. "I know. I know," Gram said.

Rachel pushed up on one elbow and looked over at Amber who was just staring up at the ceiling. Just the way Amber had been staring at the ceiling when Rachel had finally fallen asleep late into the night. "Wow," Rachel said, "I never expected this when you asked to spend the night."

"Who could have?"

"What time will she be here today?"

"I didn't ask."

"How long are you going to stay away?"

"I haven't figured that out yet."

"Well, yeah," Rachel said, "it must be hard to figure out how long you need to stay away. I mean, you don't even know how much time your mother has left. She may not have much time at all, maybe only a few hours before she is dead. And then, I guess, you can safely go home without ever having to see her."

"Cut it out, Rachel."

"What? Cut what out?"

Amber cuffed at Rachel before she got off the bed. "That's just how sorry my life is. I even have to have you for a best friend."

"Come on, you don't have to rush into her arms and forgive her but aren't you at least a little curious about why she left and even maybe what she looks like?"

"Morbid curiosity, eh?"

"Human curiosity, Amber. Just being human is okay, you know."

"Hey, you're the one who believes you were a flamingo in a previous life."

"A gazelle not a flamingo. Totally different species and you know it."

Amber picked up her makeup case and clothes as she headed for the bathroom. "Just in case you were planning on being a caring and sympathetic host, I'd love some french toast this morning."

"They're called pop tarts in this house," Rachel called out just as the bathroom door closed behind Amber.

Rachel scowled at the closed door then hopped off her bed and scurried to her mother's room. Her mother was just smoothing out her bedspread when Rachel burst in.

"What do you know about Amber's mother?" Rachel asked, flopping herself across the bed.

"Get off that bed," her mother scolded. "Now look, just look what you've done! Just because you want to live like a slob doesn't mean the rest of us do. Get up this instant."

Rachel rolled over onto her back. "Seriously, what do you know?"

"I know at times I understand why Miriam didn't want to stay and go through the type of disrespectful aggravation that I've had to put up with from my child. Now get up this instant."

Rachel sat up. "Amber told me Miriam is coming back today. She said her mother is dying of cancer."

"Oh my."

"Yeah," Rachel said. "Do you know why she left Amber behind?"

"No one can know what went through Miriam's mind when she left," Rachel's mother said, sitting down on the bed beside Rachel. "Miriam was always a…well, a little on the unpredictable side I guess you could say. So, when she ended up pregnant her senior year it was no big surprise to anyone."

"Do you know who Amber's father is?"

"No. No one would admit to it and Miriam never said. Of course, Miriam was a couple years behind me in school, but she always hung out with upperclassmen. I'm sure someone I knew would have shared it if they knew who the father was. It's still a mystery as far as I know."

"Do you think Miriam left town to be with whoever he is?" Rachel asked.

"If Miriam went off to be with Amber's father then what reason would she have for leaving their child behind all these years?"

"Yeah. Right," Rachel said.

"Poor Amber. I can only imagine what she is going through right now."

"Oh, Mom, don't let Amber see that you know about it. I promised her I wouldn't tell anyone."

Rachel's mother shook her head and stood up to resmooth the bedspread. "You, Rachel Diane, were obviously not raised right."

Rachel followed Amber to her car after their graduation rehearsal.

"Are you going to work now?" Rachel asked.

"Of course. I always work on Friday night."

"Well, I was just wondering if you maybe called your work because… because…"

"Because the mother who abandoned me eighteen years ago has suddenly shown up and is sick?"

"Well, yeah. I thought maybe you may want to go…"

"I don't," Amber said, sliding in behind the steering wheel.

Rachel waited beside Amber's car while Amber chucked her backpack onto the passenger seat and strapped on her seatbelt.

"Hey," Rachel said. "Did you bring that navy-blue blouse to my house? The one I bought you for your birthday. Cause if you did, I'd like to borrow it tonight. Eddie and I are going to dinner."

"I honestly don't even know what I grabbed."

"So, tell me," Rachel said, leaning down so Amber could see her face. "Are you ever going to be nice to me again? I'm not the one who left you behind, you know."

"I know," Amber conceded. "I know. I'm sorry."

"Okay," Rachel said, obviously pleased with an actual apology from Amber. "So, I can borrow your blouse?"

"Whatever," Amber said, shaking her head at Rachel and closing the car door.

Rachel watched Amber back out of the parking lot and then Rachel hurried to her own car. Rachel made a quick call to Eddie to cancel their date and then headed for Amber's house.

Gram answered Rachel's knock.

"Hi, Mrs. Barton," Rachel blurted out as soon as the door opened. "Amber said I could borrow one of her blouses for my date tonight. And, as you know, Amber is at work right now, so I thought, well, if it was no trouble, I could just scoot up to her room and get it."

"Well," Gram said, hesitating a moment, and then Gram shrugged and smiled, stepping back for Rachel to come in. "Of course. If it's okay with Amber, then certainly you can get it."

Rachel stepped inside the house and ever so nonchalantly tried to glance through the foyer and into whatever rooms she could see.

Gram watched her and then finally asked, "How is she, Rachel?"

"What? Oh yeah. Well, to be honest," Rachel said. "Amber didn't sleep much last night. She hasn't told me a lot, but I can see she is terribly troubled about something."

"Yes. I'm afraid so," Gram said. "Thank you for letting her stay. I hope it won't be for very long."

"Amber is always welcome at my house. You know I love her like she was my sister."

Gram's old eyes teared a little at that. "Please ask her to call me when she has time. Just so I know how she is."

"Sure. Sure thing."

"Well," Gram said, and nodded for Rachel to go on upstairs. "You know where her room is."

Rachel walked slowly, glancing, listening as she went to the staircase and started up. Then, BINGO! A voice. Two voices. One was Amber's grandfather but the other one was female. But young sounding. Too young for a mother's voice. Maybe Miriam was so weak she sounded like a child. Rachel strained but couldn't see over the banister and into the kitchen.

Rachel reached the landing and walked down the hall toward Amber's room. All the bedroom doors were closed. Rachel so wanted to open them a crack and peek in but even she didn't dare. What if someone was in there and caught her? Wait, there were three people downstairs so there wouldn't be anyone in any of the bedrooms. Right? Besides, what exactly did she expect to see? Suitcases? Medical apparatus? Still, there may be something she would see that she could report to Amber. So, Rachel decided, she should peek into the rooms on her way back down stairs. Rachel went into Amber's room and straight to her closet. Ahh, there it was, the cobalt blue top with the elastic neckline that could be tugged down over one's shoulders. Rachel still loved it. She would have bought one for herself but that would have been weird if the two of them had ever shown up somewhere dressed alike.

Rachel slipped the blouse off the hanger and turned to leave when she stopped. In the doorway was Miriam. Well, she assumed it was Miriam. The woman looking back at her appeared to be the right age, the shape of her eyes was just like Amber's eyes, and the way she looked a little vulnerable was like Amber. Which, when you thought about it, was a strange thing as Amber was the least vulnerable person Rachel knew and, Rachel assumed from the stories about Amber's mother, Miriam wasn't very vulnerable either.

Miriam frowned, and Rachel realized that Miriam was probably expecting Amber and was justifiably a little surprised to see someone very un-Amberish looking back at her. By un-Amberish she supposed it may be the black hair instead of goldish brown, maybe the olive skin of Italian ancestry rather than Amber's pale Irish/English heritage. Possibly a couple or so more pounds than Amber and, well, really nothing that looked like Miriam would expect Amber to look like at all.

"Hi, I'm Rachel. Amber's best friend. Amber is staying with me actually and she said I could borrow this blouse for a date tonight." Rachel held the blouse up as evidence. "So, I was just stopping by to get it. That's all."

"I see," Miriam said.

They stood looking at each other. Each full of questions but walking softly to leave no damage.

Finally, Rachel said she had better get going and Miriam stepped aside to let her pass. Rachel got to the top of the stairs and had to turn back. She felt she should say something. Miriam was just standing there in the hall watching her. The woman was dying for crying out loud. You can't just ignore that.

"Amber will need some time," Rachel said. "She, well, she feels things really deeply and it takes a while for her to process her feelings and make a plan. She is a big plan maker." Rachel chuckled at the thought of Amber's plan making. "But, eventually she will do the right thing. She always does."

Miriam nodded. "I understand. Thank you."

Rachel smiled for Miriam and then headed down the stairs. Gram was waiting alone by the door. Rachel was disappointed that no one else had come out of the kitchen. Maybe that mystery voice, that other someone, had driven Miriam here. Miriam may be too weak to drive. But, seriously, that voice did not sound old enough to belong to someone who could drive. Rachel would just have to plan another visit to see what that was about.

"Thanks," Rachel said leaving with the blouse and, actually, a whole lot more. She had seen Miriam. No one else in town had seen Miriam in eighteen years and here Rachel had been the first to see her. Miriam was attractive, Rachel decided, even in her weak condition. She looked tired or sad, well, obviously both. Which, Rachel guessed, she sort of deserved for abandoning her child. But maybe, Rachel thought as she got into her car and laid the blouse over the passenger seat, maybe Miriam had a secret so dark she was never able to come back home. And now that she was close to death even dark secrets didn't really mean anything because what could anyone really do to you when you are dying anyway?

Rachel thought for one crazy moment of going to the grocery store where Amber was working and buying a little something, mascara was always needed, and then waiting until Amber's checkout lane was empty. Then she would pay for her mascara and casually mention to Amber that she had seen Miriam. And then, of course, Rachel would leave quickly. That would give Amber time to get a grip on her emotions before she came home. But, where that would definitely be better for Rachel, she supposed it wouldn't be fair to upset Amber at work. So, instead, Rachel called Eddie and offered to go out with him after all. Eddie accepted, and Rachel agreed to meet him for pizza.

Rachel was sitting on her bed when Amber came in. They nodded at each other and Rachel watched as Amber hung up her jacket and put her backpack on the desk. Amber kicked off her shoes, picked up her pajamas and toothbrush, and headed for the bathroom.

"I have leftover pizza if you want some before you brush your teeth." Rachel offered.

"Thanks. I had a sub at work before I left."

"Okay," Rachel said and waited for Amber to come back.

"So, how was your day?" Rachel asked when Amber reappeared.

"Long actually."

"Too tired to talk?"

"Does it matter? Besides, with you it's mostly listening and that doesn't take as much energy."

"Well," Rachel said. "*This* listening may take a lot of listening energy. I've been here wrestling with myself all evening wondering if I should even tell you or not tell you and I, well, I think I should tell you. I think I should just come clean and tell you and then deal with however you feel about what I have to say."

"Good grief, Rachel, are you ever going to get to it or just wear me out telling me that you are going to tell me something?"

"Okay. Okay. But remember that you just asked me to tell you."

Amber waited, and Rachel finally blurted out that she had gone to

Amber's house, to get the blue blouse that Amber had actually said she could use, and while she was there, well, she saw Miriam. Rachel paused and watched for Amber's reaction.

Amber shrugged. "Okay."

"Well, aren't you at least miffed that I went there?"

"I would never have expected that you could stop yourself. You are impulsive, nosey and have no self-control at all. I may not have known how you would finagle it, but I'm not surprised that you went over there to snoop."

"Well, I wouldn't call it snooping actually," Rachel said in her own defense. "I went because I knew you would not go and secretly you really wanted to. So, I went for you to see what was going on and maybe see how sick your mother really is."

"Whatever," Amber said and laid down next to Rachel. "How long are you going to stay up?"

"Well," Rachel said. "There is more." Then she waited for Amber to ask her what the more was. When Amber didn't ask, Rachel told her that she heard another voice in the kitchen with Amber's grandfather. A girl voice. A young girl voice.

Amber didn't say anything, but Rachel could see Amber was as puzzled as Rachel had been.

"I thought," Rachel said, "that maybe someone had to drive your mother here, but I swear the voice sounded too young to be someone old enough to drive."

Amber rolled away from Rachel and lay very still.

"Do you think you have a sister?"

There was no answer. Rachel waited but apparently Amber didn't want to discuss it. "Oh," Rachel said in a quieter, softer voice, "your grandmother asked me to tell you to call her."

When Amber didn't reply, Rachel turned out the bedside lamp and lay down on her side of the bed.

"How are things going, ladies?" Rachel's mother asked, coming into the kitchen as her daughter slathered butter on her french toast and then drowned it in a puddle of maple syrup.

"I was thinking," Rachel said, "that maybe Amber and I could drive over to Canal Street this morning and see a psychic. What do you think, Amber? Wanna go? Now that we are graduating, and with all this other stuff that's happening, it may be a good idea to find out what's coming at us in the future."

"Well," Rachel's mother said, "I can tell you, Rachel Diane, that I know exactly what your immediate future holds. Not only do you not have money for that foolishness, you are giving me a few hours of work before you run off anywhere. There is a thrift sale at the Woman's Club tomorrow and you are sifting out some of the stuff you do not plan to take to college with you for the sale."

"But, Mom," Rachel whined, then darted her eyes at Amber and then back at her mother as if signaling that she needed to stay close to Amber today. "I have more pressing issues than an old junk sale."

"I don't want your junk. That you can throw away. I want nice things that you don't need any longer," her mother said, and then she turned to Amber. "Do you have any plans for today?"

Amber shrugged. "I go to work at three."

"How about, while Rachel is collecting her nice things for the sale, you and I spend a little time talking?"

Amber looked at this woman that she had so often wished was her mother. A woman who was always mothering, always dependable…always near. "Sure. I guess."

"It's up to you, of course, but sometimes, when we don't think we will ever know what we want, well, when we start to talk we just figure it out."

Amber nodded. "Okay."

Rachel slapped her hand on the table and stood up. "Well, excuse me! I guess I don't even exist. I'm just a junk collector. Don't include the junk collector in your conversations!"

Her mother scowled at her. "What?"

"I went over to Amber's house yesterday to try and get information to help her. But do you two care about that? Do you care that I actually saw her mother and that I think Amber may have a sister over there, too?"

Amber stood up from the table. "Yeah, maybe I don't want to talk right now."

"Rachel, you had no business going over there," her mother scolded. "What is wrong with you?"

"I guess, what is wrong with me is that I'm not afraid to do something besides talking. If you need to know something, then just go find it out. But, hey, never mind thanking me. You two just go have your little talk and figure it out without me. I'll be in my room rooting through garbage."

Rachel's mother walked past Rachel and put her arm around Amber's shoulders. "I know it's hard, honey, but you honestly need to talk to someone. Come, sit down and I'll help if I can."

Rachel grunted in disgust and flounced out of the room. For emphasis, she stomped up the stairs.

Amber followed Rachel's mother into the den and they sat together on the sofa. Amber sat for a few moments just picking at her thumbnail and thinking. Then she lifted her head and sighed. "I guess I just wish I could leave. Just get in my car and go somewhere until all this is over."

"All this?" Rachel's mother asked. "You mean until your mother has died?"

Amber nodded.

"Do you think her dying will be the end of your pain?"

"No. I suppose not."

"I have always told Rachel that everything short of death is fixable. After death, there is no way to go back and change anything."

"I know. But I don't think it is my place to try and fix someone else's mistakes. She left me."

"And she is here now. Don't you think she came back because of you? To try and put things right with you before it was too late?"

"I don't know anything about her, so I sure wouldn't know why she came back. Maybe she was just alone and wanted her mother to do the work of helping her die like Gram has done all the other work my mother never wanted to do."

"Miriam left because, for some reason, it was easier. Don't be like her, Amber. Don't run away. Take the time you need to figure out how you want to handle this, so you won't look back with regrets. You can stay here as long as you need to. You know that. But, even staying here, you will have to eventually face your fears."

"Fears? I'm not afraid."

"Oh, honey, you are full of fear. You don't want to go over there because you are afraid you may end up even more disappointed. You're afraid you may care about her and you don't want to let yourself be vulnerable to that."

Amber thought about the truth of that. An angry tear escaped and she brushed it away. "It's so unfair. After all this time she has to come back like this. She has no right to expect anything from me."

"I know. I know."

"And what if Rachel is right? What if she has another daughter? One she kept. How am I supposed to feel about that?"

"The only way to know is to face it and find out."

Amber shook her head. "No. I can't. I need time to think about it. All I've really wanted to do since I knew she was coming back was just get away until it's over."

"There is nowhere you can run to that this won't be right there with you. Besides, think of your poor grandmother, certainly she deserves more than that after all she has done for you and all she has already been through with Miriam."

"You're right. I can't hurt Gram. But it's just that I …feel…trapped."

"I know, honey. I know," Rachel's mother said, drawing Amber into her arms and rocking her.

Amber accepted the brief moment of comfort and then she drew away and sat straight. "Thank you. Really, Rachel is lucky to have you. I hope she sees that."

"Ahh, Rachel. We love her, don't we? But you and I both know she will never appreciate what she has. She will always be on the lookout for what she thinks she has missed. Poor thing," Rachel's mother said, "overlooking the good life she has had with people who love her. Rachel will never realize that no one's life is ever perfect."

Amber nodded, though she wasn't certain Rachel's mother was talking about Rachel now.

Rachel flung clothes and scarves and things with the store tags still on them onto her bed and then she crept down the stairs, glancing into the den to see the two of them all cozy on the sofa. Amber was so needy right now and her mother was always so happy to be needed. Well, super! Let her mother smother someone else for a change. Who needed it anyway? Rachel opened the door slowly, quietly and went out. She hurried past the three houses to Amber's house and knocked on the door.

Grampa opened the door and smiled when he saw Rachel. "Bringing good news of our girl?" he asked.

Grampa always projected optimism. Always seemed to trust that the world would eventually turn out right even though he was living proof that it hardly ever did. Aside from the deep disappointment of his only daughter abandoning her own family, he had suffered several strokes that had forced him to retire early. His wife had to go to work in the grade school cafeteria to help pay the bills. How humiliating that must be. Oh yes, Rachel had always been a little skeptical of Grampa's cheerfulness.

"Actually," Rachel said, her face reflecting a deep concern for Amber. "I'm afraid Amber is having a really hard time. She is really sad. Hardly even talking. That's why I thought that if maybe I could come and talk to Gram we could figure out a way I could help her."

"Oh good. Yes, come in. That may be a good idea," Grampa said, letting Rachel in and then calling out to his wife.

Gram came from the kitchen, wiping her hands on a yellow kitchen towel.

"Rachel was wondering," Grampa said, "if you could talk with her and maybe the two of you could figure out some way to help Amber."

"I see," Gram said. "Rachel, did you ask Amber to call me if she feels she still can't come home?"

"I did," Rachel answered. "Amber and my Mom were talking when I left so maybe she will call after that. And I know for sure that Amber wants to come home, but she doesn't know what to expect. Like how sick is her mother? Did anyone maybe come with her mother that could help Amber understand her Mom's condition? Just any information like that that I could take back to Amber to help her know what is going on here and, you know, maybe help her decide if she can come back."

"Whatever Amber needs to know," Gram said, "I'm certain she will feel comfortable asking me. I just need to talk to her. She must know how worried I am about her."

"Oh, yes, I'm sure she does. But you know Amber, always one to keep everything inside. She can be pretty stubborn."

Gram nodded and sighed.

"So," Rachel persisted, "I noticed the license plates on the car in your driveway were in-state. Has Amber's mother been here, in the same state as Amber all this time? I mean we sort of thought Miriam had gone off somewhere like Las Vegas or California even."

"Thank you for your concern," Gram said, "and for taking Amber in when she felt she needed it, but I'd rather answer all of Amber's questions with Amber. You know how distorted passing information on through several people can be."

"Oh yeah, sure, of course, but I promise I can get everything right. I'm really good about that," Rachel said. "Especially when I know how important it is to Amber. I'd do anything to help her, you know."

"I'm certain you would," Gram said.

Rachel waited, expecting the whole story to now come gushing from Gram, but Gram was silent until they all heard a noise and turned to look in the direction of the stairs. And there, to Rachel's delight, was a young girl pausing half way down. The girl looked at Rachel and frowned. Probably, Rachel assumed, she was disappointed that it wasn't her sister. Her sister. Amber had a sister? Man, Rachel had always wanted a younger sister!

"Mom thought it might be the hospice nurse," the girl said, "and wanted me to ask her to come up to her room. Mom is feeling really...tired."

"This is Rachel, dear" Gram said. "One of Amber's friends."

"Hi," Rachel said, walking past Gram to get a closer look at Amber's sister. "What's your name?"

"Grace. Well, actually everyone calls me Gracie but now that I'm getting older I think I'll just go by Grace."

"Grace, eh. That is so weird. Do you know that Grace is Amber's middle name?"

"No."

"Well, now," Gram said walking over to the girls, "if Miriam isn't feeling well, then I think Grace and I should go up and tend to her." Gram turned to Rachel and thanked her for coming to see what she could do to help Amber. "I guess all that you can really do is let Amber know that it is important to call me, or better, stop by. And, Rachel, if you don't mind, please don't tell Amber any of this. It would be wrong if she found out from anyone but me."

Rachel nodded and let herself be led back to the front door. She glanced back at Gracie before she went out. How was she going to be able to keep this information from Amber? How unfair would that be?

Amber was folding the tussled mess of clothes on Rachel's bed when Rachel walked in. "Are you sure you want to get rid of this?" Amber asked, holding up a purple top. "I was with you when you bought it and you loved it."

"Sure. Okay," Rachel said. "Just throw it in the chair. I'll take care of it later. Right now we need to talk."

Amber walked to the closet and hung up the blouse. "Have you been over to my house?" Amber asked.

"Yes, and you will never believe what I found out."

Amber turned to Rachel and sighed. "Stop. I'll find out what I need to know in my own time. Just stop the meddling."

"I'm only doing it for you. You have a right to know."

Amber picked up an orange sundress and started folding it. "How was Gram?"

"She really wants you to call. And she asked me not to tell you this stuff but it's just not fair that you don't know."

"Thanks for caring, Rachel, seriously, but I have to stand up to this myself. Your mom is right, there is nowhere I can go where it won't be following me. I just have to face it now and get on."

"You do have a sister," Rachel blurted. "She's about twelve or thirteen. She looks like you sort of. Maybe more like your mother than you do but, if you were both in a line up, anyone could tell you were sisters."

Amber swallowed the news and walked to look out the window.

"Her name is Grace. Isn't that weird that your mother gave you both that name? Grace didn't tell me her middle name. Or her last name for that matter. I was just standing there in the doorway talking to your grandmother when Gracie...I mean Grace, came down to see if I was the hospice nurse your mother was expecting."

"Okay," Amber whispered.

"You know how I always wanted a younger sister," Rachel said. "How crazy is it that you have one? I mean, we never would have dreamed that right out of the blue you'd find you have a sister."

"Having the same mother doesn't make her my sister. A sister is someone you grow up with. Someone you know. It's obvious that sharing the same DNA doesn't mean much in my family."

"Don't you want to go see her? Aren't you curious?"

"What I want," Amber said turning back to Rachel, "is for things to go back to where they were before Gram told me Miriam was coming. There were holes in my life but that was easier to live with than all of this."

"And you know what else?" Rachel went on, not able to stop herself. "The car in your grandparent's driveway has an in-state license plate. What if your mother has been close by all these years?"

Amber shook her head and walked past Rachel. "I'm just going out for a while."

"Where? Are you going to your house?"

"I don't know where I'm going, Rachel. Just out."

"Well, don't forget to call your grandmother," Rachel called after her as Amber hurried down the stairs.

Amber got into her car and the radio blared as soon as she started it. The song was a country song that she had loved but now she had to turn it off. Her boiling emotions couldn't stand any other noise. Amber backed out of the driveway and turned right - away from her house. She couldn't bear to drive by and see the things Rachel had told her. It had been her home for eighteen years and now it was stained. She could never feel the same walking in the door because her ... because Miriam had chosen to come back and add pain and death in the empty places she had left behind. Amber had, of course, fanaticized about one day running into her mother at a neutral place, the mall or even the checkout line in the grocery store Amber worked in. Miriam would be apologetic, and her tortured eyes would plead for Amber's forgiveness. In her fantasy, Amber had all the power. The power to allow her mother to be near her. The power to forgive. The power to make her mother work for the right to be back. But now, now, Amber had no power. Death and sympathy, and a life that Amber had never been a part of, had the power over Amber's life.

Amber drove randomly through the streets she had traveled her whole life. The same streets her mother had traveled every day until she had left. What if Rachel was right? What if her mother had been close by all the time? Somehow that felt worse than if she had been all the way across the country and not able to just come, once in a while, to try to see her daughter. But not even once in eighteen years?

Amber's chest hurt. She felt like she was suffocating. She pulled into a parking spot in front of the skating rink. Amber got out of her car and paced. She breathed in and breathed out. In and out. She would not cave. She would not cry. She would not scream.

Finally, after she had paced and huffed and puffed like a crazy woman, she forced herself to relax. Okay. Okay. Amber nodded, affirming that she was, no matter who came in and out of her life, the only one in control. She may have had no control when she was an infant, but she was an adult now.

Amber got back into her car and fished her cell phone out of the bottom of her purse. She pushed the Home button and waited through three rings before Grampa answered. Amber weakened for just a second at the happiness in his voice, then she asked if she could speak to Gram.

"I'll get her," Grampa said. "She will be so relieved, Amber. She has been worried sick about you. I see her checking the front window every time she hears a car. She lays awake half the night worrying about so much. It will be good for us all when you come home."

"I know," Amber said.

"Okay, hold on. I hear her coming," Grampa said, and Amber could envision him holding out the phone to Gram, his strong face wrinkling from his big smile.

"Oh, sweetie," Gram said. "How are you?"

"I'm okay. And I'm sorry I haven't called sooner but…"

"I understand."

"Gram, I'm sitting in front of the skating rink. The one on Fourth Street. Remember the rink where Lillian had her sixth birthday party. You came with me and watched me learn to skate."

"I remember."

"Well, it was that day that I realized that I didn't have any parents. Of course, I knew. I guess I just never really thought about it like that before, but now here were all these families. And they were all so happy together. And I kept hearing, 'Mom, hold my hand,' 'Dad, watch me twirl,'. Stuff like that and then I realized that I had never called anyone Mom or Dad. I had you and Grampa, but I would never have a Mom and Dad."

"Oh, Amber, sweetie, I'm so sorry."

Amber blinked away her self-pity. "It's not your fault. You have always done the right things. You have always taken care of everyone you loved. But, I just want you to understand why I can't come home right now. Why I can't see her or ever call her Mom."

"We can't undo the past, Amber. Believe me, I understand all that must be going through your mind right now. And it breaks my heart but, sweetie, I think you need to come home. Not for Miriam. You don't have to call her Mom if you can't right now. But you just need to stop hiding from her."

"I'm not hiding. I'm just making my own decisions and my decision is that I am going to get on with my life just like I have always had to… without her."

Gram paused and then said that there was more than Miriam at the house.

"I know," Amber said.

"That Rachel! I asked her not to say anything."

"Gram," Amber said. "It's Rachel."

"Yes, but I knew how upset you would be when you found out."

"It doesn't make anything easier, that's for sure. But honestly, the whole package is more than I want to deal with right now. Graduation is Wednesday and then I will figure out what I want to do."

"So," Gram asked, "you are still going to stay at Rachel's house?"

Amber forced a laugh. "Not because Rachel makes it any easier either, she is such a piece of work, but I am welcome there and that gives me time to think. Time to make a plan."

"The doctors have given your mother," Gram paused, then finished. "Only a few months. It may be sooner. You can't stay away that long. This is the only chance you will ever have to see her. Don't punish her at the cost to yourself. Trust me, one day you will wish you had talked to her about why she left you. We can all try to explain it, but I think you have a right to hear it from her."

"Knowing won't change it."

"But knowing may help you accept it, and that is the first step in letting go of your disappointments."

"I'll think about it, Gram. But right now, I just want you to know that I am doing okay. I'm working and busy with…stuff."

"Will you call again?"

"Yes, of course."

"When?"

Amber smiled. "Tomorrow."

"Call in the afternoon. Miriam wants to go to church so we are going with her and I don't want to miss your call."

"Sure. Okay. Good-bye, Gram."

Amber ended the call and dropped her phone back into her purse. Church? She hadn't expected that. But, then, of course, Miriam was dying. She would want to try and make amends to everyone now. If she hadn't gotten… sick, she would probably still be ignoring Amber and God.

Sunday morning Rachel was still asleep when Amber left to go to her house and pick up more clothes. Amber had realized that everyone would be at church and she could be in and out without notice. Amber went in through the kitchen door and paused. This smelled like Gram's house. The air was warm and faintly bacon and maple scented. It was Sunday - Grampa always had pancakes and bacon. Gram made him stick to his granola or oatmeal through the week, but she relented on one day and let him attack his frail heart with grease and sugar.

Amber thought of checking the refrigerator for left over bacon but instead hurried on to her bedroom. She gathered what she wanted and then started to go back down the stairs when she stopped. Amber went back to her mother's room and put her hand on the doorknob. Her grandmother had made the third bedroom into a nursery and had left Miriam's room untouched in case Miriam ever decided to return. Amber had explored everything in that room over the years, but she wondered what it looked like now that Miriam was actually in it again.

Amber turned the doorknob and started to push the door in but changed her mind. If she saw rows of medicines on the dresser would she have to feel sympathy for this woman who had abandoned her? If she saw slippers by the bed would she have to picture Miriam as a frail pathetic figure scuffling through the rooms? If she saw photos of Grace on the bed stand would she feel a pull to know her sister or a justifiably deserved resentment?

Amber dropped her hand and bounded down the stairs. She couldn't risk those feelings. She would get out of the house before everyone returned and she would go to the senior party at Miles Lake as though she was just like all the rest of her friends.

Rachel was ridiculously fretful all morning. She started out fretting because now that Amber was staying with her, they were not going to be able to claim they were each staying at the other's house for the night. But, Amber told Rachel to just tell her mother that they were staying at the lake house with everyone else that didn't want to be on the road with reckless teens who had consumed too much alcohol. What parent would insist their child drive home on backcountry roads in the dark of night under dangerous conditions? "Really, Rachel, this may shock you, but sometimes the truth does work," Amber said.

Next Rachel fretted because Amber didn't want to go to the party with

James. "You like him. You know you do. You went to senior prom with him. What's the difference?"

"The difference is that we came home after the prom. I don't want James to get any ideas because we are all spending the night there."

"Well, you don't have to do anything you don't want to," Rachel persisted.

"Thank you. And so, I think what I want to do is to go by myself."

"That's not what I meant. I meant you don't have to sleep with him if you don't want to."

"I know what you meant," Amber said.

"Well, he'll probably bring someone else anyway seeing as how you obviously turned him down," Rachel snapped.

Amber shrugged.

"Sometimes you don't even act human. Like you don't have any feelings at all."

"Don't worry, Rachel. I won't spy on you and Eddie."

"And don't tell Mom anything either."

"Hey, my name is Amber not Rachel."

Rachel threw a beach towel at Amber. "I only told you stuff to help you and you know it."

Amber threw the towel back. "Well, your stuff didn't help."

"Girls," Rachel's mother said, appearing in the doorway. "Are you graduating high school or kindergarten?"

"It's all Amber's fault," Rachel said, laughing and throwing the towel back at Amber.

"Yeah, right," Rachel's mother said. "Anyway, I guess you two didn't hear the phone while you were acting like toddlers but, Amber, your grandmother is on the phone for you."

Amber dropped the towel and hurried down to the kitchen to pick up the phone.

"I hate to interrupt," Gram said, "but we are not going to be home for a while and I didn't want to miss your call."

"Thanks, but I already left a message on the house phone that I was going to a senior party today and won't be back until… well, who knows."

"Okay. It's just that we are out of town and I didn't want you to worry if you couldn't get in touch with us."

"Thanks for calling and letting me know."

"Yes. Well, there is one thing," Gram said. "And you know I never really ask you to do anything you don't want to do, and I understand that you have important plans for today, so I won't ask you to change them, but, if you could… promise to come to the house tomorrow. After school. Any time really. The earlier the better actually. Just please come."

Amber sighed.

"I know it's not easy," Gram said. "But, if you can't come today, please promise you will come tomorrow."

"Can't you tell me why this is so important?"

Gram hesitated then said that she was sorry but it wouldn't work to tell her over the phone.

"My mother is dying. I already know that. What could be harder than that to tell someone?"

Amber heard her grandmother start to cry and say, "Here, you take this, I can't. I just can't."

Grampa apologized to Amber then said, "Please, sweetheart, it's just important that you come to the house as soon as you can. We wouldn't ask if we didn't think it was the right thing."

"Of course. Sure. I'll be there after lunch. The seniors don't have school tomorrow, so I can get there before I go to work."

"Thank you," her grandfather said, and ended the call.

Amber stood there stunned and, truthfully, a little frightened. She had never seen, or even heard through a closed door, her grandmother cry. She had never heard such weight in her grandfather's voice. Even when she and Gram had sat by his hospital bed after his strokes, Grampa had made light of their worry and they had, in return, pretended braveness for him. Now, apparently, there was no hiding or pretending for any of them. Miriam was back and with her ugly, selfish truths she had shattered the quiet safety of their pretending.

Amber drove herself to the lake party. She was never one to trust anyone else with control over her life anyway but tonight if she wanted to leave she didn't want to have to depend on Rachel and Eddie being able or willing to drive her. If James showed up with someone else, she wanted to choose when she felt like leaving. And, also of course, if worry ate at her mood and ruined the whole evening she would be better off just getting away from everyone else.

Bethany's parents were sitting on the back deck when everyone arrived.

They wanted every senior to pass by them and be aware of their presence. They smiled and swung back and forth on the porch swing.

"Hope there is no liquor in those beach bags," Bethany's dad would say as each group passed by him.

"Oh, no sir," they would lie.

Everyone traipsed through the kitchen, grabbing snacks on the way, then went down to the dock and peeled off their swimsuit covers. What a beautiful afternoon on the lake. The water was cold when they first dove in but by the time they swam out to the wooden raft they were merely chilly. The platform had a slide and a stack of inner tubes. It didn't take long for chaos to reign. The real world was breathing down their necks and they were happy to be irresponsible for, at least, maybe, one last time.

James was sitting on the dock when Amber, Rachel and Eddie came out of the kitchen. James had his back to the house, but Amber noticed he was sitting alone. Still that didn't mean he wasn't waiting for someone. James's shoulders were bare and impressive. He had blonde shaggy hair. His eyes were deep dark brown. His hands were broad and knuckly. Amber's heart betrayed her, and she sighed at the sight of him. Eighteen was such a dangerous age.

Eddie pulled off his shirt and handed it to Rachel as he dashed toward James but, instinct kicked in, and James leaned to the right just as Eddie charged and Eddie went flying past him into the water. Every witness to Eddie's failure laughed as Eddie's head surfaced. Eddie shook the water from his face and swam back to the dock. James reached down and helped pull him up out of the water.

"Always one to make an entrance," James said.

"His exits aren't much better," Rachel said. "Remember when he fell off the back of Rodney's convertible?"

"Hey, now woman," Eddie said, "you are supposed to be on my side."

James smiled at Amber and she smiled back. She could suddenly breathe a little better than she had since Gram's call.

Soon the dock was crowded and Amber felt herself holding James's hand. Someone in the house set speakers in the window and cranked up the music. Dancing immediately ensued and continued until the food was gone, the smuggled bottles of rum and whiskey were empty, the sun had disappeared, and the mosquitoes had joined the party. Then everyone collected their soggy belongings and said goodbye to Bethany's parents.

They backed their cars out onto the blacktop and drove six camps over and snuck into an empty camp. Everyone knew that when old man Perkins died his children had just put the camp up for sale and never bothered to come back and check on it. The water and electricity had been turned off but the solution to those problems had been figured out before this night began. Out of car trunks came lanterns, sleeping bags, snacks, drinks and, undoubtedly, other various items not on an approved parental list.

Amber waited until nearly everyone had left before she drove her car over to the Perkins camp. She had promised James she would go but she wanted to park in the back so her car wouldn't be blocked in just in case she decided to leave early.

James was waiting for her at the door. He handed her a red plastic cup. She could smell it was more than mixer. They went inside where the windows had been covered and taped around the edges so no sliver of light would leak out onto the lake. It was very late, but you couldn't trust old busybodies that sat around like self-appointed killjoys and called the police at any sign of fun. Lanterns made the rooms cozy and already couples were snuggled up together on sleeping bags and blankets. Someone was actually snoring.

"Look around folks," Fred Pierce said. "Life will never be as easy and painless as this moment. We will soon be leaving our nests and changing the world."

Everyone cheered.

"Let's drink to the 2016 Barry High class. The class of intellectual geniuses, exceptional athletes and the most beautiful girls!"

Everyone cheered and drank enthusiastically.

Then more toasts ensued. "And let's drink to smearing Davenport by twenty-six glorious points!"

"Yeah, and let's drink to having the best prom ever put on in the prom history of the planet."

"And finally getting creepy old Courser fired."

"And, thanks to Aaron, we may have the only student in the history of attendance keeping to have never missed a day of school ever!"

There was silence. "Who said that?" Fred asked.

"I did," Aaron's girlfriend said.

"Is Aaron here?" Fred asked.

"Yes," Aaron answered.

"What? What were you thinking, man?" Fred said.

"What?"

"You never missed a day of school? Ever?"

"Well, only if the school was closed, you know, for a storm day or something."

"Why? Why did you do something stupid like that?"

"Obviously," Aaron said, "you never met my mother."

Everyone laughed at that and the toasts continued. Everyone except Amber. James could feel her tighten up and pull away from him. "What's wrong?" James asked.

"I just realized that Fred is right. This is the easiest and least painful day I will ever have again."

"Ahh, come on. You of all people have it made. You are smart and everyone likes you. And when you put your mind to something no one can stop you. What have you got to be afraid of?"

Meeting *my* mother, Amber wanted to say but instead she cuddled up against James and let the premonition of disaster pass through her and move on. Let tomorrow bring what it may. She sipped from her red cup then turned her face up to be kissed by James.

Rachel rode home with Amber the next morning. They pulled into the driveway and dragged themselves up the walk to the door.

Rachel's mother opened the door. "Showers or food first?"

"Food," Rachel said.

"Shower," Amber said.

"Next question," Rachel's mother asked. "Breakfast or lunch?"

"What? What time is it?" Rachel asked, squinting at her mother.

"Too late to be dragging home for one thing. And too late to be dragging home looking like this for another."

"We are safe, Mom. Isn't that enough?" Rachel said, and stomped past her mother and into the house.

"I'm sorry, Mrs...." Amber began but Rachel's mother just smiled. "I'm glad you are both home safe and sound. I've kept sausage and pancakes warm in the oven."

"Okay, food first," Amber said.

While the girls ate, Rachel's mother remembered to let Amber know that her grandmother had called for Amber earlier and that she had promised to have Amber call her as soon as she and Rachel got home from the errand

Rachel's mother had sent them on. "Can't believe you delinquents have me lying for you. But, that sweet lady does not need to be worrying when I am here worrying about the two of you anyway."

Rachel groaned. "Please, Mom, you worry all the time regardless of where I am. You are probably worrying about me now when I am here sitting right in front of you."

"As a matter of fact, I am," Rachel's mother said. "Extremely worried. Just look at you. What mother wouldn't worry?"

Amber finished her food and got up to put her dishes in the dishwasher.

"Just leave those and go call your grandmother. She has been waiting."

Amber started for the phone and then turned back. "Would you mind calling while I am in the shower and telling her I should be there in a few minutes?"

Rachel snorted. "Yeah right. You ready in a few minutes."

"Sure, go on," Rachel's mother said. "I'll let her know."

There were two unfamiliar cars in the driveway when Amber parked in the street. Maybe the hospice nurse was there. That would certainly make it easier for Amber if someone else was there and emotions would have to be, for the moment, tempered.

Amber walked up to the door. Well, here goes. At last, after eighteen years of waiting, the time was here. Good, bad or ugly it was about to happen. Amber's heart pounded. If she were the type to give in to her emotions she may have experienced a panic attack. Amber paused in front of the door and took a deep breath. Wait. Why? Really? Why was *she* feeling like this? Why was she the one to be afraid? She had not done anything wrong. Her mother was the guilty one. Right. Her mother was the guilty one!

Gram opened the door and stepped out to hug her. "Everything is going to be fine. You will see."

Amber hugged her back. "It's just because I love you and Grampa so much that I'm doing this."

"I know."

Amber went in before Gram and saw her mother sitting on the sofa. Amber's eyes flicked from her mother to Amber's newfound sister on one side of Miriam and then to a man sitting on Miriam's other side. The man was lean and handsome. He was immaculately dressed in gray slacks and white shirt. He stood up when Amber stepped into the room. He smiled tentatively and waited. Everyone just stared at Amber and waited for…what? For her to make the first move as though she was the returning lost child and not Miriam.

"Amber," Gram said, "this is your mother and sister, Grace, and your father."

Amber frowned back at her grandmother. "Father?"

The man stepped forward. "I am so sorry that it has taken this tragedy to…"

"Don't speak," Amber snarled, lifting her hand to stop him. "Don't any of you even try to talk to me."

Amber's mother stood up now. Tear streaks glistened on her face. "Please just hear me out, Amber. That's all I ask. Hear what I have to say and then you can leave and never speak to me again. I will understand. But, please, please, let me try to explain."

"I can't even imagine the words you could find to make me understand how the three of you are here, standing in front of me like some cozy little family while all this time, all my entire life, I have…" Amber's words choked off. How could she even begin to explain to these people what it had felt like to be abandoned for eighteen years?

Amber turned to leave but her grandmother stepped in front of the door. "I will never ask another thing if you will just do this for me."

"Gram, you of all people have to understand how I feel. You have been here all these years waiting just like I have. And maybe if she had ever come back and tried to make things right… but my entire life has been waiting. And for what? So she could come back just to die in front of us? And, and look at them! Such a nice little family! It's more than I can stand. Please, just let me leave and call me when they are gone."

Amber's grandfather moved up beside Gram. "You deserve to know. Whether that changes how you feel is up to you. But for your own sake, Amber, you have to stay and get through this. This family is living proof that running away from the truth has only compounded our tragedy."

Amber closed her eyes and shook her head. "Just give me some time to process this."

"Time has already robbed us of too much," Grampa said. "Wasting more time won't change the truth. Waiting a week or a month or a year won't make it easier to hear."

"I understand your impulse to run," Miriam said. "But trust me, it's the worst choice you will ever make. What you think you are running from is always there. It is always with you and it haunts your every waking moment."

"Really?" Amber said, turning back to her mother. "You left me behind and then, free as a bird, you fly off and conveniently marry my father, and even have another child with him, and now, eighteen years later, eight-teen-years, you now want me to believe that the memory of me has haunted your every waking moment? Please!"

"I'm not a bad person. I just made a bad decision. I was young and stupid, but my plan was to come back for you. Honestly, I always planned to come for you."

"Look," Amber said, "none of that matters. So, you are not a bad person. Great. So, you had a plan that you never did one single thing to accomplish. Too bad. What all this looks like to me is that you have had the life you wanted while your first child waited and waited and waited to be wanted by her own mother. I just thank God you left me with caring and loving people instead of in an old box beside the road."

"She is a good person," Grace said, her voice cracking.

Amber looked at her sister for the first time. Really looked at the frightened face so like her own. "I'm sorry," Amber said to Grace. "I'm sorry."

"Perhaps," Amber's father said, his voice ever so patient, "it would be best if Amber and I had a talk before this all gets out of hand. Who can blame her for being upset? I am a minister, I preach mercy and grace, and still I needed time and prayer to understand. To forgive."

Amber's head was spinning. Her father was a minister? Really? What would come out next? Did she have a secret dwarf brother? Amber decided to just end it before there was more she had to hear.

"You know," Amber said, pulling in her emotions, "nothing matters here. The why or when of it all just doesn't matter. The three of you have your family and I have mine. No complaints. Gram and Grampa have been wonderful. Every child should feel such love. I'm fine. Let's just leave it at that."

"I'm afraid," Grampa said, "the camel has gotten his nose under the tent. Can't look away and pretend what's there isn't there. It's there all right and, Amber girl, you are just going to have to let the whole camel in."

Gram put her hand on Amber's arm. "Please."

"Yeah. Okay. Okay I'll hear whatever they have to say. And then I'm leaving."

"Thank you," Miriam said. "But, I'm sorry, really this is not how I planned it, but I'm afraid that I need to lie down. Amber, will you come up to my room and talk with me there?"

Amber scowled. She was not giving out sympathy cards as free passes if that was what her mother was trying to pull.

"Sure. Why not?" Amber said as her father, or whoever this man even was, turned to Miriam and lifted her up into his arms.

"Just give us a couple minutes," he said.

Grace stood up. Her face was so sad that Amber had to look away from it.

"Well, Gracie girl," Grampa said, "how about you and I get back to that game of cribbage while we wait. I think I almost had you beat."

"In your dreams," Grace said, though her voice was barely a whisper.

Amber looked after them as the two headed, just as Amber and Grampa had done a million times, walking side by side, talking the same trash, into the dining room.

"Oh, sweetie," Gram said, "he's just trying to help everyone get through this."

Amber nodded. "It's fine. Everything is fine."

"None of this is Grace's fault, you know," Gram said.

"I know."

"I hope you remember that. Grace is only twelve and all of this is hard for her to deal with, too."

"Okay."

"At the end of the day," Gram said, forcing a smile for Amber, "we will still be here for you. All that you ever had will still be here plus a whole lot more. You aren't losing anything, Amber, you are finally getting a family. Try to think of that. As hard as this is, the people in this house right now, are here to help you. We all love you."

Amber nodded for her grandmother though love was hardly in Amber's equation of how she felt about these people. And, how could it possibly be otherwise, honestly how could these strangers possibly feel love for her?

Finally, Amber's father came back down the stairs. He walked to Amber and looked down into her face. "I'm sorry. I know this time should only be about you, helping you, but unfortunately a lot has been put on our plate. Your mother is frail. She has bad days and some a little less bad. I think today she has just worn herself out worrying about you. Worrying about how much you must hate her. So, I'm asking you to hold back a little on your justifiable anger at her. I don't expect you to be dishonest about how you feel and pander to her but, if you could find it in your heart to just listen, to process it all carefully before you react, then… Well, that's all I ask."

Amber shrugged.

"She's a good girl," Gram said. "Amber will be careful."

"We have time to work on what you and I have lost. Your mother may not. That's all I'm saying."

"Sure."

"Thank you," he said.

"There is one thing," Amber said. "What's your name?"

"Oh, my goodness," Gram said.

"John Davis," he said and smiled.

"Okay," Amber said and headed for the stairs. So, she should have been Amber Grace Davis?

Miriam was in a soft pink nightgown and propped up against the pillows when Amber came into the room. "Thank you," Miriam said.

Amber stood back from the bed and looked down at her mother. All her life she had thought about this woman. Envisioned her in many places, doing many things, but never like this. Never just lying like a rag doll in the bed she would probably die in. Weak and helpless. Amber had never thought of her mother as either. The images Amber had held of Miriam were of her free spirit. Her impulsiveness. Her selfishness.

"Not a pretty sight, right?" Miriam said.

"None of this is about how we look."

"I know. Please get a chair. Please sit down."

Amber retrieved a chair from the desk and sat a few feet from the bed. Miriam nodded. "Then let's get to it."

Amber folded her hands in her lap and waited.

"Your father was a year ahead of me in school," Miriam began. "He is the only boy I ever loved. I mean I was ridiculous about him. This room had his name scribbled in hearts and taped all over the walls. I was such a pest to him that he had to finally break down and ask me out. But, then his parents moved to Wakefield his senior year. I was devastated. He played sports, he had a part time job and he needed to keep his grades up to get into college, so he didn't have a lot of free time. So, I would go there whenever he had some time off to see him instead of him coming here. No one knew we were still dating. I'm not proud of it now, but I was so young and so in love that I used, shall we say, my womanly wiles to trap him to me. I knew what a straightforward guy he was and that if I had a hold on him he would stay true to me. Anyway, short story is that after he graduated high school he took a six-month mission trip before he started college. I knew I was pregnant, but I didn't tell him. I knew this trip was important to him. This trip was so he would know for certain if he wanted to be a minister or not. He had a friend who started seminary studies and then dropped out. Your father didn't want to waste time or money. That's how he is. So, he took the time away from everything to do the work of God and see if that was where his heart was. Then, while he was deep in the jungles of South America I gave birth to you. No one here knew who your father was. Not even your grandparents. So, John never knew about you."

"When did you tell him?" Amber asked.

"When I found out what type of cancer I have. We came home from my doctor appointment and I knew chemo and radiation probably wouldn't be successful. The success rate for this type of cancer is very low. So, I knew I had to tell him about you. I couldn't die and leave this mess for all of you to work out."

"But when did you tell him? I mean how long has he known about me?"

"He has known for a week."

"I see."

"We talked, and I begged him to let me come first. I had hoped to tell you and give you a chance to know the whole story. To let you know that none of this was his fault. He never knew about you and I didn't want you to look at your father for the first time the way you just now... looked at all of us."

"Guess things don't always work out the way we had hoped they would."

"I'm sorry for my weakness, Amber." Miriam said. "Truly sorry. I know I've been a coward."

"It sounds to me like you were not too much of a coward to get what you wanted."

"I did want John. I had to be with him. When he came back from his mission and started school, well, that is when I left you. I had graduated and so I moved to Middlebury and we got married. I worked in a small bank there until John was out of school and then he had to move around to a few churches until we got back to Wakefield. I knew you were safe and well taken care of, so I just went on being the little minister's wife until it became too late to just tell him. I was scared that if he found out that I had lied he would never be able to forgive me. Our life was working, and I felt this need to be good enough to be a minister's wife. How could I, how could we suddenly show up with a child? It was just too complicated, and I never found the courage to risk losing everything by telling him."

"I see."

"Do you? Do you really have any idea how this could happen? Is there someone in your life that you would sacrifice everything for?"

"I can't see myself ever making your choices if that is what you are asking me."

"Well, someday you will love someone so much that you will do anything to be with them."

"If discarding a child is the cost, I doubt that love would survive."

"I could have gotten an abortion and no one would ever have known. But I didn't. I couldn't. Isn't that worth something? Doesn't that prove I'm not as heartless and selfish as you think?"

"Quite honestly, I don't know what I think right now. About you or my father or any of it. All I know is that I agreed to listen and I have. I have heard your side of it and I have lived my side of it. I have to sort out what I feel and what I want to do now."

"Of course. Of course, you do. But please believe that I have thought about you every day. I missed your first tooth. I wondered when you had taken your first step? Were you easy to potty train? Was your hair curly like mine or straight like your father's? Did you like math or literature? All these things that I knew you were doing and ..."

"Please," Amber said, standing up. "Please. No more. I'm going to go now."

"Will you come back?"

"I don't know."

"Okay," Miriam said. "Thank you for listening."

Amber stared at her for a second and then turned and started out of the room.

"Please," Miriam said, "don't take too long. I do love you. I always have."

John was waiting at the foot of the stairs. He watched Amber pause when she saw him and then continue down. Her face was emotionless.

"Can we talk?" he asked.

Amber shook her head.

"I'll be here when you are ready," John said as she passed by him and went out the door.

When Amber was safely in her car she checked her watch. She had a couple hours before she went to work so she called James. When James answered she asked him if he was able to see her. "I just need to talk to someone," Amber said, her voice trembling.

"Do you need me to come there? To your house?"

"No. Can we meet somewhere else? Maybe Foster's Park?"

"I can be there in fifteen."

"Thank you," Amber whispered, and then James heard her sob.

Amber had collected herself by the time James got to the park. Her face was still puffy and flushed but her spine was straight as she waited on a bench, under an oak tree, hands clasped in her lap, for him to reach her.

"I don't know how I didn't get a ticket getting over here," James said, sitting down beside her. And then he waited for her to tell him.

"We have never really talked about our families," Amber began. "I know that you live with your mother and sister. I know you work to financially help your mother. But I don't know anything about your father."

"Not much to tell. He's big on excuses but not much else."

"Do you ever see him?"

"We see him from time to time, but he is no one we can count on."

Amber reached over and took his hand.

"Look," James said, "is this something about my family? I mean, I'm nothing like my father. I'm..."

"No. I just realized, sitting here waiting for you, that I didn't really know what your family was like. I didn't want to carry on and pity myself in front of you when you may be dealing with your own problems."

"I'm okay."

"Good." Amber said. "I was just wondering, you know, I mean I don't know what you have heard about my family. Or rather, lack of one."

"Well, I know, of course, that you live with your grandparents. I don't know anything about your parents. I think, well, only because I have never heard otherwise, that they may still be alive... somewhere."

Amber nodded. "They are."

"Okay," James said and waited for Amber to continue.

"It's all such a mess," Amber said. "They have all suddenly just shown up. After eighteen years the three of them just appear out of nowhere. Nothing for my whole life and now… here they are looking at me like I'm disappointing them. Like I have to accept them all or feel… feel guilty."

"Three of them?"

"Yes. I just discovered that I have a twelve-year-old sister named Grace, a father who is a minister, apparently, and a mother dying of cancer. How is that for an instant family?"

James didn't know what to say so he just waited.

"I've always wanted a family. I've always hoped that one day my mother would come back for me. But now, now I just want them all to go away and let me go back to dreaming that the family I had hoped for will still appear some day and it will be wonderful."

James nodded.

"I want to be mad," Amber said. "I don't want to forgive them. They have no right to ask that of me."

"Sure. You're right."

"It would be so different if she just wasn't dying. Then I could make her stand up and face me. Make her have to look at what she has done."

"Wow," James said. "Your mother is dying?"

Amber nodded.

"That must be hard."

"I don't understand why her dying hurts me so much when I have always lived without her anyway? It's not like I can miss what I've never had. How can I grieve over someone I don't even know?"

"Maybe," James offered, "maybe your sadness is more about the loss of what you'd always hoped you would have."

Yes. James was right. Amber's grief was because her mother had not only ruined Amber's past, Miriam was now taking Amber's dreams to the grave with her. There could never be a happy ending for Amber and her long-awaited mother.

"That sounds selfish, doesn't it?" Amber said. "That I'm sad about what I will be losing instead of what she is facing."

"You're not selfish. It's just a lot for you to figure out all at once."

Amber sighed and glanced at her watch. "I have to get to work."

James stood up. "Are you going to be alright? Do you need me to meet you after work?"

"No. Really. I'll be okay. I guess I just needed someone to listen to me and not try to tell me what to do or how to feel."

"You'll figure it out, Amber. Don't be too hard on yourself."

"Thanks," Amber said. "Thanks for coming."

James watched Amber walk away toward her car. "Amber," he called out and she looked back. "My father is in jail."

Amber ran back to James and they just stood quietly holding each other for a moment then they parted and went their separate ways.

"So," Rachel said as soon as Amber came into the bedroom. "Tell me all about your day and I'll tell you about mine."

Amber sank down onto the bed and slipped her shoes off. "You go first. I'm sure your day was much better than mine."

"Well, okay. You remember that dreadful junk sale Mom was working? Well, she forced me to go with her. Dad got to go play golf, so I had to be her pack mule. And I will tell you, it was not fun. But, but all was not lost. I met this other totally bored kid, well, I thought he was bored at first, but he was just contemplating stuff, yeah, he said he was contemplating or meditating or something. Anyway, his name was Alfred, yeah really, Alfred just like from some old English novel. Anyway, Alfred swears he has studied the occult and he believes in reincarnation, too."

"Great," Amber said, getting her pajamas out of her bag.

"He is honestly the smartest guy I have ever met. You can't believe the stuff he could talk about. Things like hidden laws and principles of the universe. He even talked about metaphysics. I mean, what guy do we know that even can pronounce metaphysics? He said that most people confuse occult with occult arts. Whatever that means. Anyway, he doesn't believe in fate and luck... or bad luck. He..."

"What is your point, Rachel?" Amber finally asked. "That you met some new guy that has swept you off your feet because he believes he was also once a flamingo in a past life?"

"My point, Miss Haughty Pants, was that I thought my day was going to be ruined and it turned out super amazing. Today has most probably changed my life. So, no matter what happened to you today, at your grandparent's house or whatever, life goes on and can really surprise you."

Amber had to agree, life was definitely full of surprises. "I'm sorry,

Rachel. Really. I'm sorry for being so snippy. I'm glad you made lemonade out of your lemon. You are definitely a role model."

"Hey, all I'm saying is that everything happens for a reason. For the good of the universe."

Amber smiled for her friend. "I'll try to remember that."

"So, tell me, what happened with you today? You know, when you went home?"

"Oh, I guess you could say that my day was a lot like yours. I met people I had never seen before and they gave me a lot to think about."

"So, you met your mother and sister? What did they say? Don't you think your sister looks like you? Well, maybe not exactly but she does look like she could be your sister, right? I mean, maybe you two even have the same father. Wouldn't that be something? I mean if you were real sisters and not just half-sisters. But I guess that doesn't make any sense. Why would your mother not come back for you if she was with your father?"

Amber headed out of the room. "I'm going to change and when I come back I want to hear more about Albert."

"Alfred. Alfred. His name is Alfred."

When Amber came back into the room she saw Rachel sitting cross-legged on the bed, slouching over her laptop.

"Look, Amber, he is on Facebook! Come look at this. Here is his page. He's kinda cute, right? I mean in a… a wizardly kinda way. I'm going to friend request him. Just look at all this neat stuff. I read some of his posts. Listen to this one someone wrote to him. 'You have changed my life. I have always believed that something existed that we could not see or prove. I have read the books you suggested and admit that I was shocked when I ended up believing in God." Rachel stopped reading and frowned. "God? Like I guess she means God. The church God. How did she get that out of the occult?"

"I wouldn't know." Amber got in under the bed covers. "Read me some more," she said so that Rachel could continue on her mystic tirade and not bring up Amber's day.

"Here, his post yesterday says that we need to train ourselves to think positive thoughts. He said it is a natural law, proven throughout history, that those who consciously think positive thoughts bring about a light to dispel darkness."

Rachel sighed and looked up from her screen. "Oh, Amber, I want to be a good light in the darkness."

"Don't we all?" Amber said.

"There, I just sent my friend request. It looks like he posts stuff every day. He has a few books listed that I will, of course, need to get. I mean, this is exactly what I've been looking for, right? It's like the cosmic forces have finally noticed me and have now sent me the key to the door of secret knowledge. Alfred is my key. I was meant to be dragged to that junk sale."

Rachel closed the lid of her laptop and lay back on her pillow. She drew a sigh all the way from the tips of her toes. "My real life is just beginning. This day has changed my life."

Amber turned over on her side. "Yeah, I know how you feel."

"No really, Amber, all that palm reading and astrology and séances and all that crazy searching we have done has led me to this day. The mystic forces have finally found me."

"Well, I hope they are kind to you," Amber said.

"Me too," Rachel said, her voice suddenly a little doubtful. Rachel knew there were dark forces as well as light. She had better talk to Alfred about that.

Tuesday was pretty much a waiting day. Finals were posted. Classes consisted of joking around and disinterested teacher rhetoric. Those graduating had nothing to do really except get through the day. It suddenly occurred to Amber to wonder if Mr. Perfect Attendance had gone all crazy and actually taken senior skip day off yesterday, or if he had been the lone senior wandering through the empty class rooms.

James met up with Amber at lunch and they went off campus to get a burger and fries. Amber watched James stop by the counter to get napkins and straws. Then he brought the tray of food to their booth.

"What is this?" Amber asked, pointing at the ice cream sundae.

"I just thought you needed a treat."

Amber watched James set out their food on the table and then stab his straw into his drink. Amber wondered if she loved James. Well, more specifically, if she was in love with James. She thought she may be, but she didn't feel like Miriam described her love for Amber's father. James wasn't an obsession. He wasn't always on her mind. She had never written his name all over everything. Amber wondered now, for the first time really, how she would feel if James had to move away.

"What is it?" James asked, smirking at her.

"What?"

"You're staring at me kind of weird."

"Oh. Sorry."

"You know," James began, "I was thinking about your mother. Will she be able to come tomorrow to your graduation? Is she strong enough?"

Amber withdrew. "They don't have tickets. I only got two for my grandparents."

"I may be able to get you some more. I don't think my sister is going to be able to make it and Pete said he had an extra if I knew of anyone who needed it."

"Thanks, but I don't want them to come."

"I see," James said. "But, what if they do? What if they find a way and show up?"

"There are a lot of people who will be there. Some I hope to see and some I don't. I can't control everyone."

"How about your sister?"

"James, I don't have any family except my grandparents. That hasn't changed just because these people have interjected themselves into my life. My parents have not done one tiny thing to contribute to my education. They don't need to be a part of my graduation."

They both unwrapped their burgers and took a bite.

"Would you want your father at your graduation?" Amber finally asked.

James nodded. "I'd be okay with that."

"Really?"

"Amber, some people are more victims of themselves than other people are victims of them."

"What do you mean?"

"My father doesn't want to hurt me. He doesn't want to hurt my Mom and sister. He just... well, the choices he makes ends up hurting us, but it hurts him most of all. He is just weak, but I don't think he is mean."

"Excuse me but that sounds selfish if he does things that he knows will hurt his family."

James shrugged. "I don't think he thinks like that. He just gets out of jail with good intentions and then does something stupid again and goes right back in. I don't think he thinks about how it affects us. I think he is really sorry that his, that our, lives have turned out like this."

"You don't sound angry at him. How can you not be angry?"

James laid his hamburger back on the paper. "I've seen him cry, Amber. My father cried in front of us. I know he wishes he could be different. But he can't help himself and we don't know how to help him, so we just have to accept that he is who he is and live around him."

Amber thought about that. "My situation is completely different," she finally said.

"You can forgive anyone you choose to," James said.

"They managed eighteen years without my forgiveness. I think they can live the rest of their lives without it."

James reached across the table and put his hand over hers. "My mom has a sign in her kitchen. It says that we must forgive. If not for their peace, then for our own."

"What does that mean?"

"It means," James explained, "that if people have hurt us and we remain angry over it, then we don't have peace. So, if we forgive them, even if we don't believe they want or deserve forgiveness, then we let it go and get on with our own happiness."

Amber pulled her hand away. "I guess I will just have to find another way to be happy."

James picked up his hamburger and studied it as if trying to decide where to bite it. "And what if you can't?"

"If I can ever forgive them, I know that I can't do it now. So, please don't get any tickets for them. I don't want my graduation to be ruined by knowing they are out there watching me, pretending I'm their daughter." Amber said. "I honestly think that I'd rather not even go if I knew they were going to be there."

"Okay. No tickets. But I hate seeing you like this. Maybe you need to find someone to talk to that can help you."

"I'm talking to you."

James chuckled. "The one bit of advice I gave you, you smacked it down."

"Well, that just means you have to try harder."

"Okay. I'll go home and read more of Mom's signs."

Amber started in on her ice cream sundae. "Have you really forgiven your father?"

James shrugged. "Most of the time. But we are all entitled to a little slippage as long as we are trying."

John was waiting by Amber's car when she got out of school. She hesitated when she saw him then continued on.

"You never came back."

"I had to work last night."

"I see. Well, is there somewhere we can go to talk now?"

"What is the point? My... Miriam told me why she did what she did and how you never knew until now. What else is there to say?"

"I believe you and I have a lot to talk about. Granted you have grown up without your parents but I have lived for eighteen years without knowing my daughter. I understand how you feel. I do. I felt the same at first. But, I also know that we, you and I, have to move on from this point because we can never change the past. All we have to work with is now."

"The truth is," Amber said, looking away from her father, out over the school parking lot, "I don't want to talk about it. I just want to get on with my life the way it was."

"In that life that you had before we came, did it include you wishing your mother would come back for you? Did you ever wish you had a family that very much wants you? Are you telling me now that you want us to let you go back to just wishing for us when we are right here in front of you?"

Amber shrugged.

"Can you give me an hour? A half hour?"

"Fine. Fine. Okay."

"Is there a place you will be comfortable talking?"

"It used to be my house."

John let that slide. "Well, is there another place?"

Before Amber could answer Rachel appeared. "Hey, Amber," Rachel said, glancing all the while at the man with her. "Are you coming straight home? I have some new dresses we need to try on for tomorrow. Mom sent me a text that she has been shopping today."

"I don't know when I will get to your house," Amber answered.

Apparently Amber was not interested in introducing Rachel to this man so, of course, again, Rachel had to take the lead. "Hello," Rachel said, extending her hand. "I'm Rachel, Amber's best friend. She is actually staying at my house for a while."

John shook her hand and introduced himself as John Davis.

"And you know Amber how?" Rachel asked.

"Rachel," Amber cut in. "I'm okay. I don't know when I will be home. Just tell your Mom not to plan on me for dinner."

"Well, she might ask where you are going and who you are with."

"Really, Rachel. I'm okay."

Rachel looked doubtful, but Eddie pulled up beside Amber's car and stopped. Rachel started to get in his car, then hesitated, a horn blasted behind them, Eddie grumbled something, and Rachel got into his car. "I'll see you at home," Rachel called out the window as Eddie's car pulled away.

"I don't really know where we can go to talk," Amber said. "This isn't a big town. Everyone knows everyone's business."

"Would you mind then if I took you to Wakefield? We can talk in the office at my house or the church. Whichever you are comfortable with."

Amber scowled. "Wakefield. Right, Miriam has been in Wakefield all this time. It just feels so much worse that she has been that close and never once..."

John nodded. "I'm sorry. I know it's hard. But, I believe I have the help you need."

"What? Are you going to try to tell me that God cares?"

John smiled. "Actually, you are surrounded by loving fathers. Let us help you."

"I may as well tell you that I do not go to church. I'm not saying that I'm against it. It's just something we, my grandparents and I, never did."

"Then we can go to my house if you'd rather."

Amber thought about that. She was not ready to see their home. To walk in their door and see the pieces of their life...their furniture and family photos and...and where they took care of each other. "No. I guess the church will be fine."

Amber buckled up and looked straight ahead on the drive to Wakefield.

"I can see that you don't feel like talking about yourself, so I will just start," John said. "I know your mother told you a little about how we have all ended up here. So, do you have any questions about that before I start rambling?"

"Maybe one," Amber said. "Didn't you think it was strange that Miriam never visited her family? I mean as close as she was."

"She told me she did visit her parents periodically. Of course, with my work, I am busiest on weekends when most people are off. The holidays also carry extra work for me. So, when your mother told me she went to visit her parents while I was working, I had no reason to doubt her."

Amber was quiet, thinking about that.

"I wasn't looking for problems, so I never questioned whatever she told me."

"Okay."

"Anything else?"

"What did you find in South America that convinced you to become a minister?"

John glanced over at her. Obviously, it was not going to be an easy task to get to know his daughter. "Okay. We can start there," he said. "What I found was that God is here for all of us that want him and invite him into our life. Coming from my comfortable religious background it was easy to take that for granted. I went to church. I sang the songs and tried to learn from the sermons, but I didn't really get it. I had to go where God was absent to see the hunger for Him. To see the joy after lives were opened to knowing Him."

"Okay," Amber said.

"I, of course, found the primitive living conditions, the lack of proper sanitation and agricultural progress that I had expected to find, but I also found... I found a people who were spiritually needy. They met us with such hope. Not just for the food and medicines but also, when you looked into their expectant faces, you could see how they longed for what we could teach them about our merciful and caring God. I came to see for the first time how God could actually change lives. I was suddenly, instantly, excited to be a part of introducing these people to the truths of the gospel."

Amber thought about that. "And did they believe in God by the time you left?"

"Those that wanted to, yes. Of course, just like anywhere else there are those who welcome you for just the things you are bringing them and those who want more than the shoes and food. I was young, it was my first mission, but I left that village a changed man. In teaching them I discovered things I hadn't understood before. Things about me and them and my religion. It was my first mission, but it wasn't the first for the group leaders that I went with and they knew how to approach the initiation of biblical teachings. I saw miracles happen. And I found that these impoverished, forgotten people were open to accepting miracles where we, in our supposedly civilized society, are hesitant to acknowledge them."

"Miracles?" Amber said. "You actually saw miracles?"

"Yes. I mean we didn't cure the blind, but I saw lives change in miraculous ways. Hope and feeling loved heals a lot of problems."

Amber looked out the window. "I suppose."

"Surely," John said, "you are not suggesting that you live without hope and love?"

"Let's just say that I was learning how to live my life without dwelling on my losses until you all appeared and reminded me exactly what my losses were."

"We are hoping you choose not to continue to live with those losses. We are hoping you, like us, are eager to make up for lost time."

"How can I ever make up for a life time of waiting only to find that it was just because of one person's selfishness? The one person who, in the whole world, was supposed to put me, her child, first."

"Your mother made poor decisions, but she has paid the price for them."

"I find that hard to believe. Unless, unless you mean that God is punishing her with this cancer."

"No. That is definitely not what I meant. God does not punish us for making mistakes. He died on the cross to make us flawless. He loves us because of, and despite of, our humanness. He forgives when asked for forgiveness. What I meant is that your mother has suffered all these years by carrying her shame and regret over a secret that could have been told."

"She said she was afraid she would lose you if she told you and, apparently, you have always been more important than I was."

"I don't think she ever thought of you as lost. I think she truly believed that someday she would come back for you."

"Again," Amber said, "she was selfishly thinking of just what she wanted. Do you think she ever once tried to imagine how Gram had to explain to a little girl why her own mother didn't want her? Did Miriam even wonder what she had done to her parents by just walking away from them and breaking their hearts, to say nothing of dumping them with the responsibility of her child?"

"I have wrestled with these same questions," John said. "It was hard to accept that Miriam could keep this secret from me all these years. If you weren't my child I could almost understand her hiding you but…"

"And yet you have forgiven her?"

"Forgiving her was not a choice. I forgave her because I love her and because it's God's command that we forgive others as he has forgiven us."

"Okay then," Amber said.

John looked over at her. "It isn't as easy as it sounds. Please know that."

"Well, I don't know God's commands so it's definitely going to take me a little longer than you. If I can ever forgive her."

"Forgiving is a process, but you have to want to start it to achieve it."

"Meaning?"

"Meaning you can choose to dwell on what you didn't have instead of being grateful for what you do have."

"So, my pity party is over, is that what you are saying? Now just pretend that I don't feel what I think I feel and smile some fake and empty smile for you all. Fine, I can do that. What does it matter to me what you all think of me anyway?"

They rode in silence for a while then Amber asked him if they could turn back. John said they were almost to his church and he'd really like her to see it.

Amber looked out the side window until John pulled into the church parking lot and turned off the car.

John stared at the white clapboard church in front of him. "You asked me what I learned from the people in Peru," John said. "I learned that they came to us wanting to trust us. They wanted to believe that we could make their lives better. Better for their health and better for their souls. They were surrounded by disappointments and burdens we, in our comfortable life, could not even imagine, but they trusted us when we offered them help."

"I don't need help. I can figure this out by myself if all of you would just give me time."

"Amber, the cancer is in your mother's pancreas. Do you know how serious that is? The doctor recommended surgery then chemo and radiation but your mother just wants to give up. She is afraid to try, afraid to go through all that torture, as she puts it, and then die anyway."

Amber looked at his face now. He was right, she was not the only one damaged by Miriam's selfishness.

"I'm telling you this because if she doesn't change her mind and try to fight this, then you may not have the time you need to figure it out by yourself."

"Okay. I understand."

"Good, let's go inside and I'll show you around."

Before John had opened the car door an elderly woman approached the car and wrapped on his window. John smiled at her and she burst into tears.

"Fred's in the hospital. The ambulance just took him away."

John glanced back at Amber and told her he would only be a minute then he opened the door and got out.

Amber watched as he walked a few steps away from the car with the lady. They stopped and talked. The old lady drew a hankie from her pocket and wiped at her face and nose. Then Amber watched as her father took the lady's hands in his own and they both bowed their heads in prayer. When the prayer was over the lady looked up and thanked him. Then she gathered her courage and went back to her car.

Amber got out of the car and walked up to him just as a group of teens burst out of the church and hurried past them.

"Pastor Davis," each teen called out to him on their way by. A few smiled and nodded at Amber.

"I hope you are all ready for your part on Sunday," John said as they passed.

"Oh, we will be. We may just be so awesome we take over the whole sermon."

"That is my plan," John said. "In fact, I'm not even writing a sermon for this Sunday."

Everyone chuckled and dispersed in their own direction.

John led Amber up the steps and into the sanctuary. "I would have introduced you, but I thought it would be better if I do it when I have the time to explain things rather than just announce that you are my daughter and then let the stories build on their own."

"Whatever," Amber said, looking around at the simple décor.

"Everything we need to get the job done is here," her father said as if reading her thoughts that his church was pretty bare bones. "Come, my office is back here."

Amber followed him past a couple closed doors to his office. His desk was neat, but the walls were covered with calendars filled in with different colored markings, there were stacks of bulletins in a corner chair and plaques of biblical verses tacked everywhere. Amber smiled, thinking of James's mother's kitchen. Yes, look, here was one about forgiveness.

Amber strolled around the room, reading the notes on the calendars, reading the encouraging words, picking up the photos of Miriam and Grace and then putting them down.

"How do you write your sermons?" Amber asked.

"Pretty much like all the term papers I used to hate. I choose my topic and research the bible and these file drawers of scraps I have collected from various sources then I try to organize my ideas into a coherent message, throw in a little humor and end on a positive note."

"Bet your first one was scary."

"To be honest, they are all scary. I can't bore the congregation. I can't espouse my personal views if they may offend someone. I can't come off as too stern or too weak. It's a balance that I pray I can reach each Sunday."

"Do you actually... you know, pray about your sermons?"

"Most definitely. I don't want to be getting the word of God wrong."

Amber smiled. Unfortunately, she was starting to like her father. Rather, starting to like John.

Amber sank down in the chair in front of his desk. "Why did you want me to come here?"

"I felt getting you out of your house and town would help remove the extra weight of the emotions I saw when you walked into your grandparent's house."

"It wasn't my grandparents or their house that was upsetting to me."

"I know."

"So, what now?"

"Exactly," John said sitting on the corner of his desk. "What now? We can't go back so we have to start from now."

"I mean, what exactly do you want from me?"

"Well, I'm hoping for your help."

Amber frowned.

"I know you do not owe us anything. We can't expect forgiveness so soon. We can't expect it at all. That is totally your call. But I think part of your mother's decision to give in to this death sentence without trying to do everything she can to help herself is, well, it's a self-punishment for all the damage she believes she has done."

"That doesn't make any sense," Amber shot back. "Shouldn't she be more afraid of dying than finally telling the truth?"

"Well, there are a couple things here. First, Miriam isn't as afraid of dying as some. You see, when you have faith then death isn't as frightening.

We grieve for the people and times we will miss, but if we believe, not just talk the talk, then spending eternity with our Heavenly Father doesn't seem as terrible as if we believed we will simply cease to exist anywhere. And, though you cannot know it, your mother is insecure in many ways. Miriam has never seen the simple beauty of herself. She wears herself out being an over achiever in everything she does. She can also be so insecure she feels a certain... jealousy of my congregation. She has accused me of putting her and Grace in second place. But, people come to me in their time of need, they are vulnerable and scared, and when I can help them get through their bad times, well, Miriam has, unfortunately, chosen to see their gratitude as something more. I can see now where that insecurity is probably what has kept her from telling me the truth about you."

"What? How could knowing about me be a threat to your marriage?"

"It wasn't you personally that she was afraid to admit to, it was the lie that she started and didn't know how to get out of. I believe that she has always intended, at least in her own conscience, to come back for you. But when we were finally married we needed the two incomes and, more important, we had to be who we presented ourselves to be. No parish would accept a new pastor who presented himself as good and moral and then they would see that children suddenly appeared that he couldn't explain. They would see that I lied and then, without credibility, I would have never succeeded."

"I see," Amber said. "So, at first she left me so you could have time in South America to decide if you wanted to be a minister. Then when you did decide, she didn't tell you because that would ruin your career, and then when you had a successful career she couldn't tell you because you would be upset and leave her for some overly grateful woman in your congregation?"

"Let's hope it's not that simple. But yes, Miriam has a problem with over dramatization and guilt. I knew before we had Grace that she somehow blamed herself. Each month she would be depressed when she wasn't pregnant. That is why she said she wanted to name our daughter Grace, because she felt God had finally given her what she desperately wanted but did not deserve. I didn't understand it at the time, why would Miriam feel she didn't deserve a child but, of course, it's clear now."

"So," Amber said, standing up and moving away to the window, "you are asking me to convince the woman who abandoned me to save her own life?"

"I think you are the only one who can."

"It's unfair. You know that don't you? It's unfair to make me responsible for her life when she never took responsibility for mine."

"I agree. But here we are. God works in mysterious ways, I'm afraid."

Amber stared out the window at the green grass and the neat houses across the street. For some reason, here, right now, she wanted to do what John asked. She knew it was the right thing. But she was afraid to make a promise she may not be able to keep. "I'll think about it," she said.

"Thank you. Now can I take you to dinner? What is your favorite food?"

Amber shrugged. "Anything I guess."

"Have you ever tried Greek?"

Amber smiled. "Gram isn't that adventurous."

"There is a Greek restaurant by the hospital. If it is okay with you, I'd like to check on Mrs. Thompson's husband before we head back. Her daughter was meeting her at the hospital, but I think I need to stop by his room and see what I can do for them."

Amber shrugged. "I don't have a curfew."

Amber lay in bed staring into the darkness. Now what? As hard as it felt before, at least it was somehow easier to be angry than to care. John had reached over in the dark car and gently laid his hand on her arm. "I don't think for one minute that you are having a pity party for yourself. I know your feelings of betrayal and sadness are real. Justifiably real. And it breaks my heart. But, I hope you can be honest enough with me to not hide behind a fake smile. I want us to work together to fix this. Okay?"

And Amber had nodded. But in all honesty, she didn't know how she was ever going to be able to do what John asked. She may feel kinder toward him, but she just couldn't let go of her mother's betrayal. In fact, the more she learned about Miriam the less she liked her. Oh, why couldn't her mother just have been abducted and stricken with amnesia and never have known all these years that she had abandoned her daughter? Amber could almost have forgiven that.

"So!" Rachel said, coming into the room and turning the overhead light on in Amber's face. "Who is that man?"

"John Davis."

"Yeah, right, like I'm going to let you get away with that."

"Apparently he is my father."

"OH YES! I knew it! I just knew it!" Rachel squealed and jumped on the bed then settled into an attentive position.

"Get your dirty shoes off the bed," Amber said, pushing her away.

"Hey, it's my bed."

"Yeah but tell me when you ever washed any of the bed linen."

"Stop stalling," Rachel said, slipping her shoes off and getting back on the bed.

"He is the minister in the Community Christian Church in Wakefield. He didn't know about me until just a week ago."

"What?"

"I believe him."

"Okay, maybe, but I'll be the judge of that. Go on."

"His congregation seems to really like him."

"Blaa blaa blaa!"

"What, Rachel? I just met him. We talked. We had dinner and then he brought me back to my car."

"Seriously? After all we have been through, that's all you are going to share? And you think your mother is selfish."

"He asked me to help talk my mother into getting treatments for her cancer."

"Well, first, that is a lot of nerve. And second, why wouldn't she get treatments?"

"It's complicated apparently."

"And did you agree to it? To talk her into it?"

"I don't know. What can I say? I mean how much credit will she give my opinion when she has never given my thoughts or feelings any credit?"

"That's right! These people have a lot of gall to show up and ask anything of you."

"Yeah, that's what I thought."

"But?"

"But he has a way of explaining things that makes me feel sorry for her even though she doesn't deserve it. I think I want to do what he asked to please him more than save her."

"Yeah, he is really good looking."

"Rachel, he is my father. Let's not judge everyone by your standards."

"Yeah, right. I forgot he was your father. Hey, Amber, you now know who your father is. All these years you wouldn't even talk about having a father and now here he is in the flesh and blood."

"I know. It gets crazier by the minute."

"Hey, are they coming to your graduation?"

"He asked about that at dinner. I told him, right now, I would rather they didn't come. I just want tomorrow to be about my high school graduation."

"Seriously? Come on, Amber, you know I wanted to see them all again. I mean, remember I have seen each one separately but I can't wait to see what they are like together."

"Well, I hope you can live through your disappointment. By the way, I tried on the dresses your mom bought when I got home and have picked out the one I want to wear tomorrow."

"What? That's outrageous!"

"Before you get all crazy on me, why don't you look at them and see which one you want. It may not even be the one I like."

As usual, Rachel was easily distracted and after some drama about the dress decision they were able to get some sleep.

Graduation turned out to be as long as it had actually felt in rehearsal. Well, a little longer even because there are always those parents who feel they are the exception and can scream and hoot for their particular graduate after specifically being asked not to. That is always a great example to set for young people heading out into a world of rules and regulations.

When it was finally over, and Amber met her grandparents outside she was happy and sad and, surprisingly, a little excited by the speeches about the future. This known part of her life was over, and the next step could be anything she could dream. Well, within reason. Community college was safely in her grandparent's budget but still even that first modest step would lead to the rest of her life.

Gram was still clutching her damp wadded hankie and Grampa beamed proudly.

"Our baby girl," Gram said, hugging her.

"What are your plans now, big woman of the world?" Grampa asked.

"I don't know. Maybe go to lunch with James and then come home and hang out for a while. If that is all right?"

"Well," Grampa said, "Gram has made lasagna, homemade bread and beautiful custard pies. She has been chopping and baking all day."

"Oh, my favorites," Amber said.

"So, you think you can come home for lunch? And bring James if you'd like. Even his parents. I'm sure Gram made enough to feed half the neighborhood."

"I'll see what James is doing. But of course, I will be home. Who else would I rather spend my special moments with than you two?"

Gram hugged her again. "Thank you, sweetie."

Grampa fished his phone out of his pocket and began the picture taking. Amber's friends stopped by to pause in their frenzy and more pictures were taken. Finally, James appeared and Amber asked him about coming to dinner at her house.

"Sure. Whatever you want," James said. "My mom and I were just going to go out somewhere, where ever we didn't have to wait an hour to get in."

"Well, now, this is just grand," Grampa said, taking a picture of Amber and James.

"I'll ride over with James," Amber said. "We have to go find James's mother and I want to see Rachel and her parents, so we may be a few minutes behind you."

"Take your time," Grampa said. "You're the star today. We won't start without you."

Amber gave them another hug and turned to leave when Gram told her to invite Rachel's family too. Amber rolled her eyes at James. Yeah, right. That would really send the whole day down the rabbit hole.

Rachel and Eddie were waiting by James's car when James and Amber got there.

"Hey, Amber, we bumped into your grandparents," Rachel said. "They said you were looking for me."

"Yeah, I sort of lost track of you. I just wanted to let you know that I'm... we're going to my grandparent's house for a while and then we can catch up with you two later if you want."

"Why later? Your grandparents invited us over for lasagna. Eddie loves lasagna. Right, Eddie?"

Eddie nodded.

"Great," Amber said. "That's just great."

"I told my parents to go on over and we would wait here for you and James."

"Great," Amber repeated.

"Sure, what are best friends for?" Rachel asked.

"And after we eat we can go to Lisa's house," Eddie said. "I think she's having a real party."

Rachel elbowed Eddie in the ribs and Eddie looked surprised. "What?"

"Well, now, let's get this started then," James said, opening the passenger car door for Amber.

Amber sighed as she got into James's car.

"Well, John... my father, warned me," Amber said, watching Rachel and Eddie fishtail out of the parking lot, "that God moves in mysterious ways. I think this must be one of them. I mean can you even imagine Rachel interrogating my parents... wow, that sounds weird. For the first time in my whole life I just said 'my parents'."

"Well, look at it this way," James said, "at least Rachel will keep all the attention off of you."

"Yeah, maybe Rachel can be an asset after all. Who would have dreamed?"

Miriam was resting in Grampa's recliner when the four graduates came in. Miriam stood up and came toward them. "Thank you for coming," Miriam said, smiling hopefully at Amber.

"This is my home," Amber replied.

Miriam nodded. "Yes. Still, I know this is not easy for you, so I want you to know I appreciate it."

Amber ignored that and said. "Miriam, this is James and Rachel and Eddie."

The three nodded at Miriam and Amber moved past them to go to the kitchen. Gram and Rachel's mother were busily counting out plates and silverware when Amber came in.

"There are too many people for the dining room table, so I have John and your Grampa getting the folding table and chairs from the garage. I just should have anticipated this and been ready."

"Seriously, Gram, as long as it's your food no one will care where they sit."

"Oh, you are so sweet." Gram said, and then shooed Amber out of the kitchen.

Amber went back into the living room to see Rachel and Miriam sitting together on the sofa.

"I know Amber would never admit it," Rachel was saying, "but, as her best friend, I know she is wondering about, you know, how you are doing? Are you going to find a doctor here?"

Miriam smiled up at Amber as she came into the room. "How nice of Amber to worry about my health. Just tell her I've put it all in God's hands now."

"Seriously?" Rachel squeaked sitting back from Miriam. "Don't you think you should at least try to do something medically before, you know, you just turn it over to God."

"Let's just say, Rachel, that its time I stopped calling the shots. It seems, in trying to figure things out on my own, I have made a terrible mess of everything."

"Wow," Rachel said. Then she thought and asked. "But aren't you a little worried that... you know, that God may not be exactly happy with you either?"

"Oh, I'm certain He is not. But all I can do now is show Him that I am trying to make it right by the people I have hurt. I must do that before I die." Miriam looked up at Amber, her eyes misty.

Amber turned away and went to her sister who was sitting alone on the bay window sill. "Are you okay?" Amber asked her.

"Why can't you just forgive her? Why do you have to be so selfish?"

Amber sat down next to Grace. "Have you forgiven her?"

"For what?"

"For knowing you had a sister, and grandparents, so close and never telling you?"

Grace looked out the window.

"Look," Amber said, "this is going to take time to figure it all out. Let's not, you and I, be angry with each other."

Grace looked back at Amber. Her chin trembled. "My mother is going to die. That's all I care about."

Amber glanced over at their mother luring Rachel into her web. How could Amber ever be expected to forgive this woman who would choose to hurt both of her daughters? What if there was a chance the cancer could be stopped? What if the suffering Grace was going through wasn't even necessary?

"Don't give up hope," Amber said.

"I'm praying for her," Grace said. "But sometimes God has other plans."

"Look," Amber said, "here is Grampa and your dad with the folding table. How about you and I get the table cloths and set the tables for Gram?"

Grace nodded and slid off the windowsill.

"And," Amber continued, "keep praying. Maybe God will surprise you."

Grace nodded and smiled a little.

The four graduates survived the dinner and went on to Lisa's house for the real party. It wasn't until Rachel and Amber were in bed with the light out that Rachel said anything about Miriam.

"You know your mother told me the doctor wants to do surgery. Wants to cut off the part of her pancreas that has the tumor on it."

"You don't say."

"But," Rachel went on, "I guess she doesn't want the surgery. That's crazy, right? To not even try."

"I guess it's her life. She is the only one who can decide that."

"Well, maybe someone should try to reason with her." Rachel said. "Try to talk her into at least trying."

"Didn't you?"

"Oh, yeah, of course. I told her I thought she should try it. But she just looked real sad and said that maybe it was best if she just gave up. She said she had caused everyone a lot of pain and it may be best if she just wasn't around to cause more."

"Well, that is very generous of her."

Rachel sat up and turned the bedside lamp on. "Seriously, that's all you can say?"

"Who am I to argue with her? She never cared about how I felt about anything anyway."

"Oh, stop it. You may be exactly the one person who can talk her into it. If you show her you forgive her and want her to live, then maybe that will make the difference. Maybe you can talk her into trying."

"But I don't forgive her."

"Fine. But can't you pretend if it will save her life?"

"Did she put you up to this? To talk me into begging her to try and save her own life?"

"No. No one puts me up to anything. I just thought, when I saw how sorry she is about leaving you behind all these years, that she would now want to please you and so you could use that to get her to have the surgery."

"You're very clever."

"I know."

Rachel waited but Amber just closed her eyes and pretended sleep.

"Well," Rachel said, "okay, she did ask me to plead with you to spend some time with her before. . . before she dies."

Amber had decided at the dinner table, because of Grace, and because John had asked her, that she would talk to Miriam. Amber really doubted that she could be convincing in her plea when her heart definitely wasn't in it, but at least she would get that obligation behind her.

"You know, Rachel, I think you have just talked me into doing it."

"Great. I can't wait to tell Miriam."

"When do you think I should talk to her?"

"Well," Rachel said, lying back down and shutting off the light, "give me a chance to set it up and I'll let you know."

"I shall await your word."

Word came the next afternoon. Amber was helping Rachel's mother clean out the garage so it could be scrubbed down and repainted when Rachel appeared and told Amber that Miriam was waiting in Gram's back yard.

"She is all set up in a lounge chair in the sun," Rachel reported.

"If she is that weak maybe we should wait," Amber said.

"No. No. She is ready and thankful to me for helping this along."

"Helping what along?" Rachel's mother asked, brushing a loose curl out of her face.

"Oh, I just talked Amber into reasoning with her mother about having surgery to try and save her life."

"If Miriam can be saved then why is hospice involved?" Rachel's mother asked.

"Oh, she was just meeting with them to get set up for when she would really need them. She gave them her doctor's information and stuff like that."

"Well," Rachel's mother said, "you certainly are well informed."

"Someone has to be. Amber would piddle around being mad until it was too late to save her own mother if I hadn't gotten involved."

"How awesome," Amber said, "that if she lives it will be all because of you, Rachel."

"You know, that is true. I have tried to stay positive about all of this.

And, remember, Alfred said that positive things happen when we project positivity."

"Alfred?" Rachel's mother asked.

"Oh, you wouldn't understand," Rachel said. "Now get on over there, Amber. She is waiting."

Miriam clicked off her cell phone when she saw Amber approaching. She smiled and laid her phone on the small table by her lounge.

Amber sat across from her mother.

"Thanks, I know this is not easy for you."

"First," Amber said, "stop thanking me."

Miriam looked wounded. "Okay."

"John told me," Amber began, "that your doctor advised surgery and you refused."

"It's hard to fight against something you feel you deserve."

"I'm not going to debate that." Amber said. "But, it's not very smart or courageous to just accept defeat when it may be fixable."

"Like your feelings about me?" Miriam asked.

"No," Amber said, not allowing Miriam to redirect the conversation. "Like your death. No matter what is between you and me, you do have four people who will be heartbroken if you let yourself die. Don't you have any sympathy for them?"

"Oh, they will all go on no matter what happens to me. Trust me, I am not that irreplaceable."

Amber had no patience for Miriam's melodrama. "What exactly do you want from me? Really, what do you want me to say?"

"I'd just like to find a way to at least be friends before I go. That's all. I just want to know you and show you that I'm not evil. I'm just …"

"Selfish?"

"I was going to say sorry. I'm just sorry that things turned out the way they have. I have always planned that we would be together again someday. I have dreamed about it every day since I left you. Please, if you don't believe anything else I say, please believe that I never thought we would be apart this long. It just happened. Time just kept slipping by. And now, it seems," Miriam said, her eyes pleading with Amber, "our time is running out."

"How long did your doctor give you to make up your mind about the surgery?"

"What do you mean?"

"Is there a point that it would be too late, the cancer too big, to expect a recovery?"

"I don't know what you think you know about pancreatic cancer, but it is very serious. Nearly always fatal."

"I don't know anything about it. But John seems to think that there is a chance it can be cured if you choose to have the surgery."

Miriam fluttered her hand. "Oh, John hears what he wants to hear. The doctor never promised us hope of a cure."

"Okay. Subject closed. What next? What do you want from me so I can let everyone know that I have tried, and you have convinced me that it would be hopeless, so we can all get on to the next step."

"You do hate me, don't you?"

"Actually, I have never thought of it as hate. I guess because when I stopped thinking about you, stopped looking for you, I was probably too young to understand why I should hate you. I just knew that you chose to leave me behind like some unwanted puppy that you knew someone else would feed and look after."

Miriam was silent. Just sitting there in the lounge chair studying Amber. Amber stiffened her back and stared back.

"You have failed as a mother to me," Amber finally said. "Try to grow up and be a mother to Grace. Don't abandon her like you did me. If there is a chance surgery will cure you, then have it. Have it for Grace so she won't wonder someday why you didn't even try to stay in her life."

Miriam covered her mouth to stifle her sob as Amber stood up to leave.

Miriam looked away from her and Amber turned and went into the house.

Gram and Grampa jumped back from the window when she entered the kitchen.

"I love you two. Do you know that?" Amber said, standing there in front of them.

"Of course, dear," Gram said. "We love you, too."

"I know things didn't look very good out there, but if there is any hope of her having the surgery, I think she is considering it now."

"Really?" Gram looked doubtful.

"Just help me understand," Amber said, "how she got to be so selfish."

"Now, dear," Gram said.

"I'm sorry, really. But I never asked you about her because I knew it would hurt you to talk about her and how she had left us. But now she is back, and I really want to know if she has always been like this."

"Like what exactly?" Gram asked.

"Like she will use anyone to get her own way. Like she pretends to be so innocent when she is conniving to get her own way all the time. I seriously don't know how the four of you can love her at all."

"Maybe you are just seeing her through your disappointment. Miriam isn't bad. She was, we admit, probably spoiled as a child. We did try to give her whatever she wanted. She was our only child. We loved her. But she is a woman now. She is facing something very difficult and we can't judge her actions right now."

"Maybe now, when she has so much at stake, is exactly when she should be showing her true colors. If she isn't selfish, if she isn't a childish brat, then now is when she should stand up and be a woman and a mother."

Just as Amber finished her tirade, Miriam opened the door and came in.

"Oh dear," Gram said.

"She is right, Mom," Miriam said. "This isn't exactly how I expected our conversation to go, but Amber is right. I will stop saying I'm sorry for my mistakes and start fixing them. I am going home. Grace and I will go back today. I will call my doctor and see what he has to say about the surgery."

"That is wonderful," Gram said. "Well, not that you are leaving, of course, but that you have decided to go through with the surgery and treatments."

"There can never be any promises with this type of cancer," Miriam cautioned.

"Still," Gram said, "we can hope."

"Yes, Mom, we can hope. And pray."

Miriam glanced at Amber and then passed by her calling out to Grace. Amber scowled, how could a glance feel like a slap? But it did.

"This is good news," Gram said. "Miriam is back and there is hope."

"Well," Grampa said, ever the optimist, "you can go get your stuff and come home now."

Amber nodded.

"Need any help?" Grampa asked.

"No. No. I can manage," Amber said. "I can handle whatever I have to."

Rachel flopped on the bed as Amber placed her clothes in her duffle bag and zipped it up.

"I was just getting used to your snoring and cold feet," Rachel said.

Amber dropped the duffle bag on the floor and sat down on the edge of the bed. "Thanks for letting me stay. It helped."

'Wow, what a ride this has been. We will never forget our graduation that's for sure. Not only are we headed for college, well, I am, you get to stay home and go to community college, but we are both moving on, and on top of that, you have finally found your family. Seriously, the high drama!"

"Glad you enjoyed it."

"It's not a secret that I have always had to be the positive force in this friendship," Rachel said.

"Yeah, it must have been a real struggle to remain positive when you always got exactly what you wanted."

"Hey, I deserve everything I get."

Amber smiled at her friend. "In my next life, I want to be you."

"Ah ha! I knew it. You do believe in reincarnation."

Amber sighed. "I don't exactly know what I believe in to be honest."

"Like what? What do you mean?"

"You and I," Amber said, "we have always been searching for something to believe in. Some mystical magical something that we could believe explained the world and . . .us. But, seriously, nothing we ever explored really made sense."

"Oh, it all makes sense to me."

"Really? Which crazy idea do you think makes sense?"

"Well, not just one. All of the things we have tried make up some of the whole."

"That's stupid."

"No really. They are all connected. The heavens, the underworld, the ghosts and sorcerers. Even witchcraft and fortunetellers all are connected. The same cosmic force runs through them all and through us. Connecting us all as one."

"Seriously," Amber said, "do you ever even listen to yourself?"

"Unless you have a better explanation, I am sticking to mine."

"Maybe," Amber said. "Maybe there is a better one."

Rachel sat up. "I'm listening."

Amber shrugged. "I don't know. I was just thinking out loud. Never mind."

"No. No. If you know of something we haven't looked at then I want to know what it is."

Amber stood up and picked up her duffle bag. "I'll get back with you about it," she said.

"And until you do, I'm sticking with this new direction that Alfred is taking me. The more I read the more I love it."

"Well, be careful. That one girl on his Facebook page said it lead her to God."

"Oh, who knows what she meant by that?"

"Not me," Amber said. "At least not yet."

Gram, Grampa and Amber sat at the dinner table. Amber had the feeling all evening that they wanted to tell her something, but they weren't sure how. Miriam and Grace had been gone three days now and though the atmosphere felt shadowed and foreign somehow, Amber was certain that in time they would be able to slip back into their old patterns.

"Chicken potpie," Grampa said, scraping the last of the chicken gravy off his plate. "No one makes it better than your grandmother. Right, Amber?"

Grampa was never good at small talk. That was probably the fourth time he had complimented Gram on her chicken potpie. And each time he had boomed out chicken potpie like Amber and Gram weren't aware of what they were eating.

"Please," Amber finally said, "just say it. Just open the door and let the elephant out."

Grampa pretended to look like he was surprised. Like he didn't have a clue what Amber could mean. But Gram laid her crumpled napkin on the table and looked over at Amber.

"Your mother is having her surgery tomorrow," Gram said.

"Great. Why should that be so hard to say?"

"Well, dear, she has asked that. . . that just Grampa and I go to the hospital."

Amber shrugged.

"We just didn't want to hurt your feelings," Gram said.

Amber sat back in her chair. "I'm glad actually. I wasn't sure how to get out of going to the hospital without hurting yours and Grampa's feelings.

Now I don't have to worry about that. Miriam has taken the awkwardness out of the whole situation. She doesn't want me there and I don't want to be there. Everyone is happy. Great."

"It's not great," Gram said. "This should be a time when families come together."

"Well," Amber said, sliding her chair back, "don't surrender your hope. If she defeats the cancer, then there is always time for our family to come together. How about that? And in the meantime, everyone knows exactly where they stand."

"She just thinks you hate her. She is trying to let you out of. . ." Gram's words trailed off.

"I appreciate that. Really, I do. And please don't you and Grampa worry about it. I hope the surgery is successful and that she doesn't lose all her hair in chemo and all that stuff. Really. I wish them all the best."

"Amber, sweetie," Gram said. "Don't be like that."

"Like what?"

"Pretending you don't care. Pretending you are so tough."

"Gram, I am no different than I was before they all showed up. My life is the same. I have graduated. I have a job. I am going to college in a couple months. It's all good. Everything in my life is exactly as it was going to be before they came. I haven't lost anything that I had. It's all good."

Gram glanced helplessly at Grampa. Grampa looked down at his empty plate.

Amber walked over to her grandmother and laid her hand on Gram's shoulder. "Go tomorrow. I'm working until close so don't worry about getting back for me. Be there, for the first time in eighteen years, with your daughter when she needs you. I'm fine."

Gram patted Amber's hand and nodded.

"Now you two," Amber said, "scoot and let me clean the kitchen. You have dawdled so long trying to get up the courage to tell me that now you are going to miss your favorite show."

Grampa glanced at the clock and stood up to leave.

"You go," Gram said to Grampa. "I don't feel like watching TV."

So, Grampa left the kitchen and Amber and Gram moved silently clearing the dishes, loading the dishwasher, wiping the table and stove. When they had finished Gram asked Amber to come out on the porch and sit in the swing with her for a while.

Gram reached over and took Amber's hand as they swung back and forth. "Selfishly, I wouldn't change a thing about raising you. I know it wasn't right for you to grow up without your mother, but I haven't for one moment wished for you to be anywhere else but with us."

Amber smiled in the dim night air. "I couldn't have been better taken care of. Please never worry about that."

"I know you and your mother will need some time but what about your father? How did it go the night you were with him?"

"He's okay. But I can't see anything really happening with us. I mean his loyalties are understandably with his family. You know?"

"You are his family. You are as much his daughter as Grace is."

Amber sighed. "Whatever. All I'm saying is that I don't think he wants me out of his life like... well, all I'm saying is that it is too late to try and make any fatherly bond with me."

"Nonsense. Your father is your father and he is very hurt and disappointed in missing your first eighteen years. He hopes you want a chance to get to know him as much as he wants to know you."

"Okay," Amber said.

"Really he asked me all about you. He wanted to know everything he missed."

"Oh, good grief, tell me that you didn't spill everything?" Amber said in mock dismay.

Gram chuckled. "The things I told him made him smile with tears in his eyes."

"You have that way with people, Gram. We all want to cry when you tell us things."

"Amber, be good."

"Okay. Okay." Amber said. Then she grew serious. "What about him being a minister?"

"What do you mean?"

"I don't know anything about God really. I don't even know what to ask John if I wanted to talk to him about it. It seems like I should find out something if we are ever going to be able to talk."

"Yes. Yes," Gram said. "I'm afraid we did let you down there. I just never grew up in a church and so I guess we neglected to think of that with you."

"Hey, no regrets. As you just said, it's never too late for some things. I can figure it out."

"You know," Gram said, "my friend Sadie is very religious. We can talk to her and see how to get us up to speed."

"We?"

"Of course, no fool like an old fool so I'd better get to work so I don't end up an old fool."

Amber laughed and hugged her grandmother. "Poor Grace, she doesn't even know what she has missed not knowing you all her life."

James was waiting outside the grocery store when Amber came out at nine o'clock. Amber smiled and walked over to his car.

"Well, this is a nice surprise," she said.

"Just hadn't seen you for a while and I was wondering how things were going."

"Same old fun."

James nodded. "Okay. You hungry or anything?"

"Not really but we both know I never have to be hungry to want a hot fudge sundae."

"Done," he said and opened his passenger door for her.

"I'll meet you there. That way my car is half way home and we don't have to come back for it."

James shut his car door. "Always the practical one, Amber."

"Hey, I have a wild and crazy boyfriend. How much more chaos can a girl stand?"

"You're right," he said, trying to look cocky. "Besides, if I had to waste the extra gas to drive back for your car I probably wouldn't be able to afford whipped cream on your sundae."

"Life is full of tough choices and sacrifices," Amber said, then got in behind the steering wheel. Amber started her car and backed out of her parking spot. She smiled as she saw James waiting for her to follow him. Just like he thought she didn't know how to get to Shirleys. There was a commercial on the radio and then the Christian station started playing a song. This music was all new to her so she didn't know what it was, but it was not actual choir music, more like soft rock, so she would try to like it. Amber had searched for a radio preacher to listen to on her way to work but the only one she found was just exhausting. He talked in just words, words that didn't reach her, monotone words that made her change the channel. *We must love our Lord Jesus Christ. Must commit our life and soul to him now! There is no other way to our Father in heaven, my friends. No other way to salvation!* She couldn't imagine her father talking to his congregation like that. She actually wished she could find her father on the radio and hear what kind of stuff he would say about faith and God and all that before she saw him again. If she ever saw him again.

Amber turned onto Baker Street as the song changed to one the DJ said was titled, *You Raise Me Up*. She frowned as she listened to the lyrics. Her eyes actually misted from the sudden ache it touched inside her. She turned the radio up as she followed James into the parking lot of Shirleys. James got out of his car and waited for her by the door, but she couldn't move until the song was over. She saw him start toward her car, so she held her hand up to stop him. She didn't know how this song could reach her so deeply but she didn't want to move until it had finished. And then, when it had ended, she quickly turned off the radio. She didn't want to hear anything else. She just wanted to feel what it had done to her. *I am strong when I am on your shoulders. You raise me up to more than I can be.* What did that really mean? She had to find a way to hear it again.

James started toward her car now, so she blinked her eyes to clear them and got out.

"You okay?"

Amber shrugged. No, she wasn't, not really, but how could she ever explain why when she didn't even understand what had just happened to her. "I just wanted to finish listening to something on the radio."

"Oh. Okay. Well, let's get in there. We have forty minutes before they close and it looks pretty busy tonight."

Shirleys was busy every night at this time. The owners were smart to stay open an hour later than most of the other businesses in town because when the young waiters and waitresses and retail people got out of work they were always hungry for food and fellowship.

James found a booth in the back corner and they slid in opposite each other.

James smiled at her. "Hard day?" he asked.

"Miriam had surgery today."

"That's good. Right?"

"Yes. I suppose. If they can get all the cancer cells."

"Right."

The waitress came over and got their order.

"Why didn't you take the day off and be there?" he asked.

"Two reasons. She didn't want me there and I didn't want to be there."

"Wow. Really?"

"Gram and Grampa went over. Gram texted me that the doctor felt optimistic. The tumor was on the outside, so they didn't have to take much of the pancreas."

"So, now what?"

"Chemo and radiation, I'm told."

"No, Amber, I meant what about the two of you?"

"I don't know. The more I know her, the more I dislike her. I'm sure she feels the same."

"Hey, here's a new saying for you," James said, *"We are all broken... that's how the light gets in."*

"Who said that?"

"Hemingway. At least that is what it said on the paper Mom had taped above the sink."

"That's a good one," Amber said. "But I'm not sure there is a light that can fix my mother and me."

The waitress appeared with the hot fudge sundae and James's hamburger.

"I like your mom," Amber said, lifting her spoon to scoop up the cherry on the top of her sundae.

"Yeah," James said and then sighed.

"But?" Amber asked, knowing there was something more he wanted to say.

"It's just that it's so hard to love someone so much when you can't help them. There is nothing I can do to fix her life. And she deserves it to be fixed."

Amber nodded. "It was a lot easier on us before we decided to talk about our parents."

"I know. I thought it was the parents who were supposed to worry about their kids."

"Messed up world," Amber said, and they moved on to talking about easier things.

Amber lay awake in the darkness. She was glad she supposed, no, no, of course she was glad that Miriam's surgery had gone well. But, in all honesty, she was a little miffed that Miriam had made such drama about it. Why hadn't she just had the surgery to find out if they had gotten all the cancer before she came back into everyone's life all weak and pitiful and declaring she was going to make things right before she died? Miriam had probably never believed that she was actually going to die. Amber could be easily convinced that Miriam had just used this as an excuse to get the lie out in the open and still have everyone forgive her because she was so ill. That would be the ultimate self-centered act of self-centeredness!

There was a light knock on Amber's bedroom door and Gram opened it a crack.

"You still awake?"

Amber sat up. "Yes."

Gram left the door open so that only the light from the hall illuminated the room. Gram sat on the side of Amber's bed. "Well, I was a part of something very moving today."

"Pray tell, what was it?" Amber said, playing along with Gram's story.

"Exactly, Amber, it was prayer. Before Miriam went into surgery John had us all stand around her bed, holding hands, and he said a prayer. Not just words. He didn't recite anything. It was like he was actually talking to God and he believed God was listening."

Amber was quiet.

"And then he paused, and Miriam asked God for His forgiveness of her sins and pleaded for a chance to live," Gram said. "And then we all said Amen and I, somehow, felt more hopeful."

"It sounds very moving," Amber said because she didn't know what else to say to something like this.

"Oh, it was. It was. I mean it didn't feel like just going through the motions in a last desperate attempt to save Miriam. John was so sincere it brought tears to my eyes."

Amber nodded. She wished she could have been a shadow in the corner to see that for herself.

"Maybe we have been missing something," Gram said. "So tonight, instead of watching TV with Grampa, I sat out on the porch and read the Bible."

"And?"

"Well, dear, I'm afraid we are going to have to get some help. Everything was okay for the first couple parts. Genesis, I knew about. The next part was okay but then I got lost."

"Maybe we can read it together."

"That would be nice."

They sat quietly together thinking about what Gram had witnessed and then Amber remembered.

"You know, Gram, something happened to me today, too. I heard a song tonight that I can't stop thinking about. I looked up the lyrics on line when I got home. It was like just what I needed to hear but I didn't know I needed it."

"Did you write the lyrics down? Can you read them to me?"

Amber nodded and reached for her notebook on her nightstand and opened it. "When I am down and oh my soul so weary. When troubles come, and my heart burdened be. Then I am still and wait here in the silence until you come and sit a while with me."

"Oh, that is lovely," Gram said.

"But there is more. This is the part that really got me. 'You raise me up so I can stand on mountains. You raise me up to walk on stormy seas. I am strong when I am on your shoulders. You raise me up to more than I can be."

Gram sat back from her listening and sighed.

"I know," Amber said. "It just gave me hope when I was feeling... I don't know, maybe just sad and lonely. I mean I don't want to be petty and melodramatic but not going to the hospital with all of you today really bothered me. It was like one more thing I was missing out on in being part of a family. Don't get me wrong, I did not actually want to be there, but I felt somehow alone all day because I wasn't there. That is silly, I know."

"Nonsense. It makes perfect sense. Our heart and head don't always agree. It will take time to get them to come together. But you are working on that."

"Well, trying to understand John's faith doesn't mean I will ever be able to understand his love for Miriam. But, if I can just get the faith part maybe that will be enough."

"From what I suspect, when you get the faith part the understanding and forgiving parts will follow."

Amber fell back against her pillow. "Remember when you would sit on the side of my bed because I had a bad dream, or I thought I was wronged because some other kid didn't pick me in a game? Don't you wish life could still be that easy. What happened to us, Gram?"

"Good stuff. It's all good stuff. You'll see."

Rachel came in and flopped down on Amber's sofa. She dropped her book bag on the floor beside her. "I only have a few minutes. I'm meeting Alfred at the coffee shop."

"Then I'm greatly honored to have these few minutes with you," Amber said sitting on the love seat opposite Rachel.

"Well, I've told Alfred about you, about us, and how we are always trying to find some answers to the universe."

"Actually, I'm not shooting that broad. I'd like to find the answers to my personal space."

"Whatever. Anyway, Alfred said you could come with me to meet him. He meets a few times a week at the coffee shop with a small group of... well, he said some of them are pagans actually."

"Pagans?"

"Yeah, you and I have so much to learn. Pagans, because I've researched this, believe in many gods. I guess you get to pick which one you want depending on what you are searching for."

"Seriously, have you gone that far off your rocker?"

"Hey, Amber, you don't know anything about what I'm learning so don't be so quick to judge."

"Just because someone made up something doesn't make it true."

"Well," Rachel huffed, "Occult and Paganism is not anything new. It has been around for centuries."

"So."

"So, what?"

"So," Amber continued, "just because there have been gullible groupies for centuries does not prove there is truth in their teachings and rituals."

"I don't get you," Rachel said, sitting up to look into Amber's face. "You used to be interested in all of this with me."

"We were kids, Rachel. It was all in fun. It felt exotic and a little dangerous, but we never believed that spirits actually moved the Ouija Board, or that the omens we worried about ever produced any proof that they were warning us about anything horrible that really happened."

"Well," Rachel said, standing up and snatching up her book bag. "I'm sorry I stopped by. I find Alfred and his friends very interesting."

"I'm sure they are but I just don't want you to get swept up in something that ends up hurting you."

"Knowledge is never harmful."

"Books are written by people. Books are not necessarily truth. So, all I'm saying is to proceed with caution."

"Well, I would rather find the wrong answer than never find any answer which is just how you're probably going to end up."

"Look," Amber said, standing up, too, "did you ever consider looking into going to church? I hear people have found answers there."

"Actually, I have not. My Aunt Peggy is a slave to her church and she has dragged her kids into it, too. And, trust me, you do not want to be like her. She is so pious and self-righteous."

"Because church made her that way or is she just like that?"

"Who knows," Rachel snapped.

"So, tell me, do you know any other pious and self-righteous people who do not go to church? Like maybe Tammy Sims?"

"Oh her! She is just conceited, and no one likes her anyway."

"Still, church didn't make her that way."

"Well…well," Rachel stammered.

"Well," Amber continued for her, "sometimes pious, self-righteous people go to church and sometimes they don't. Sometimes very nice and humble people go to church and sometimes they don't."

"Well, everyone knows that church goers are judgmental."

"So, you personally know this "*Everyone*" that seems to know what every single person that attends church is truly like and yet couldn't possibly have met every single person that attends church. Stereotypes usually aren't a true picture. In fact, I thought you were always against stereotypes because you said they were made up by people to put down those they don't like or understand."

"Well, some are."

"And some people just use stereotypes to make themselves comfortable in justifying their choices."

"What do you mean?"

"Maybe that you don't want to go to church because your aunt does and she is judgmental. So therefore, if everyone in church is like your aunt then you are justified in never giving it a try."

"Why are you so suddenly all about church? Are you just trying to please your newly discovered father?"

"Actually, I do want to understand why John chose God as his life's work. I mean, going to church is one thing but choosing it as your only and forever job?"

"Well," Rachel said, heading back toward the front door, "you go check out the church and I'll go check out all of Alfred's spiritual discoveries and we will talk again."

"That's what I like about you." Amber said, following her. "There is no path you fear to tread."

The grocery store doors swished closed behind Amber at eleven-fifteen a.m. She much preferred the evening shift to the morning one but now that school was over she was put on full time and that included mornings. The evening shift was nice because she had been doing it for a couple years and had really gotten used to the regulars that stopped on their home from work and were happy to chat a moment. And, strangely, she even liked the habitually late ones who flew in just before the doors were locked and kept apologizing even though the next day they would keep one cashier waiting to close out her register past nine o'clock.

Amber headed to the back of the parking lot where employees were required to park when she paused and then continued a little slower. John was, again, waiting by her car.

Amber smiled and nodded.

"We missed you yesterday," John said.

"I was asked not to come."

"I know. And that is why I'm here. Miriam asked me to come over and apologize. She was afraid of the surgery and, of course she was emotional and, I guess, she just wasn't thinking clearly when she told your grandmother that."

"Please don't apologize for her. If you want to believe that she is sorry then fine, but please don't try to convince me of that. It isn't fair to either of us that she even asked you to come and apologize to me for her."

"First, I do believe that she regrets her words. And second, I look forward to any excuse to come and talk with you. I know it is going to be all uphill for me to reach you, but I must warn you, I am a persistent climber."

Amber shrugged. "Fine. Okay. Just tell Miriam not to worry about it. Tell her I really don't need her apology."

John frowned a little at that and then let it go. "Actually, I also wanted to invite you to come to my church Sunday. If you're free and would like to."

Amber rubbed at the back of her neck. "I don't know."

"Is your hesitation about me or the church?"

"Actually, I've been thinking about going to church. But I haven't figured out where I want to go just yet."

"Then it's me?"

"No," Amber said, frowning. "It's not you. I've actually been thinking… about what your sermons would be like. But, I guess my hesitation is just all the other things about going to your town and your church. That's your life with… them."

"Them? You mean your mother and sister?"

"Yes."

"And not you?"

"Yes."

"Well, if you allow us to, we can make it our life with you, too."

Amber fished her keys out of her pocket. "Thanks. Maybe someday."

"I'm working on a sermon specifically inspired by you."

Amber was intrigued and, despite herself, she relented. "If I come, please don't mention me or notice me. Just let me be there like anyone else."

"Sort of sneaking in the back and getting out quick before you're noticed?"

"Exactly."

John nodded. "Okay. Deal. But then you must promise that you will tell me what you thought of my sermon."

"Will a text do?"

"I will accept whatever is comfortable for you. Only please be honest. And if you have questions, I'd love to be the one to help you find answers. You could say that's in my job description."

"What time Sunday?"

"I do three services. Eight, nine-thirty and eleven. However, all the same sermon so I'd recommend you come to the early service so if you really like it, well, then you can listen to me two more times." He winked and smiled. "I actually get really good at it by the third sermon. So, if you'd rather sleep in, then just come at eleven and catch my best act."

Amber smiled back. "Thanks for coming all the way over here."

"I'd go anywhere. Just know that."

Amber unlocked her car and opened her door. Then she turned back to him. "I'm just wondering, when did you know Miriam asked me not to come?"

"When everyone was in the hospital room except you. I asked your grandmother where you were, and I believe she was embarrassed to tell me what your mother had said. I thought of calling you, but I didn't want to bring you into a situation that would be uncomfortable for you until I had time to talk to Miriam."

"Just so you know, I had already decided that I didn't want to be there." John nodded.

"No offense to you, but life was just easier when I didn't know about all of you."

"If you can give me the chance," John said, "I will do everything in my power to change that."

And that was it. John, her father actually, had driven all the way over just to spend a few minutes in the parking lot talking with her. How incredible was that? Miriam could do whatever she wanted now but she couldn't erase the fact that Amber not only had a father, but she finally knew who he was. The fact that he was a minister felt different than if he had been, say, a cop or construction worker or a teacher. John was a man of God. How do you ever just call him Dad?

Sadie sat on her overstuffed flowered sofa and smiled at Gram and Amber. Sadie was a spinster, though that did not immediately account for her strong faith, it did make it easier to understand that a woman who never filled her life and heart with a husband and children may have had ample time to spend studying the bible and loving her God. Amber remembered the many nights Gram would finish cleaning up their dinner dishes after she had been in the school cafeteria all day. Gram would make a cup of herbal tea and sink down in a chair at the kitchen table. She would sigh and push off her thick-soled shoes and rub her tired feet together. Sadie on the other hand, had never worked in the real world. She was the only child of a doctor and so had inherited her house and, apparently, enough investment money to keep her comfortable.

"So," Sadie said, looking pleased that they were there, "what can I help you with? What do you want to know?"

"We don't really know," Amber said.

"Everything," Gram said. "We need to know everything."

Sadie laughed. Her laugh was easy and delicate. "That is a lot for me to accomplish in an hour or two."

"What we mean," Amber said, "is that we don't really know what we don't know. Like, I've been wondering what the difference is between God and Jesus. I mean I think of God as this all powerful, all knowing spirit being and Jesus was half God and yet a man. Jesus walked the earth. And yet Jesus is...I guess, as important as God. Right?"

Sadie sat back in her chair and thought for a moment. "Let me try to explain. I believe there is one Father and one mediator between the Father and man. That mediator is Jesus. We could say that the Father is the will and Jesus is the action. Together they are God. Along with the Holy Spirit, of course. Now, God could not be seen by man, so Jesus was sent to be born in human form, with human emotions and a human perspective. He didn't come to judge or punish, Jesus came to save us from the pit of sin we had made of the world. He brought the new covenant, a new agreement, shall we say, between God and man."

"So, Jesus is not God?" Amber asked.

"I know it's difficult to get your mind wrapped around this. So, first we have to struggle to not think in human terms. Jesus was with the Father and the Holy Spirit from the beginning. The three are the trinity that make up God. One way I discovered from my reading to try and understand how they can appear separate and yet be one is to think of them as colors. We all know that the color white contains all the colors of the rainbow. And, we know that the colors of the rainbow are made up of the three primary colors. These primary colors are in the color that is white light. Now these three primary colors can also exist apart from the white light, but white light could not exist apart from these three colors. So, God is the combination of the Father, the Son, and the Holy Spirit."

"That sort of makes sense. But I have to think about it some more," Amber said.

"Yeah," Gram said, "me too."

"So okay," Amber said, "after we have figured out who God is, what's next?"

"I don't know what you mean, dear," Sadie said.

"Well, I'm just not sure what we are expected to do. You know, go to church and read the Bible I suppose. But that just doesn't seem enough."

Sadie nodded. "That could be just going through the motions if you don't look any deeper than that. It is, of course, the best way to begin one's spiritual journey."

"Oh dear," Gram said, "a spiritual journey. I hope it's not a long journey. I may not have much time left."

"Oh, Gram," Amber said, reaching over to pat Gram's hand, "you will live to be a hundred."

"Now, I'm not sure I'd like that," Gram said, as though Amber could be serious.

"Well," Sadie said, "for me it has been a lifetime journey and I'm still not ready to be judged."

"That's the thing," Amber said, leaning forward. "This judgment thing. Once we start this spiritual journey and, say we get lost, say we never really measure up to God's standards... well, does He punish us more harshly for failing than if we had never even started trying?"

"Punish? No. No. God loves us. He is in the love business not the punishment business. I mean if you truly love someone you don't want to punish them. Right? God loves us, He even loves the quitters and the sinners. He is always just waiting and hoping His wandering flock will find their way and all come back to Him of their own free will. And because He loves us, all He really wants is for us to love Him back."

"My goodness," Gram said. "He's been waiting for me all my life and I haven't even known."

"Oh," Sadie said, smiling, "He has been waiting."

"So, how do I find Him?" Gram asked.

"He promises that if you search for Him, you will find Him."

"Have you found Him?" Amber asked.

"I have in my own way. Yes. I would say that I enjoy a personal relationship with our Heavenly Father."

"Personal relationship?" Amber had to ask. "Like a two-way relationship? Like God really knows you personally? So, if you are good and He knows it, He rewards you personally?"

"Well, now," Sadie said, frowning, "if you are only good to be rewarded then, no, He will probably be disappointed in you. He isn't Santa Claus who is loved for what he can give you. He is real. He takes you seriously and He wants you to take Him seriously."

"Tell me," Gram said, "has He talked to you? Is that how you know what He wants?"

"I wish He talked to me. But no, not like you mean. He does communicate through His word though. The Bible is His word and if you read the Bible with an open mind and heart then the Holy Spirit will help you understand what God wants you to know. Well," Sadie paused and chuckled, "and a teaching Bible doesn't hurt when you're first starting to read the Bible."

"Teaching Bible?" Gram asked.

"Yes. The one I have has explanations for the passages at the bottom of each page. There is a lot about the ancient times the Bible talks about that we couldn't possibly understand in today's world. And when Jesus talks in parables, He liked to preach in parables, well, they can get past you if you don't have a little help with them."

"This is a lot," Gram said.

"It is," Sadie said. "But the reward just grows and grows with your effort."

Gram nodded. "You do seem happy enough about it all."

"Indeed. I've had my God moments. And when you discover God moments, when you understand what I've tried so clumsily to explain, then you will look back at your life and see the little miracles God has sprinkled along your path to lead you right where you need to be."

"Have you had little miracles?" Amber asked.

"Well, yes. Yes, I most definitely have. One was the love of my life. Most people don't know about Henry, but he and I were very much in love. Henry lived in Branberry and I rode over with my father to check on him one time. My father was a doctor, Amber. I don't know if your grandmother told you that."

"She did."

Sadie seemed pleased with that. "Back in the day, as us old folks like to say, if the patient couldn't come to the doctor's office, handicapped assistance wasn't always what it is today, then the doctor would have to go to the patient's home when they needed him. Henry was like that. He was what you may call a cripple. His family farmed, and Henry turned over on a tractor and broke all kinds of bones. He was in a wheelchair but his mind and heart, and his good looks I might add, were not crippled. After a couple times of going with my father to check on Henry, well, let's just say that I never let Daddy go out there without me again. I was young. Only seventeen but my heart knew what it liked. And it liked Henry."

"Well, anyway," Sadie continued, "it didn't take long for Henry to realize why I always came with my father. As I said, Henry's brain was not broken.

My father started letting me go out to the farm without him and I had this dream of marrying Henry one day. I know most young girls wouldn't choose a crippled-up man but that's only because they never knew one as good as Henry. I knew if I married him there would never be a day I would regret doing it. But then my dream was shattered. I'll spare you the painful details, but Henry got a blood clot that traveled to his heart and he was gone before I knew it."

The room was silent as they each processed Sadie's story.

"I'm sorry," Amber finally said. "But how is that a miracle?"

"I will admit," Sadie said, "that it took some time for me to find the answer to that. I was as devastated as any young girl could be. But, in time, my father helped me to see the beauty of what had happened."

Amber shook her head, not even seeing a flicker of logic in that.

"Daddy explained that Henry was more broken than I realized. He had survived the accident but the inside of him was never going to be right. In fact, Daddy said Henry's kidneys were slowly shutting down. Aside from the constant pain Henry was in from all the broken bones, he was slowly dying of many other things. So, the blood clot was a blessing because it stopped his heart and ended his suffering, to say nothing of sparing him from the undignified way he could have died from all the other reasons."

"Still," Amber said.

"Right," Sadie went on. "The real miracle, aside from the merciful way he died, was that God allowed him just enough time to know love before he was taken. Henry and I had such sweet moments. Just to think, if I had not gone with my father that day, and I can honestly say that I had never once asked or agreed to go to visit patients with Daddy before, then I would never have met Henry. And he would have died without ever knowing that he could be loved by a true and grateful heart. God gave us both a beautiful gift."

Gram sniffled and rummaged in her purse for a tissue.

"So," Amber said, "your father knew Henry was going to die and he still let you fall in love with him?"

"It was God's will. None of us could have known at first but looking back Daddy and I could see that it was. And you are right, Amber, my Daddy would never knowingly take me where he thought I could be hurt. But when he realized what was happening, the deed was done. He probably thought then, after Henry's death, that I would mature and love again. Only I never could. I just never could love another man. Maybe," Sadie said, sighing and looking now out the window, "maybe I would never have found love anyway. Maybe without Henry I would never have known love at all."

"Oh my," Gram said, trying to blow her nose now in a muted, lady-like manner.

"Oh, I'm sorry," Sadie said, coming back from her distant thoughts. "This was not meant to be a sad story. I find it a beautiful memory and I am grateful I have it."

"I have a lot to learn," Amber said.

"And God will be there helping you," Sadie assured her.

"Well, what do you think, Gram?" Amber asked as she drove them home.

"I think there is not one more crack of a space left in my heart to fill. I have gone from simply worrying about you being all grown up and starting college to now. . . now I don't know what to do with all the new thoughts and worries inside me. I swear I don't have room for one more new thing to happen to us."

"Really," Amber agreed.

"I mean, Miriam is back, that's good. But she has cancer, that's bad. I have another grandchild and a son-in-law that I've just found, that's good. But I've missed so much. That's bad. You are going through so much turmoil that I can't solve for you and now Grampa is starting to show signs of over-doing, those are bad. Then there is God appearing when I hardly have time or energy for Him." Gram sighed. "I fear I'm just too old for all of this."

"Nonsense. You are at your best when you have your basket full of problems to solve."

"That is ridiculous."

"Admit it, boredom has always been your enemy."

"Well, fortunately I have had you and Grampa to keep me from dealing with that."

"So, Gram, what do you think?" Amber asked. "Do you think that Sadie believes that God really orchestrated what happened to her and Henry, or is she just trying to believe that so she can accept how her life turned out?"

"She believes it," Gram said, nodding her head. "I have no doubt that she truly believes everything she told us."

"Do you believe it?" Amber asked.

"It's strange, because I have never had thoughts like this, but yes, yes I do believe that God touched both their lives. How else can you explain why Sadie went to that one appointment with her father and how it ended up being what both Sadie and Henry had needed?"

"I don't know."

"Do you believe her story, Amber?"

"I believe it happened as she said but I'll need time to figure out how I feel about her explanation for it."

"Well," Gram said, "why don't we just stop by the book store on our way home and see if they have one of those teaching Bibles? We can't wait for our own miracle before we start this spiritual journey. I'm not getting any younger."

Amber smiled and put her blinker on to get over a lane and turn onto State Street. Of all the spiritual journeys that she and Rachel had ever pursued, this one felt different. Amber had always believed that whatever game she had played with Rachel, she actually knew that they were not real. She had never really believed in witches and fortunetellers but now, now she wasn't sure how she felt about God. Could there really be a God out there that knew her? Knew her from birth and had been watching over her, waiting for her to stop pitying herself and trust that He had the big picture all planned out for her? Would God really help her if she just looked for Him and asked Him for help?

Rachel knocked once on the door and then walked into Amber's house. "Hello. Hello."

"I'm in the kitchen," Amber called out.

Rachel appeared in the doorway, her book bag bulging and her hair in a tangled bun on top of her head. Rachel had on purple leggings and a long pink sweater. She wore black pointy-toed flat boots that Amber frowned at.

"Where did you find the pixie shoes and what happened to your hair?"

"Actually, the boots are new and very comfortable. And about my hair. . . well, I'm not primping any longer. This is the real me and that is what the world needs to see. My hair is not naturally smooth and shiny so why pretend? Who am I trying to impress?"

"I see," Amber said, putting the top slice of bread on her sandwich. "And does the new you eat regular food, or does she need seeds and compost?"

"I have already eaten, thank you very much."

"Great. Well, how about something to drink?"

"If you have grapefruit juice, that would be fine."

"Sorry, grapefruit juice interferers with my grandparent's medicine."

"Water will do. Without ice."

"As you command," Amber said, smiling at her friend and going to get a glass from the cabinet.

Rachel dropped the book bag onto a kitchen chair and then dropped herself down onto another chair.

Amber set the two glasses of water on the table and sat down opposite Rachel.

"So, what have you found out about church?" Rachel asked.

"Actually," Amber said, "I intend to go to my father's church this Sunday. Then I will report back to you. What about you? What has prompted this pure and natural you? I mean you are not even wearing make-up!"

Rachel reached over and pulled a book from the bag. "Alfred has me reading about Paracelsus. He was one of the world's greatest alchemists as well as being a philosopher and physician. He is revered by the Occult as well."

"Okay," Amber said, and bit her sandwich.

"Here, let me read you something that will help you understand what I need to do. What Paracelsus said is, 'He who wishes to learn Occult Truth must first of all divest himself of all intellectual pride, prejudice, preconceptions and the opinions of others for all these bar the door to the entrance of Truth.'"

"Wow, that is lofty."

Rachel shook her head and rolled her eyes to the ceiling. "You are not even trying."

"What?" Amber said. "You are so full of yourself. Tell me, how are you divesting yourself of your intellectual pride when you are obviously very proud that you are becoming so superior with all this new secret truth knowledge? And don't pretend that you have gotten rid of all your prejudices and preconceptions. Also, not wearing make-up or combing your hair is one thing but, Rachel, when all is said and done I doubt that you have really stopped caring about the opinion of others. I bet you care a lot about Alfred's opinions."

"I never claimed I was where I need to be yet. I'm just beginning. And Alfred explained that I do not have to stop listening to the opinions of others, I merely have to be suspicious of their motives and then evaluate their remarks for the truth."

"Great," Amber said, taking another bite of her sandwich. "So, what exactly are the truths you are evaluating opinions to find?"

"I don't know yet. No one has been specific but when I am worthy I know I will find them."

Amber laid her sandwich down. "What if, when you change everything about yourself, when you think like they want you to think, and sacrifice what they want you to sacrifice, what if you just end up finding their truth is God?"

"God? What? Why are you saying that?"

"Remember that girl on Alfred's Facebook page who said her quest had brought her to God?"

"Yeah. I guess I better ask him what she meant by that. I'm certain God isn't the hidden truth. I mean everyone has heard of God, how could that be the hidden truth?"

Amber shrugged.

"So anyway," Rachel said, deciding to change the subject, "how is it going with your new family?"

"Miriam has had her surgery. No one can say yet if she will be cured or not. But she did ask," Amber said, deciding to brighten Rachel's day with gossip. "Miriam asked Gram to tell me that she didn't want me at the hospital with all the other family. And then she asked my father to come to me and apologize for her."

Rachel nearly spit her water across the table. "That is outrageous! What a slap in the face. Tell me you didn't accept the apology."

"I told him that I did accept it."

"Really? You accepted her apology?"

"Why not? I don't care that she didn't want me there. I didn't want to be there anyway so what do I care if she thought it was her idea. Miriam is not going to use me the way she uses everyone else."

"Well, you know," Rachel said, "she is not at her best right now so maybe you shouldn't judge her yet. Let her get through the cancer scare and then see how she is."

Amber shook her head. "No. No. Now is when she should be the nicest to those around her. I mean if you were dying would you want to leave this earth with everyone hating you?"

"No," Rachel said. "I suppose not."

"I think just because I didn't gratefully rush into her arms when she finally appeared, and I didn't fall apart when she said she was dying, well, I think her true colors showed up then. If any of the others really look at how she has handled this, they would have to see that she is still thinking of only herself."

"You are so harsh."

"Maybe. But that is how you get when the person who is supposed to be your greatest protector has abandoned you for a happy life with her real family. She has probably been worried sick that I would try to track her down some day and now her cancer scare was the perfect opportunity to get the truth out while everyone would have to be sympathetic to her."

"Well, then, now that I know how you feel about your mother..."

"Miriam," Amber corrected her.

"About Miriam," Rachel said, correcting herself. "So, tell me, how do you feel about your father and sister?"

Amber shrugged. "I find that I like my father. Well, aside from the fact that he believes Miriam and forgives her for everything she has done to all of us. I don't understand that."

"I want to find that kind of love," Rachel said, obviously ignoring the blatant evil of Miriam.

"You could love someone who, without remorse, hurt other people?"

"How do you know she isn't remorseful? You have hardly spoken to her?"

"Anyway," Amber said, getting up to clean up her lunch items. "So far I'm afraid that I am not impressed with your new psychic insights."

"I'm just saying, why put yourself through a whole bunch of anger and resentment when you may find out that she isn't so bad. Maybe she just made mistakes that she honestly regrets."

"And maybe you should start combing your hair again."

Rachel got up and followed Amber around the kitchen as she put away the mayonnaise and luncheon meat and wiped the counter and table.

"What about your sister?"

Amber stopped wiping the table. She sighed. "I don't know. Gram was right that none of this is Grace's fault. I understand that and yet . . ."

"Why don't you drive over and just spend some time with her? Just the two of you and see what you feel then."

Amber continued cleaning the table. "I'll think about it."

"I can go with you, if that would be easier."

"Really, Rachel, when would that ever be easier?"

"I could bring my crystals and wrap the three of us in a rosy aura that would protect us from evil thoughts and angry words."

"And would you comb your hair and cover that big pimple on your forehead?"

"What?" Rachel shrieked, and rushed to the hall mirror to examine her forehead. "Oh, you horrid, horrid creep. If there is a god, he will get you for this."

"Sorry," Amber said. "I was just seeing how advanced you were about not caring what others thought of you. You failed miserably. Miserably."

"Well," Rachel said, stomping back into the kitchen. "I came over to share my new knowledge with you and invite you to Alfred's meeting, but I have changed my mind. You are way too uncivilized."

"Do you think going to church will help me?"

"I doubt it."

Amber followed Rachel to the door. "Thanks for stopping by," Amber said.

"Yeah, I've always enjoyed self-inflicted pain."

"I'll be nicer next time."

"Right. And I also believe global warming is real."

"At least we agree on something," Amber called out as Rachel sashayed to her car and left without a backward glance.

Amber and James sat in his car in her driveway trying to decide what to do with a Saturday that they both had off from work.

"You want to go target shooting?" Amber asked, knowing that James often went to the range with his friends. "It's time I learned how to shoot. Not knowing how to use a gun is a lot more dangerous than knowing how to handle it. Didn't someone tell me that? Oh yeah, it was you."

"Sure," James said, reaching down to turn the key.

"But what? Do you want to do something else?"

"No. I guess not."

"Oh, come on, spill it. I know there is something. What?"

James looked out the windshield and then turned to Amber. "Saturday is visitation day at the prison. I feel like I should go see my Dad. I haven't been since I graduated, and, well, he wrote me this letter about his hopes for me. He poured his heart out and I just can't ignore that."

"Wow. Sure. Of course. Maybe we could do something when you get back."

"Well, I was hoping you would come with me. I've told him about you, so I thought . . ."

"Yeah, great. I'd love to come with you if you want me to."

James laughed self-consciously. "I know jail isn't exactly the place you should take a girl on a date."

"It's the right thing to do. I'm glad you want me to meet your dad."

"Truth is, I want him to meet you."

"Oh."

James leaned over and gave Amber a quick kiss.

The ride to the county jail was pleasant. They rode with the windows down and the music up. This was a good thing. Amber was actually happy to be going to meet James's father. She had wondered about him ever since James had confessed that he could forgive this man who had mangled all their lives with his selfish behavior.

Amber looked at James's profile as he drove. Her heart did smile at the sight of that face.

"If you don't mind me asking, why is your father in jail? I don't mean it to be judgmental. I just think I may understand him, and you, better if I know what he keeps doing to get himself back in jail."

"No problem," James said. "My parents got married right out of high school and my dad tried a few jobs then decided to just go into the Army. Then he . . . he got injured and came home after a year. His right arm is pretty useless, and he lost sight in his right eye. He was on a lot of pain medicine and, well, it's a common story I guess, but his spirit was broken and he sank into depression. I was a new baby so my Mom had me, a job, and a broken husband at the age of twenty. I guess my grandparents helped a lot, but eventually they just wanted Mom to leave him. I mean, it's one thing to see someone giving up but another thing to watch them pull your child down with them. I understand why they couldn't watch it any longer and stopped helping us. I guess they thought that Mom would eventually be forced to give up on him and come home. But Mom just couldn't. No one knew the pain my father was in. Not the pain in his body or the pain in his soul. It was more than just his injuries. He had seen stuff. He had lost friends. Mom said she had to hide his boots because he would just set them beside each other and stare at them." James paused and glanced over at Amber. "You've seen the pictures of the fallen soldier's empty boots with their dog tags draped over them?"

"Yes."

"Anyway, bottom line, Dad was addicted to pain meds. So, when the VA would refuse to renew his prescriptions he found someone who could help him with that. He'd be angry that he couldn't get off the pills, but he still wanted them. And so, when Mom didn't have the money for him to get them he'd borrow, shall we say, other people's possessions to get the money."

"I see."

"Really? Can you understand?"

"Yes. I can see now why you are so forgiving of his weakness. He was caught in a trap that he found himself in because he chose to serve his country and then he was just forgotten, just cast aside when he was of no more use or value to them. It's so sad. We see this over and over."

James nodded. "I knew you would be able to see more than just what he has done since he came home so broken."

"Ahh, your mother's kitchen sign that Hemmingway wrote. What was it?"

"We are all broken … that's how the light gets in."

"Right. Your mom is so smart."

"There are those who would disagree with you."

"Like your grandparents?"

"Yeah. I know that still hurts Mom. There is so much she has had to carry."

Amber reached over and laid her hand gently over James's. "And so much you have had to carry. I'm so glad you are sharing this with me."

"And one more thing to share. I'm a junior. Dad goes by Jim, but he insisted I go by James. Guess he agreed that Mom could give him the gift of naming his son after him just as long as I never identified myself as being a copy of him."

"Got it," Amber said.

Amber sat beside James in the courtyard as the prisoners gathered in small groups with their visitors. The sun was broken into dusty streaks as it fell through the mesh canopy covering the picnic tables.

"There he is," James said, standing and waiting for his father to come across the courtyard.

Amber watched this thin man come striding across the cement, his James-smile broad and his blonde hair combed back from his face. The two met and Jim wrapped his left arm around his son in a hug so tight they both grunted from the effort.

"What a surprise. What a great surprise." Jim said, nodding at his son's face.

"Dad, this is Amber," James said, reaching down to touch Amber's arm.

Amber stood up and held out her hand. Jim reached with his left hand to shake hers.

"What a pleasure. Thanks for coming."

They stood awkwardly assessing each other for a moment then all sat down at the picnic table.

"I got your letter, Dad. Thanks."

"Pearls of wisdom from a failure. Don't know how much you should listen to me but I had to try, you know. I owe you so much and I couldn't just let this big moment in your life happen without at least trying to explain how I felt."

"It was good, Dad. Really."

"Well, it's not like I don't have a lot of time to reflect on life and regrets and dreams for my son."

"Mom has to work today or she would have come with us."

Jim nodded and looked away from their faces. "She's a saint. I'll never know what I could have done to ever deserve that woman."

"Mom said you only have four more months and then you could get parole."

"Could is the word, son. I can't blame them for not trusting me again but this time I swear will be different." Jim sighed at his spotted track record and then turned his attention to Amber. "So, you like this big goofy kid?"

Amber shrugged. "I have a soft spot for nice guys."

"Yeah, he is handsome, too. Right? Looks just like his old man."

"Yes," Amber said, knowing they were embarrassing James. "Can't keep my eyes off him."

"Yeah, my good looks and with two good arms and both eyes. He's a winner."

James frowned.

"He is a winner," Amber said. "In fact, I think James would still be a winner even with one arm and one eye."

Jim looked stern. "So, what are you trying to say? That I can't be?"

"Oh no," Amber said. "I apologize if you thought I was inferring that. I certainly have no right to judge what you have been through or how you have had to cope. I was just saying, envying actually, James's way of finding peace with his disappointments."

"Disappointments that his old man has caused him?"

"For crying out loud, Dad!"

"What?" Jim said. "I'm just trying to understand what's going on here."

"All that's going on," James said, "is that I asked Amber to come with me today so I could thank you for your letter. She doesn't care about your handicaps."

"Well, of course not, just look at her. What could she know about handicaps anyway?"

"Actually," Amber said, "none of us should judge what anyone else is going through by the looks of them."

"Well, well, now, aren't you are a frank little one. If I may be bold enough to ask, what exactly are you going through that could be so difficult?"

"Dad!"

Amber stared into Jim's eyes. "It's okay, James. Seeing how your father has let his struggles override his compassion for his family is a real eye opener for me. I'm not the only one who has a selfish parent. They appear to be everywhere."

"Selfish parent? You can't even begin to know what I have suffered through."

"And apparently, you have no idea of what others have suffered through because of your choice to pity yourself rather than put them first. I'm glad I came. I'm sorry for James, but I'm glad I got to see I'm not alone."

"So glad my misery could be of assistance to someone," Jim said.

"Please, you two, this is not how this was supposed to go."

"Well, okay," Jim said, shrugging. "I'm sorry. I'm sorry about a lot of things and you can believe that or not."

"And, I'm sorry. Really, James, I don't know what got into me. I was just sitting here one minute thinking how lucky you were to have both of your parents, your mother who takes care of you every day and a father who thinks about you and writes meaningful, heartfelt letters, but then he tried to make you feel guilty because you are not wounded when you are wounded only in a different way. And, well, I guess my anger about his not seeing that, and about my own parents, just bubbled over. I'm sorry. Really. I apologize to both of you."

"Yeah," Jim said, "that was wrong of me. I'm sorry, James. I'm grateful every day that you haven't turned out like me."

"Dad, you are not a bad person. You just didn't get the help you needed when you needed it most, and it has taken you some time to figure out how to handle that."

"Yeah, I've been trying, as the song goes, to learn to accentuate the positive and eliminate the negative. But, as it turns out, that's a whole lot harder than it sounds."

"Only until you start trying, Dad. Then I hear it may get easier."

"You know, since I wrote that letter telling you how to live your life," Jim said, turning to his son, "I have started taking computer classes. You know, just in case I do get out. It seems that a one armed, one eyed ex-con can still be useful."

"Computer classes, Dad, that's great."

"Yeah, my counselor said that with the Internet I can find a place for myself, a job where maybe I can work from home and not have to squint and hunt and peck in front of anyone else. Also, I found this site on line where wounded veterans can go to get help finding a job that fits their injuries. It's some sort of charity funded site, but hey, I'm the one who got shot up for my country so who am I to be too proud to take help from my countrymen?"

"That's great," James said. "Mom will be thrilled."

"Of course, I'm not out yet so don't go getting all hopeful."

"Dad, I've never stopped being hopeful."

Amber smiled. Light may be sneaking into all their broken places.

James and Amber stayed for a few more minutes. Jim relaxed and joked about prison life. Amber did her best to be amicable. She was still a little prickly over Jim's total lack of understanding or regret for what he had put his family through, but it wasn't her place to project her sensitivity about family wounds on to James's relationship with his father. She shouldn't be so protective of James's feelings when James seemed content to accept whatever his father offered.

"Before we go, Dad, is there anything you need? Anything I can bring you?"

"Yes, there is son," Jim said, grinning now. "You can bring this sharp-tongued young lady with you the next time you come. It's kind of refreshing to be scolded by someone besides my lawyer and the judge."

Sunday morning Amber drove herself to Wakefield. She had thought of inviting Rachel to come to church with her. Amber had no doubt that Rachel would be willing, out of shear curiosity, to come with her, but Amber decided she needed to do this on her own. She didn't want the distraction of thinking of anyone else, wondering if they were okay with being there, wondering what they may think of her father's sermon, wondering if Rachel would want to discuss what Amber was still trying to figure out. No, she had to come alone. She had to sit in the back and just see what it was all about.

Amber chose the nine-thirty sermon. She didn't want to be in the early service in case there weren't as many parishioners to blend in with. She didn't want the eleven o'clock service because she knew her father would be finished and may want her to stay and talk. She felt she could get in and out unnoticed if she was there when there was the confusion of people coming in and leaving at the same time. Good grief, it was so much work just figuring out when she wanted to sneak into the church.

Amber chose the very last row and slid into the seat furthest from the aisle. Which, of course, is exactly where one would look if one were looking for the lone parishioner trying to hide. Amber nodded at the smiles she encountered on her scurry from her car to her seat.

At last, all were seated and her father walked from the back of the church to the front. He wore a dark gray tailored suit and a pale pink shirt. She didn't know what she thought of that. First, she had assumed that all clergy wore robes and second, she didn't picture a religious leader wearing pink. Maybe some shade of serious blue or white, but definitely not pink. He did look good in it, though. Maybe Miriam had chosen his clothes.

Miriam. Amber tried to close her mind to thoughts of Miriam. She knew they would not be kind and this was certainly not the place to come with your black heart exposed. Gram had assured her that Miriam was released from the hospital but definitely was in no condition to be sitting through a church service. Gram had also offered to come with Amber but accepted that Amber needed to do this alone.

Amber sighed as her father, *seriously, this man standing in front of everyone was actually her father,* turned and smiled at his congregation. Amber still had trouble imagining herself with a father. As no one ever knew who her father was, Amber had not even tried to put a face on him or think of him ever appearing in her life. She was not one of those abandoned children who had plotted her whole life to one day search down her parents. In fact, the older she got the less she even wanted her mother to find her. It had all seemed too late to even worry about it until now… now, here was this man, this Godly man, asking her to let him be her father.

"Good morning," John began. "Welcome to church." John spoke for a few moments and then turned it over to the …band? Amber frowned as five people appeared in front of the congregation with their guitars and keyboard. Two women joined them and then one woman asked for all those who could stand for Worship to please do so. Amber stood. Wasn't there supposed to be a choir?

The music started and the words to "How Great is Our God" appeared on a screen behind the pulpit so that everyone could sing along. Amber didn't sing but she could see how much most of the congregation enjoyed praising their God in song. There was one more song before one of the women asked everyone to be seated as she read off the church announcements. John appeared again as the band and their instruments dispersed. John stood between the aisles and bowed his head in prayer. Amber bowed her head and tried to concentrate on John's words of praise and his requested blessings for his congregation, but her mind kept struggling between trying hard to be sincere in accepting this prayer and her feeling like a fraud. John did, as Gram had told her about his hospital prayer, speak to God as though he was just talking to Him, as though he knew God was listening. Then John asked each person to share what was on their heart with God in a silent prayer. Amber didn't know what to share, what kind of things she should even be asking or telling God. Here, in His house, it was pretty good odds that He was listening, and she didn't want to draw more attention to her religious ignorance. So, instead of praying, Amber snuck a peek at John as he raised his hand and was, apparently, silently blessing each section of the congregation. She froze when his raised hand was pointed over her section of the pews. She actually held her breath but then he moved on and she was disappointed that she hadn't felt any mystical rush from his blessing. Too much time spent with Rachel.

After the prayer, John invited everyone to stand and welcome each other. Oh no! How could she be invisible when everyone beside her and in front of her was extending their hand and welcoming her? Thankfully, that ended, and they moved on to the business of prayer request cards, visitor cards and the offering. At least she knew about the offering beforehand. She had her money folded in the front pocket of her purse and was ready for the collection basket.

Then it was finally time for the sermon. John thanked the congregation for their help in extending God's word and work to those not fortunate enough to be in His church this morning. John walked up to the podium and opened his Bible. Amber prepared herself. He had said that his sermon was inspired by her. What could that be?

"Our scripture today is about Saul and comes from Acts 26:9 - 11. Hear the word of the Lord," John said, and then he read - "I myself was convinced that I ought to do many things in opposing the name of Jesus of Nazareth. And I did so in Jerusalem. I not only locked up many of the saints in prison after receiving authority from the chief priests, but when they were put to death I cast my vote against them. And I punished them often in all the synagogues and tried to make them blaspheme, and in raging fury against them I persecuted them even to foreign cities."

Amber followed the words on the screen behind her father. When he finished she felt tears in her eyes. Was this what he said was about her? Was inspired by her? Did he think she was like this Saul, punishing them and opposing them when they were righteous and she was not?

John closed the Bible and laid it on the podium. "While Saul was on his way to Damascus to hunt down Christians, he was met by the bright light of the resurrected Jesus. When Saul had fallen to the ground, Jesus said, 'Saul, Saul, why are you persecuting me?"

Persecuting? Did John think Amber was deliberately trying to be vengeful? Amber swallowed and suppressed her desperate desire to flee. Just get up and leave before she had to be humiliated further.

"But," John went on, "Jesus told Saul to rise and stand up. Jesus told Saul that He had appeared before Saul to appoint Saul as His servant and witness. Jesus wanted Saul to open people's eyes so that they may turn from darkness to light. Turn from Satan to God so that they may receive forgiveness of sins and a place among those who are sanctified by faith in Jesus."

"Well," John continued, "why Saul? Why would Jesus appear before someone whose driving purpose was to crush anyone who believed in Jesus? If Jesus was going to bestow the honor on someone to be His messenger, to spread His word, then wouldn't you think that Saul would be on the very bottom of His list of potential prospects?"

The congregation was silent. Waiting for the reason. Amber was afraid that what came next may wound her even further and yet she couldn't leave. She had to hear why Jesus had chosen Saul.

"Of course, all of us who have read the Bible know the story of Saul becoming Paul and of how this enemy of Christianity went on to become one of the ultimate missionaries of God's word. Paul traveled to many countries, preaching the Good News of Jesus and establishing numerous churches. And so," John said, "I remind you of Paul's story because I was recently asked what I found on my first missionary trip that convinced me that becoming a pastor was what I was meant to do. Jesus had not stopped me in my tracks one day and instructed me in this calling. I was a believer, and an all right kind of guy, but I was not entirely convinced that I was worthy of being a spokesman to God's flock. I went on that missionary trip to figure out what I wanted to do. I had hoped for my own middle of the road encounter with Jesus so I could be certain, but it never came. What came, what was given to me was seeing a Saul miracle. I'm going to tell you the details so you will understand that God does not use just the pure and worthy. God lifts up the Sauls, the dark and unworthy and, in opening their eyes, he opens ours."

Amber was hooked.

"After high school, I went on a missionary trip to a small community in South America and there I met my Saul. A young boy who resented the missionaries coming in out of the blue and trying to control the hearts and minds of these people who had struggled on by themselves for generations. This young man resisted the gifts, any offer of medical assistance and especially the invitation to fellowship. He was strong willed and had his own followers. They would torment the other villagers when they would accept needed supplies and spiritual guidance. His thugs bullied the young men and women into rejecting the missionaries' help.'

'I struggled with my feelings about this young man. I prayed for guidance in what to do for the village and I prayed for God's emergency help with my anger at this boy. Instead of being happy I was investing six months of my life to help these people I was, instead, becoming discouraged and believed that this trip was a waste of my time. I believed that I had failed and was just looking forward to the end of my time when I could leave and get back to my own life.'

'Then, one day, probably three months into my mission, Rafael walked into our tiny church when I was there alone. I was, in all honesty, a little concerned for my safety. It was no secret to Rafael that I judged him one notch above a heathen and, also not lost on him, was the fact that I was not an intimidating specimen in any physical or courageous form. So, there I stood with only my faith that God would let me live through whatever was coming and then preparing myself for whatever was coming. Rafael walked straight up to me. He looked me in the eye. His eyes were dark and intense and piercing. We just stood there for several minutes before he spoke. 'Do you believe in these miracles you talk about?' I nodded. 'Then come with me,' he said and turned to walk out of the church. So, of course, the thought crossed my mind to just run for it as soon as we got outside, but I couldn't. I was powerless to do anything but follow him. So, there we went, Rafael and I parading out of the church, down the center street of shacks, straight to his home. Rafael stopped and stood by the door so I could enter first."

John paused for effect. "Now give me credit here, friends, and please acknowledge that I did walk into the unknown. A lot of different terrors could have been waiting for me in there. But, in the dim light of the open door, all I could see was someone laying on the bed in the corner. I went closer to the bed and saw a frail older woman asleep there. I turned to Rafael and he motioned for me to take the chair by the bed.'

'I sat down and Rafael sat on the end of her small bed. After a few minutes of her ragged breathing, I asked him if it was his mother. He nodded. I sat back in my chair with my hands in my lap. 'She is dying,' Rafael finally said. 'I'm sorry,' I said. 'She is afraid,' he said. I nodded. Then he said, 'When she wakes I want you to convince her that this heaven you profess is real and she can go there."

John walked out from behind the podium. "If you have ever considered yourselves a tough sell for me, let me assure you that you are not. You have come here to God's church seeking Him, I did not get dragged to your bedside where I was forced to convince you in the space of one meeting that God is real, that He loves you, and that He will make a place for you in His Father's house.'

'So, back to my story. Rafael and I waited for his mother to wake up. I was actually afraid to have her wake up because what did I really know about convincing anyone? Who was I to take on that responsibility when I was in this backwards, forgotten place just trying to make up my own mind if I even wanted the job or not? Anyway, she did wake up. Rafael told her that I was from the new church and I wanted to tell her about my God. I know I was more frightened than she was at that moment. Where do I even begin? So, I took her hand and I closed my eyes, and I asked the Holy Spirit to join us. I asked Him to fill the room and help me find the right words to open this dying woman's heart so she could receive the full love and acceptance of our God."

The church was quiet.

"Well, I found the words," John said. "Once I started I told her all that I knew. I started with Genesis and then skipped through to the birth of Jesus. I told His story. If I was not yet educated on interpreting and explaining the Bible, I knew enough to help this desperate woman. Her hopeful eyes spurred me on and I found what I had hoped I would feel when I shared His word. In the end, she asked if I would baptize her so she could be accepted into Heaven. I told her I could not, but that I would have our Pastor visit her as soon as possible. Then she looked to Rafael and asked him to be baptized with her. She said that she didn't want to go to Heaven if he was never going to be there with her. She wanted to die knowing that she would see her son again.'

'Well, Rafael had just been trapped in his own web. He wanted me to give peace to his dying mother but he was not expecting that he would be asked to accept this new religion for himself. Here he had convinced his peers that they should be against our church and now his love for his mother may force him to cave in and actually be baptized as a Christian.'

'I left them to figure it out but when I walked out of that simple house I felt like I was leaving God's church. I had found what I had come to find. I actually felt the Holy Spirit directing me to the words I needed to say. I felt Rafael's mother's spirit absorbing my message. Her desire to be baptized was not just a safety net in case I was right, it was a burning desire to belong to God. To accept Jesus as her savior. I can tell you that nothing after that experience could have stopped me from serving God.'

'But, my story aside, the point I want to make is about Rafael and Saul. Like Saul, Rafael eventually chose baptism. Our Pastor initially refused to baptize Rafael until he was convinced that Rafael was entering into this baptism for the right reason. Appeasing his mother did not meet the necessary threshold for entering into a permanent relationship with God. Our Pastor had to be convinced that Rafael was making the commitment as sincerely as his mother was. Let us remember that baptism isn't about God's commitment to us, that had been taken care of at the cross, it is about our commitment to God. So, I am pleased to report that Rafael not only ended up wanting baptism for himself, for God had opened his eyes and his heart, but Rafael came to believe that he, like Paul, had been chosen to be a servant and witness for God. Rafael has become a minister and is now traveling from village to village convincing other rebellious young men to believe in Christ."

John smiled with the memory of God's victory. "So, great feel good story, right? But I haven't answered your questions about why God would choose someone like Saul and Rafael to build his churches. Certainly, there were more worthy candidates."

Amber listened completely to the rest of her father's sermon. She loved it. She loved the easy way he spoke to his congregation, the way he called them friends, the way he anticipated their questions and then answered them. She loved the way he invited you to believe that God was real and alive and wanted to have a personal relationship with you.

While the final song was being sung, Amber slipped out the door and was going to her car. She had so much to think about now. Though the sermon was interesting and uplifting for anyone, she felt it had been directed toward her. That her father was answering so many of her questions. She just needed to be alone now and think about it. But when she crossed the street to her car she saw James coming up the walkway to the front of the church.

"James?"

James stopped and then smiled and came toward her.

"What are you doing here?"

"Well," he said. "You came to my father's place of employment, so I felt I should do the same for your father."

"I see."

"So, how was it?"

Amber shook her head at the indescribable fullness of her experience.

"That good? Great. Want to catch the next sermon with me?"

Amber nodded. "I do. I want to hear it again and listen differently this time."

James frowned. "How does one listen differently?"

"Oh, well, I just meant I want to hear it like anyone else, not hear it like I was afraid that what he may say would somehow... hurt my feelings."

"Okay. Great. And, oh yeah, I have a new saying. I don't know where this one came from but I liked it. It is not necessary to move mountains to move mountains. It is necessary only to move pebbles."

"Good one," Amber said.

"Yeah," James said. "I used to be annoyed when I saw Mom taping up a new mantra on the wall. Like, what good are words to change anything? But, I was wrong. They aren't just words. They are the thoughts that come after the words that can change things. I guess that's how she has been able to carry on through all her disappointments."

Rachel and Gram were on the back-porch swing when Amber got home.

"So, how was it?" Rachel asked, finishing her last sip of iced tea. "We thought you would be home hours ago."

"I stayed for both services."

"Really?" Gram said. "I thought all three sermons were the same."

"They are but I could listen to this one a hundred times. There was so much there to think about."

"Good," Rachel said, though Amber wasn't certain Rachel meant it by the tone of her voice.

"Can I refill your tea?" Amber asked, reaching for Rachel's glass. "I'm going in to get me some."

"Sure," Rachel said. "But hurry, we are dying to hear about everything."

"Did you have lunch?" Gram asked, as Amber opened the door to go back inside.

"Yes, James and I stopped on our way back because he had to go in to work and needed to eat."

"Humph!" Rachel said. "Isn't she Miss Big Pants?"

Gram smiled. "We may all live through this yet."

"Well," Rachel said, "we don't know if that is true about Miriam. I mean, have you heard any more about the cancer treatments?"

"She can't start any chemo or radiation until her surgery has healed, of course. But we are all hopeful."

"I'll include Miriam in my spiritual ritual tonight."

Gram seemed interested. "Spiritual ritual. What is that?"

"Well, I am just starting so I'm trying to figure out what I want. I mean there are several directions I can go. Paganism is so individualized. There are different practices and beliefs, but basically whichever one I decide on will expand on my love of the earth and all things that dwell on it. My divinity is feminine, a goddess. I haven't found the right statue of her yet. I mean, I could have a male figure, but I see the earth as a woman who provides and nourishes and comforts us. So, I'm building a shrine in my room with a feminine slant. I haven't gotten it completely figured out but it has the basic earth elements. It has a crystal, a candle, incense, a small vile of holy water a friend gave me that came from a well near Stonehenge. I just must go to Stonehenge one day. That is my dream."

"My," Gram said. "What does your mother think of this?"

"Oh, Mom, you know she has a very limited imagination. She cannot see out of the box she is in."

"So, I can assume that she is not appreciating your new adventure?"

"She said I'm so immature that she is afraid to let me go off to college on my own."

Gram chuckled. "Need any help?" she called into Amber.

"Nope. Got it."

"I'm trying to choose a name for my goddess. I like Parvati. That is a Hindu name meaning Divine Mother. She is the embodiment of the total energy of the universe. The goddess of power and light. Now, that is who I want watching over me. But, I also like Cybele. That's Greek for Earth Mother. Maybe I should just start small and then move up into the universe when I'm more experienced with that type of power."

"Cybele is nice," Gram said as Amber pushed open the screen door and came out with the drinks.

"Whose Cybele?"

"A goddess Rachel is naming. It means Earth Mother."

"Really? I mean, really, Rachel?" Amber said, handing her the tea.

"Yes. Really, Amber."

"You are making up a goddess? And then what? When you get her invented will she then be real?"

"See," Rachel said, pointing her finger at Amber. "I was right. Just like Aunt Peggy. You go to church one time and now you're judgmental!"

"Oh right," Amber said, leaning against the porch railing. "Like I've never questioned anything you've ever done before?"

"Maybe, but not with that tone."

"Oh, now who is being judgmental? Besides, you've never invented your own religion before, Rachel."

"Girls. Girls." Gram said. "Let's pretend you two are best friends."

"I just get annoyed with hypocrisy," Amber said.

"What? I'm not a hypocrite. I believe everyone should be free to find peace and what makes them complete."

Amber groaned.

"What's wrong with that? Really, Gram, do you think what I just said was groan worthy?"

Gram smiled at her girls. "I'm just content that you both are healthy and beautiful and are here with me at this moment."

Rachel and Amber groaned.

"So," Gram continued, "what was your father's sermon about?"

Amber grinned and looked at Rachel. "About how God made the earth and created all living plants and animals."

"That's nice," Gram said.

"No, it's not," Rachel snapped. "She just said that because of Cybele."

"Well, did Cybele create the earth?" Amber asked.

"I never claimed she created it. I just meant that she revered it and so I could honor her."

"I revere the earth. Why not name your goddess Amber?"

"Because I couldn't possibly foster an aura of peace with any deity that reminds me of you."

"Fair enough," Amber said. "Actually, Gram, John's sermon was about the apostle Paul, who was, I might add, an actual living breathing person. And about why John became a minister."

"Now that sounds interesting," Gram said.

"It was," Amber said.

"So," Rachel asked. "Why?"

Amber looked thoughtful. "Because of the Holy Spirit."

"Holy Spirit?" Rachel drew her chin back. "Well, now that sounds mystical."

"Yeah, throw in a little witchcraft and it could almost be Pagan."

"Hey, don't dis witchcraft."

Amber smiled at Rachel. "You know I love you anyway, right?"

"One does not get credit for succumbing to the unavoidable."

Amber sat at her desk, staring out the window with her phone in her hands. All evening the thought of texting John had nagged at her. What could she say to him about his sermon? Did he want her to just say that it was good and she liked it? Or did he want her to explain how she understood what he was trying to say to her and then list her new revelations? She wished she had taken a tablet and pen with her when she went back to hear the sermon again. There were so many moments when he said something so true and specific that she wished she had been able to write it down. Bible references that she needed to think about and even research. Questions about God's forgiveness. Had God actually forgiven all of the horrible things Saul had apparently done to God's innocent people? Amber needed to talk to John about that. It seemed impossible somehow. Unfair somehow.

And then the heartache of Rafael's love for his mother. Amber could imagine the sacrifices Rafael's mother had made for him. The troubles she had endured because he was so rebellious and ungrateful. Sacrifices that Rafael was forced to own when he was faced with his mother's death. Amber shook her head at the weight of that. But then a new thought occurred to her, certainly John couldn't think that Amber and Miriam could ever have such a bond that neither of them would want to spend eternity without the other. Of course, Amber could see clearly that Miriam and Grace had that relationship, but John couldn't expect Amber to own the unearned sorrow of losing a real mother. Certainly, the loss of Miriam could not alter Amber's future when it had never altered her past.

Amber sighed and laid her phone down. That was a lie. Miriam had definitely altered Amber's past. And now she was seeping into Amber's future with John and God. Did they both expect forgiveness from Amber for all the heartaches and disappointments Miriam had caused her? That felt impossible. Totally unfair.

Amber's hand was still on her phone when it vibrated and signaled a text. She lifted the phone and looked at the message. It was from John. Amber opened the message.

"I was so pleased to see you in church today but I'm wondering, did you come back for the second sermon because you enjoyed it or because you were trying to understand it?"

"Both," Amber typed.

"Any specific questions?"

"I guess I'm confused about Jesus's forgiveness. I know that you told us that He did, but why would He forgive Saul when Saul would never have repented if Jesus had not blinded him and then given Saul his sight back? Forced regret is not the same as sincere regret."

"Very astute." John typed. "Let's say a child was playing hide and seek. She hid behind a big bush when she saw a bird's nest. She pulled the branch down just enough to see if there were eggs in the nest. Two eggs rolled out. One landed safely but the other one broke. She picked up a big leaf and worked hard to return the unbroken egg to the nest without putting human scent on it just in case the mother bird could tell and reject the egg. Her intentions were never to break the eggs. Her intentions were innocent and then she did her best to repair the damage. Should she be forgiven by the mother bird?"

"But Saul knew what he was doing?" Amber typed back.

"Saul knew what he was taught in his Jewish studies. He was a Pharisee who was filled with religious piety and believed that his persecution of the Christians was actually doing the work of God."

"So, Jesus forgave Saul because Jesus understood that though Saul was wrong, Saul believed he was doing something right and then tried, for the rest of his life, to repair the damage?" Amber typed.

"Like the child acknowledging the broken egg was an unintended consequence of her actions and she was sincerely regretful, Saul was faced with the truth that his actions were wrong. Jesus was exactly who his followers had professed he was. Jesus of Nazareth was the Jewish Messiah and the Son of God. So, for the three days of his blindness, Saul refused food and water and just prayed to God. He was sincere in his regret."

"Okay, I understand. But one more question."

"I'm ready."

"Would God forgive someone with no regret for what she had done?"

"Amber, your mother does regret her choice to leave you."

"Now that her broken egg is on the ground for all to see, is that forced regret or sincere regret?"

There was a pause before John answered her question.

Amber waited, a little frightened for having asked that. She knew that how her father answered her question would determine if she would believe him about anything else he told her.

"I pray for us both that she is sincere. But our struggle with doubt does not bar her from God's grace."

Amber read his words. Okay, he was really who she had hoped he would be. He preached God's word but he was human. He was her father, he understood her struggle and he would be honest with her about all things.

"Thank you. And by the way, I truly loved your sermon."

Amber came in from work and dropped her purse on the hall table. She bent over and untied her shoes then slipped them off. Ahh, eight hours on her feet behind a cash register was enough. Amber glanced in at Grampa watching TV as she headed for the kitchen.

"How was your night?" Grampa asked, as he shut off the TV and got up from his chair.

"The usual," Amber said, pausing to see what he wanted to say. "How was yours?"

"We went over to visit Miriam and John."

"How nice," Amber said.

"Yes. It was. What a shame we lost all those years of family visits."

"Where is Gram?" Amber asked, changing the subject so she wouldn't have to be lead down the disappointing path of discussing Miriam's choices. She had always hated disagreeing with Grampa even when he was wrong.

"Gram was just tuckered out, so she went up to bed about an hour ago. I told her I would wait up for you."

"Oh, you don't need to do that. I'm a big girl now, Grampa."

"Now, we will decide when we want to stop waiting up for you."

"Well, if I'd known I was keeping you up I would have come straight home. I went with James for a snack after the store closed."

"No worries," Grampa said. "I wasn't working too hard while I was waiting."

"I was just headed to get a drink. Do you want anything?"

Grampa shook his head and followed her into the kitchen.

"Did Gram ask you to tuck me in, too?" Amber asked, smiling as she got a water glass out of the cupboard.

"No. But I was supposed to be sure you got this letter from Gracie before I went to bed."

Amber sat her glass down on the counter and came to take the letter.

"Is something wrong?"

"No. Gracie just asked us to be sure you got this. She reminds us a lot of you. A little serious for her age."

"Being an only child can do that to you," Amber said. "Well, I guess that isn't true. Look at Rachel."

"Okay, the delivery has been made so I guess I will go upstairs."

Amber gave him a hug and he turned and scuffled out of the kitchen. Amber opened the envelope with unicorns stamped on the flap.

"Dear Amber,

I know we have been strangers all of our lives, but I want to know you and I want you to know me.

I will tell you some stuff about me so you will know me a little. I hope you tell me stuff about you.

I love unicorns. I know they are not real but it's okay to like things that can't be seen except in our imaginations.

I love God. I know I can't see Him either, but He is real. God loves us all, and when I pray I believe He hears me.

Yellow is my favorite color. It is hard to be sad when you look at yellow.

Oatmeal raisin cookies are my favorite. I think they are kind of healthy for a treat.

Vanilla is my favorite ice cream. Some of my friends think it is boring but I like the kind with the tiny dots of vanilla beans in it.

I like to wear dresses more than jeans. Most of my friends think dresses are too fancy but I don't care what they think.

I don't like homework, but I like good grades, so that is my quandary. (This is a new spelling word so I wanted to use it for you)

And last, I have always wanted a sister.

I hope we can be friends some day and sisters after that. I know we didn't start off very good but I have been so worried about Mom that I haven't thought of anyone else. Maybe you can come by some day and see me. We can talk in my room if you want.

Love, your sister, Grace

p.s. I am a little angry with Mom that she didn't tell me about you and Gram and Grampa. Maybe when I get older I will understand why she couldn't."

Amber held the letter in one hand as she wiped the tears from her cheeks. Every single line was heart wrenching. Did Miriam even have a clue what she has done to them all?

Amber folded the letter and sat staring at the air. To be honest, Amber had been so busy being angry at Miriam, and trying to figure out how she felt about her father and God, that she hadn't even once seriously thought about Grace. Oh, she had thought about how unfair it was that Miriam had another daughter that she had kept, a daughter that Miriam apparently did all the customary motherly things for, a daughter that had the family that Amber had always wanted. But Amber had not seen Grace as Grace. Amber hadn't tried to imagine who Grace was or how she was handling all of this drama at twelve when Amber was hardly able to deal with it at eighteen.

Amber stood on the broad front porch of her... parent's house. How strange to ever even think of coming to her parent's house. The house was, of course, the picture-perfect house that one could dream of growing up in. It had straight white clapboards with tall windows along the front of the house. There were blue shutters on both the bottom and upstairs windows. The porch railing had flowerboxes overflowing with blue petunias. Amber hesitated a moment, suddenly wanting desperately to change her mind and leave without having to see any more, but she couldn't. She had to do this for Grace.

Amber pushed the doorbell button and waited as she heard footsteps hurrying toward the door.

Grace yanked open the door, her face beaming. "Hi! I'm so glad you came!"

Amber smiled back. Grace was dressed in a yellow sundress and her hair was pulled back in a bouncy ponytail.

"Who is it, Grace?" Miriam called from the living room.

"It's Amber, Mom." Grace said, as she stepped back so Amber could come inside.

"Amber?" Miriam said, coming into the foyer, pulling the belt of her satin robe snug. "How unexpected."

"I wrote her a letter and asked her to come visit me," Grace said.

"I see," Miriam said, forcing a smile. "I almost thought, for a second, that she may have come by to check on her mother after my surgery."

There was a pause as if Grace and Miriam were waiting for Amber to ask Miriam how she was feeling.

Finally, Amber looked from Miriam to Grace. "It's so beautiful out today, maybe we can sit outside and talk."

"Sure. Okay. But first I want you to come up and see my room. I want to show you all the stuff I like."

Amber nodded and started to follow Grace to the stairs when Miriam stopped them. "Just a moment, girls. I'm trying to understand what is going on here. Grace, why didn't you tell me you had written a letter to Amber?"

Grace shrugged. "I don't know. I just thought it was okay, so I gave it to Grampa to give to Amber."

"Well, I would have liked to have seen it first," Miriam said.

"Why?" Amber asked.

"Because," Miriam said, looking directly into Amber's face. "I am her mother and it is my responsibility to know about things like this."

"What things like this?" Amber asked incredulously. "Grace just wanted us to spend some time getting to know each other. You may not like me but that doesn't mean Grace and I can't get along."

"Please, don't take that tone with me," Miriam said. "And Grace knows she is supposed to talk to me about things like this. Don't you, Grace?"

Grace looked down at the floor and nodded. "I'm sorry."

"What?" Amber said, her face hardening. "She has to be sorry for writing to her sister?"

Miriam returned the hard look. "And this is exactly why I need to be aware of what is going on in my own house. I can't have you undermining me behind my back."

"Oh right, I forgot, you are the pillar of being upfront and honest."

Miriam turned to Grace and told her to go up to her room. "You and I will talk about this later."

Grace looked at Amber, her eyes watering. Amber smiled and nodded that it would be all right.

Grace ran upstairs and closed her bedroom door.

Miriam turned back to Amber. "This is exactly the thing I wanted to avoid. I don't want Grace getting hurt by all of this. She is a sensitive girl and has had a lot to deal with. My cancer and then discovering you. I need time to help her figure it out before she just jumps into a relationship with you. I don't even know you. I don't know what kind of things you may say about me to her."

"I had hoped that she and I wouldn't talk about you," Amber said.

Miriam shook her head. "You are so full of hate. I'm afraid you need time to get that under control before you spend time with Grace."

"I see," Amber said.

"Good," Miriam said. "I'll talk to Grace and, after I get my strength back, maybe we can set something up for the three of us."

Amber just stood staring at Miriam and shaking her head.

"And to think," Amber finally said, "my whole life I actually thought I was missing something by not knowing my mother. When you first appeared, I thought for a while that Grace was the lucky one to have had a mother taking care of her. But now I see that I was the lucky one. I would have suffocated being controlled by you. Thank you so much for leaving me behind."

Miriam nodded. "And thank you. You keep making me glad that I did choose John over you."

"What?"

"Believe me, I agonized over leaving you. You were a demanding baby but still I grieved – yes, don't make that face at me – I grieved over leaving my baby, but I believed that in the end our lives would all work out. I believed we would someday be together as a family. But I see now that that was just a foolish dream. You are so filled with hate and jealousy…"

"Jealousy? What do you have that I could possibly be jealous of? Certainly not your compassion or loyalty or honesty!"

"How dare you judge me? You don't know me, you just know what you want to think I am so you can hate me. Well, I won't have it. I won't have you bringing your selfish poison into my home. My family."

"Well, guess what, Miriam! Prepare yourself because that is exactly what I intend to do."

"Get out and stay away from us. You hear? Stay away from my husband and daughter until you grow up and learn how to treat people."

"I'm your daughter, remember? So, I may never be capable of growing up and learning how to treat people," Amber said, her voice so cold it startled Miriam. Then Amber turned and stalked toward the door. In all her life Amber had never talked to anyone like that. She had never even wanted to say those things out loud to anyone, but Miriam had shown her true colors and Amber was suddenly ready to take her on.

Amber reached for the doorknob to leave when the door opened and John stood there. He smiled at Amber then the smile pulled into a frown.

"What's wrong?" he asked.

"A lot," Amber said.

"Do you want to talk about it?"

"I'll tell you what it is," Miriam said, stepping forward. "She just said the most horrible things to me."

John looked from Miriam's indignant face to Amber. "Okay, I guess we should talk."

"I'm a little too old to be put in time out," Amber said. "Besides it wouldn't change how I feel."

"See," Miriam said, crossing her arms.

"Let's go to the church office and see what we can figure out," John said to Amber.

"What?" Miriam shrieked. "Don't you want to hear my side first?"

"I just did," John said. "We can discuss the rest when I come home."

"No. If you want to talk to her then do it here. What can be said that I shouldn't hear?"

John walked over and looked patiently down into Miriam's face. "Everything is fixable. Just relax and we will work on it."

Miriam's chin quivered and tears streamed down her face. John smiled and wiped them away with his thumb. "Go get some rest and stop worrying. Everything is in God's plan."

Miriam nodded. "Please don't be long."

Amber fought the urge to just walk away from all the drama but, for some reason, she didn't want to walk out on John. She didn't want to disappoint him even though he was obviously taken in by all of Miriam's pathetic fake victimization.

John and Amber left the house and walked silently to the church. When they had gotten in his office, and he'd closed the door, Amber told him that some things are just the way they are and there are no words that can change them. "Besides, I'm fine now," she said. "Really."

"Being too strong to let your tears show doesn't mean you don't have them."

"If I had tears," Amber said, "they would be tears of anger not hurt."

"I see, so you're just angry?"

"I feel entitled to that, yes," Amber said.

"Would you rather not be angry?"

"What I would *rather* is just to go back to my life. She told me to stay away from her family and right now, to be honest, that is exactly what I want."

John sat back in his chair. He folded his hands in his lap. "I can tell you that there is no escaping to back before we all knew. So, that said, let's figure out where we go from here."

"I don't know what you want from me. Am I not supposed to have any feelings about what Miriam has done, what she has said to me?"

"Of course, you have feelings. No one can blame you for being angry about how your mother has handled all of this. My objective isn't to tell you to stop being disappointed, my objective is to help you live without bitterness and anger. I'm certain neither of those words described you before we came into your life. I just want to help you get back there."

"Okay," Amber said, sitting down. "I'm listening."

"First some words to think about," John said, opening a notebook in front of him. He turned a few pages and lifted out a sheet of paper. "Some wise words I keep close by," he said and then read, "Bitterness is the only poison one can drink with the mistaken assumption that the act of drinking it will harm someone else." He paused and looked up at Amber.

Amber chewed the side of her lip and thought about that. "Okay. I get that."

"The way you are feeling is hurting you. You have to forgive your mother for your own sake."

Amber shook her head. "I don't think I will ever forgive her no matter how that makes me feel."

John studied her, and she looked away to the window.

"My greatest hope," he said, "is that you and your mother find peace with each other. But if that takes time, I at least hope you both can find peace with yourselves."

Amber looked back at him. "You said that you forgave her because you love her and because God commands you to. Right now I do not see myself ever loving her and God hasn't spoken to me. I'm sorry but I can't just forgive someone who isn't even sorry."

"Are you unhappy whenever you think of her?"

"Yes."

"Forgiving her may not make you feel happy but it will stop you from feeling unhappy. If you decide to forgive her and start thinking of her as you do everyone else, without prejudice and anger, then you will be free to work your way through this."

"I can't unhear what she just said to me. She said it."

"Tell me, have you ever had a disagreement with, say, Rachel?"

"Of course. You've met Rachel."

"Have you forgiven her and moved on?"

"Of course. But there is no way to compare our petty disagreements to this."

"You can decide to do anything you want."

"Why should I want to decide to forgive her?"

"So you can stop feeling unhappy."

Amber sighed. "She doesn't deserve it."

"Maybe not. But you do."

"So, it's just that easy?"

"No. But it's a direction to walk toward. If you want to feel happy you will find a way."

"It just feels so unfair," Amber said.

"Don't a lot of things in this life?"

Amber was quiet, thinking about what he was trying to tell her. "I know you want me to just say fine, I forgive her but, to tell you the truth, that makes me feel more unhappy with myself than I am with her."

John chuckled. "You both are hard cases. Look, at least think about it for your sake. And when you said that God hasn't spoken to you about forgiveness it's just because you aren't listening." John lifted his worn Bible. "This is God's word written for us and it is full of forgiveness help. In fact, let me leave you with these words." He opened the Bible and thumbed through the pages. "Ah, here it is. 'Those who nursed their bitterness remained invalids. It was as simple and horrible as that."

Amber sat still, stunned by the impact of the truth of those words.

John stood up. "Let's go get an ice cream. I've never been able to share that parental moment with you."

Amber nodded and stood up.

"And here," John said, opening a file cabinet and pulling out a sheet of paper, "take this. Read it when you feel like it. I think everyone should read Mother Teresa's wisdom often."

Amber took the paper and folded it and slid it into her purse. "Do you think we could take Grace with us? I was supposed to spend some time with her today before…well, before… you know."

John smiled. "There is nothing I would like more than buying ice cream for my daughters."

James and Amber sat close together on the back-porch swing. The sun was just slipping behind the tall maples when James sighed and gently squeezed Amber's hand. She looked up at him and gave him a quick kiss.

"Mind if I join you two?" Gram asked, stepping out onto the porch.

"Of course not," Amber said, scooting closer to James so Gram could fit her little self on the swing.

"It's just such a lovely evening that I can't settle down inside the house."

"Right," Amber said, as they began the slow steady swinging back and forth.

"Thanks again for dinner, Mrs. Barton," James said.

"Always a pleasure to have you here," Gram said.

Amber smiled. This moment was perfect.

"Did you get to see Grace today?" Gram finally asked after a few moments of contented swinging.

"Yes, I did. She and I had hot fudge sundaes with John. And you know, Gram, Grace doesn't like nuts on her sundae either."

"How about that," Gram said. "But I didn't know that you were going to see your father, too."

Amber's contentment withered. "Me either, but he showed up just as Miriam and I were..."

"Were what, dear?"

"Don't even ask. You don't want to know."

The swing stopped. "Oh my!" Gram said.

"Yeah," Amber said, "it wasn't pretty. Miriam appeared, and things went downhill fast from there."

"I'm sorry to hear that," Gram said.

Amber smiled for Gram. "It's okay. I'm certain Miriam is grateful we have finally drawn our lines in the sand. I know I am."

"Really? You are grateful that you two are moving apart instead of together?" Gram asked.

"I'm grateful we are honest about how we feel instead of her pretending she regrets abandoning me."

"Amber, none of us can know what was going on inside Miriam's head when she made that fateful decision. She was so young."

"I'll concede that, but it really doesn't matter now anyway. As John said, we can't change the past. We just have to figure out how to best deal with the present."

"Well," Gram said, "thank the good Lord you at least like your father."

"And my sister. You know, Gram, Grace told me about a whole other family I have that I never knew about. I have another grandmother. John's Dad died six months ago. Grace really loved him. Grace said John has two sisters and so I have cousins. Five cousins. Three boys and two girls. Isn't that crazy? I have all these people that I never knew."

"Oh, Miriam, Miriam," Gram whispered. "What have you done?"

"Are you going to meet them?" James asked.

"Someday. Right now we are taking it slow. Today was the first day I really got to sit with my sister and father and just talk. We decided that we would do it again next week. John is working on Miriam and me in the hopes that we can, one day, sit as a family and talk peacefully. I personally can't see that ever happening, but John is a Christian, and an optimist, so I guess he can't help but to try to save us."

"Well," Gram said, "if your father is working on it then I feel better. You and Miriam are both so stubborn that nothing would ever change if it was left up to just the two of you."

"Hey now, don't compare me to her."

"Amber," James said, "we love you, but you are stubborn."

"Only when I'm right," Amber said.

Gram and James laughed and Amber had to poke James in the ribs with her elbow.

They all swung quietly for a while then Amber asked her grandmother if she knew anything about Mother Teresa.

"Just who she was," Gram said.

"John gave me something to read that she had written."

"Did you read it?" James asked.

"No, I just remembered I had it. He gave it to me just before we left his office."

"Well, get it and read it to us." Gram said. "We'd like to know what Mother Teresa said."

"Yeah, sure. I'll be right back."

Amber dashed into the house and Gram looked at James. "I think she will be all right," Gram said.

"Yeah, it's probably Miriam we need to worry about."

Gram chuckled then sobered. "Yes. I do. Of course, I do. I hope they got all that cancer. Miriam still has a tough road with chemo and radiation. I just want the next few months to be over so we will know."

"At least," James offered, "there is hope now. When she first got here it seemed she was sure she was going to die."

"I've thought a lot about that," Gram said. "I think Miriam was just frightened of the cancer and frightened of telling us about her secret and so she thought we would, well, accept it better if we believed she may be dying. Thank God, she eventually decided to have the surgery. I think she would have just let herself die if we hadn't all forgiven her. Well, all except Amber."

"In Amber's defense," James said. "Amber has paid the biggest price for Miriam's decisions, plus she has never had the emotional history with Miriam that all the rest of you have."

Gram smiled and patted James's hand. "You are a good boy. I'm glad Amber has you."

Amber was back and settled in between James and her grandmother. She unfolded the paper. "Now, John said this was something I needed to read to help me with forgiving. I told him I could forgive when there was genuine remorse. He asked me to just read it, so here goes. People are often unreasonable and self-centered. Forgive them anyway." Amber shrugged. "Mother Teresa certainly knew who I would be dealing with."

"Just read," Gram said.

"If you are kind, people may accuse you of ulterior motives. Be kind anyway. If you are honest, people may cheat you. Be honest anyway. If you find happiness, people may be jealous. Be happy anyway. The good you do today may be forgotten tomorrow. Do good anyway. Give the world the best you have and it may never be enough. Give your best anyway. For you see, in the end, it is between you and God. It was never between you and them anyway."

Everyone sat in silence when Amber had finished reading.

"Wow," Amber said. "Just wow."

"Yeah," James said. "I need a copy of that for my Mom."

"That's a tall order," Gram said. "But she certainly left us good instructions on how to head in the right direction."

"Hey," Grampa said through the screen door. "I thought you said something about apple pie."

Gram chuckled and pushed herself up out of the swing. "Be kind anyway, eh? Guess I'm being tested right away. Imagine the day he would think to cut his own piece of pie."

"So," Rachel said, standing proudly in front of her altar to Cybele. "What do you think?"

"I think," Amber said, turning her head this way and that to see the altar from all angles. "I think you have put a lot of thought into this and a lot of money."

"Well, yes. I can't risk skimping on something this important."

"Oh right. Cybele will know if you don't honor her with the very best. No simple cross for her."

"Well, I think it is perfect," Rachel said.

"So, tell me, how do you do whatever it is that you do to honor her?"

Rachel smiled. "Well, first I light the incense. I have chosen a woodland fragrance obviously. And then I sprinkle the tiniest droplets of the holy water Jessica gave me on my forehead to get my mind centered and focused on the earth. Then I ring this little bell and recite the chant I have written for Cybele. I'll read it to you later. Then I bow my head and think of all the things I can that would please Mother Earth. Things like not wasting her bounty. I have started a compost pile in the backyard instead of just letting Mom throw away her vegetable parings. I think about watering the struggling little plants I saw in Mrs. Jenson's yard. Mrs. Jenson plants and plants and then ignores the poor little things. I swear, sometimes, at night, when my window is open, I swear I can hear those poor little flowers crying for moisture. Mrs. Jenson sees me watering them but she never comes out and says anything. But then, I'm not doing it for Mrs. Jenson anyway. I'm doing it for the poor little flowers."

"Nice," Amber said.

"So, I think about stuff like that for as long as I can and then I put on this music that's very mystical and tinkly and just seeps into my soul and makes me nearly want to burst with hope and love and peace. I sometimes flit and twirl around my room and sometimes I just sit on the floor with my eyes closed and concentrate on the music. It's all so wonderful. Really."

"And I'm just asking this for information, I'm not judging, but at the end of the day do you think this really helps the earth?"

"Oh yes, I've talked to the other Pagans about this and they totally agree that every ounce of positive energy that we expel for the earth goes into making every living thing stronger."

Amber nodded. "Good to hear."

"Finally," Rachel said, sitting down on the edge of her bed, "I have finally found what makes me whole."

"So it appears."

"And you?" Rachel asked, showing Amber that this new and better Rachel was now totally attuned to the happiness of all around her. "Is the church giving you all that you need to be whole?"

"Well, not yet. I'm afraid I haven't really thrown myself into understanding it yet the way you have Paganism. I mean I have only been to church once, but I did really enjoy that. My father did the sermon and it was something I wished I could hear over and over. There was so much to think about."

"Yes. We have a universe to acknowledge and explore now that we are aware of it. Well, more aware I mean. We have, of course, always been aware of it."

"I'm sure the universe understands that," Amber said. "Besides I think the church is a little more structured than what you are doing. I mean I can't just make up stuff."

"Oh, I'm not really making this stuff up. What I chant, what I think, is all spoken to me by Cybele."

"Sorry, I didn't know that."

"That's okay. How could you?"

"Right," Amber said. "So now that I have seen your temple how about we go and do something?"

"Well, of course, I'd love to but I'm meeting Alfred and our friends in half an hour. We are discussing the difference between the Occult and Occult Arts and how we need to educate people on the difference. We don't want to all be lumped in together. I mean, we may start practicing the Arts, but even if we don't, we can study Occult and consider ourselves members of the Occult."

"When you say, 'our friends' does that suggest that you and Eddie are now you and Alfred?"

Rachel giggled. "No. I guess you could say that I'm not really seeing Eddie any more. I mean we are friends, but he doesn't even try to understand what's important to me, so we have, shall we say, drifted apart. No hard feelings, just heading in different directions."

"So, you and Alfred?"

"Really, Amber, why do I have to be with someone? I am complete as myself and yes, I will admit that I do enjoy Alfred's company, we do spend a lot of time together, but I won't say we are a couple."

"But would you want to say you are a couple?"

"No. I am just a free spirit right now and I am happy with that."

"How about that!" Amber said. "You are not even close to the girl I have known since second grade."

"And that's a good thing. I can't believe how shallow I used to be. I mean, you know how I was always trying to be popular and have the right look and be like everyone I thought was so special. Well, now Alfred has taught me that I stand alone, and I am a model for others to emulate not the other way around."

"Awesome," Amber said. "So, what is the difference between Occult and Occult Arts?"

Rachel beamed at the question and went to her backpack and took out a folder. "I have been taking notes for our session today, so this is what I have – this is from Lucifer, Vol. 1, p.7 – Occultism is not magic, though magic is one of its tools. Occultism is not the acquirement of powers, whether psychic or intellectual, though both are its servants. Neither is occultism the pursuit of happiness, as men understand the word; for the first step is sacrifice, the second, renunciation. Occultism is the science of life, the art of living."

"Okay," Amber said, leaning against the door casing. "I don't have a clue what that means."

"This is saying that the tools of the Occult are the Arts. Like magic and witchcraft and mind control. As Pagans we do not have to necessarily engage in these Arts. But we could if that would bring us closer to being one with the universe. We pretty much believe in animism which is the living spirits in inanimate objects and plants. Like Cybele. We worship the self, earth and an all-encompassing Mother Goddess. We do not practice in Spiritism, which is where they try to communicate with a spirit or someone deceased. Those days are over for me. Of course, I never believed all that anyway."

"So magic and witches but no dead people?"

"Don't be so crude. I am serious here."

"Sorry, just trying to keep up."

"Okay, let me start from the beginning then. Occult means hidden secret or knowledge. It is about the inner nature of things rather than science really. Though science can be a part of it. Where science is only external, occultism is mostly about the inner nature. That's why we can draw deeper than the scientific reasons for things. Alfred says that divinity is inseparable from nature. We believe that everything in the universe has a life force or spiritual energy."

"Everything in the universe?"

"Yes," Rachel said and then frowned. Rachel knew that Alfred had said that but now, even to her, that seemed impossible. She had better put Amber on the defensive rather than have Amber questioning her. "Anyway, Alfred says that religion is faith and the Occult is knowledge."

"Really?" Amber said. "Maybe I could ask John about that."

"Sure. Do that. Alfred also says that Occultists don't pray to their gods, they communicate with them. He said we don't sit and hope for a miracle, we create the miracles we need."

"Interesting," Amber said. "I can see why you like listening to Alfred."

"I do."

"What does your Mom say about all of this? The shrine and your communicating with asteroids?"

"Make fun if you want. It just shows your ignorance."

Amber shrugged. "Guilty. So, I guess I had better let you get going. I'm really glad you are so happy, Rachel. I know you have been looking for something like this for a long time."

Rachel smiled. "Thanks. I am. And to think, I may never have found it if Mom hadn't dragged me to that horrid junk sale."

"Karma, right?"

"Wrong," Rachel said. "Alfred said that karma is just a figment of the imagination of those who do not know the true hidden laws of nature. Alfred said we don't believe in karma just like we don't believe in the church's belief of sin and punishment."

"Paganism is pretty easy to live with then. I guess you had just better hope he is right."

"Oh, he is," Rachel said.

Gram smiled when Grace opened the door. "Hello, sweetie," Gram said and walked into Miriam's house with the warm casserole dish wrapped in two kitchen towels to protect her hands.

"Mmm, that smells great," Grace said. "I'll go get Mom."

"Is she resting?"

Grace nodded. "But she has been lying down for a couple hours. I'm sure she won't mind."

"No, no, let her rest. Maybe you and I could have some time to talk while we wait."

"Yeah, sure."

"Okay, let's put this in the kitchen and then maybe we can just sit outside until she gets up."

"I can get us some lemonade. Is that good?"

"Perfect," Gram said, following Grace into the large white kitchen. "I'll just put this in the oven on a low temperature to keep it warm."

Grace went quietly about getting the glasses and the lemonade.

"How do you work this stove?" Gram asked, looking at the line of options.

Grace left her work and came to peer over Gram's shoulder. "I'm not sure. Mom never lets me touch the stove."

Gram looked at her. "Really, at twelve?"

Grace shrugged. "It's just how she is. She is very protective. She said she was afraid I'd burn myself or catch the house on fire." Grace laughed. "One time, when I was eight, I did melt a plastic dish in the microwave."

"Oh, we've all done that," Gram said, poking at the control panel. "There, I think I have it." Gram straightened her old back and stretched a little. "That should be good for a while. When does your father get home?"

Grace bit her lip and thought. "That depends. I think he has a meeting tonight so maybe eight o'clock."

"Fine, then we have plenty of time."

"Oh, Mom and I don't wait for him to eat dinner. Mom says I need a consistent meal time and bed time and so we just save some for Dad if he is late getting home."

"Okay. Let's get that lemonade and sit out on the back porch."

Grace poured the glasses full. "Oops, I forgot. Do you want ice?"

Gram shook her head. "It just falls when I drink and splashes lemonade all over my face."

Grace giggled. "Me too. That's why Mom always makes me use a straw."

"Sounds like your mother has everything covered."

"Yes, she takes really good care of me," Grace said and then she looked sad. "Do you think that she will be okay? I mean do you think the doctor got all the cancer?"

Gram nodded. "I do."

"Yeah," Grace said. "Me to. I pray about it every night."

"There you go," Gram said, "sounds like you have taken care of your part."

Gram and Grace carried their lemonade out to the back porch. "We better sit around the corner," Grace said in a hushed voice. "Mom's room is right above us here and we don't want to make too much noise."

Gram followed Grace to the front of the house and they sat in the blue rocking chairs by the door.

"Ahh, this is so nice," Gram said. "I'm so glad you and I are getting to spend a little time together."

"Me too. I guess I just think sometimes that you are, well, like you only belong to Amber. But you are my grandmother, too."

"I am. Just as much your grandmother."

"Did Amber tell you that she and I had ice cream with Dad?"

"She did. She was very happy about that. And she was happy that you both like your sundaes made the same way."

Grace smiled. "That was a good day. Well, in the end. It didn't start out good, that's for sure."

"Well, it ended well, so that is all that matters."

"Yes, I was so glad Dad came back for me. I was in my room, really angry with Mom for not letting me talk to Amber when Dad opened the door and told me to come with him on a date with his daughters. Wasn't that funny? A date with his daughters!"

"He is a good man," Gram said.

"Oh, he is. Sometimes Mom gets really mad at him, but he just fixes everything and we get back to being happy again."

"Well, I'm glad he fixed this for you and Amber."

"Oh, it may not be really fixed. Mom said that we can't think that Amber can just traipse in and out of our lives at her whim, but Dad said for me not to worry. He said that Mom will see everything better when she is healed."

"We will hope for that," Gram said, sipping her lemonade.

"Well, well, well," Miriam said, opening the front door. "I thought I heard voices out here."

"Oh, we're sorry," Grace said.

"It's okay. I was awake." Miriam came out onto the porch. She was wearing a simple pink beltless sheath.

"You're dressed!" Grace said.

"Yes, time to move out of my bathrobe and back into the world."

"That's great," Gram said. "You must be feeling better."

"We'll see, Mom," Miriam said.

"Well, can you join us or do you want us to go back inside where it is more comfortable for you?" Gram asked.

"I just need Grace to bring around one of the big chairs with the cushions and I think that will be fine."

Grace bounded out of her rocker and hurried to get her mother the chair.

"I just brought by a chicken casserole. It's in the oven," Gram said.

"Oh, Mom, I told you that you don't have to feed us. John can cook and the church women are bringing around enough food to feed an army."

"Well, I wanted to. You always liked my chicken casserole."

Grace was back and Miriam eased herself down into the chair. "It is a beautiful day," Miriam conceded. "It's nice to be back among the living."

"Mom," Grace shrieked. "Don't say stuff like that."

"It's just a saying, Grace," Miriam said. "So, what were you two talking about?"

"We just got out here, actually," Gram said. "So just general chit chat."

"Yeah," Grace echoed. "Just nothing really."

Miriam looked doubtful but didn't push the issue. "Are you here because Amber tattled that I'm a big meanie?"

"I'm here because I'm your mother and I want to help you while you are going through this."

"It's cancer, Mom. Not, *this*."

"I know," Gram said.

"Okay, I just don't want people tip toeing around me or pretending that what I have is some little sniffle that I will bounce back from. It's cancer and no one can know the outcome yet."

"Got it," Gram said. "I'd just like to help you while you are trying to be cured of cancer."

Miriam nodded, satisfied that there was no whitewashing the severity of her disease. "So, what did Amber tell you?"

"We don't have to talk about Amber," Gram said. "I'd like to just sit here with you two and find out all the things I have missed."

"Like what, Gram?" Grace asked, hoping to get the conversation rolling in another direction.

"Oh like, what was your favorite Christmas present?"

Grace and Gram jumped into the game of asking irrelevant questions until Miriam had had enough and asked Grace to go get her a glass of iced tea and maybe a couple of Mrs. Darbin's sugar cookies. "Would you like something, Mom? Mrs. Darbin makes the best cookies."

"Oh no, I'm fine. I guess I'd better be going soon anyway. I have a casserole warming in my own oven and your father will be ready to get into it after smelling it all afternoon."

"Can I have a cookie, too?" Grace asked, pausing at the door.

"Of course," Miriam said. "But just one. You ate a good lunch and it's almost dinner time."

As soon as Grace disappeared inside Miriam shook her head. "I bet she gobbles one in the kitchen before she comes out with her one cookie."

"Kids will be kids," Gram said.

"But sneaking behind your mother's back is sneaking behind your mother's back."

"Miriam, apparently you are forgetting who you are talking to. I was your mother when you were twelve so maybe I could remind you of a few things about you at that age."

"A parent's job is to teach their children not to repeat the mistakes they have made."

"And it's also to look away once in a while and let them learn from making their own harmless mistakes."

"We have disagreed on many things, Mom."

"And we are all paying the price for that now."

Miriam lifted her chin and narrowed her eyes. "Is this why you came over today? To lecture me?"

"As you said, you and I have often seen things differently. I came to bring you something that I had hoped would help and show you that I want to be in your life now. But, since I have been here, you have treated me, and Grace, like naughty little children. I'm a grown woman, Miriam. I love you, but I won't be talked down to or scolded just because you don't feel well."

"You know, Mom, this isn't how I wanted things to turn out either,"

Miriam suddenly looked frail, looked sorrowful. "I have missed you and Dad. Really. These years have not been easy for me either. And whenever I thought about going home and telling you and Dad about why I did what I did and how my life is now, well, I thought it would be good. I thought we would all be happy and we would have time to fix all the mistakes and just get on like regular families. And, when I first contacted you, and you and Dad were so happy, well, I felt that was how it was going to be. But I didn't factor in how angry and mean Amber would be."

"Maybe because you were just always so busy thinking about how you wanted to feel and not about how you must have made a little girl feel when she learned that her mother had simply walked away and left her."

"I didn't just simply walk away. Why won't anyone believe me? It was not easy and I have wanted to fix it every day for all these years. Seriously, I'm not as horrible as you all want to think. I have feelings, too."

"Then prove it and start acting like a mother to Amber."

"Amber won't let me."

"Just like the cookie, you know your children may not be doing exactly what you want but you don't give up. You keep putting yourself out there until they believe that you really mean what you say."

"How, Mom? How can I reach Amber?"

"By trying. What are your plans? To just sit and wait for the next fight or are you going to reach out to her and ask her to let you start over?"

"She would never agree to that."

"Maybe not the first hundred times you ask."

Miriam smiled weakly. "See why I had to leave home - you are relentless."

"I like to think of it as I'm right."

Grace pushed the door open with her foot and carried out the tea and cookies. She handed the tea to her mother and two of the cookies.

"You can have another," Miriam said, handing one of the cookies back.

"No, no. One is fine," Grace said, refusing to take the cookie.

"Really?" Miriam asked.

"Oh yeah, I don't want two."

Gram winked at Miriam and the three of them settled in their chairs to talk about irrelevant things.

"I'm so pleased to see you again," Sadie said when she opened the door to Amber.

"Thank you," Amber said, stepping inside Sadie's house. Sadie's house was instantly comforting, like stepping back in time to a quieter and simpler life. Actually, Sadie herself felt like an old soul who'd been reincarnated into this modern, fast paced, often vulgar, world. Amber guessed Sadie had just lived within her safe walls and had been content with her books and garden and memories. Lord knows that it wasn't safe to listen to the radio or even watch mainstream TV anymore if one was at all delicate and naïve.

"Can I get you something?" Sadie asked. "Tea perhaps? I have regular and decaffeinated. I'm afraid I can never drink caffeine this late in the afternoon as it either keeps me awake all night or gives me fitful dreams when I do doze off."

"I'm really okay but, thank you."

"Good. Good," Sadie said as she led Amber through the dim, overstuffed house to the sun porch crowded with ferns and peace lilies and spider plants hanging in every corner. "Let's sit here where we can look out at the pond. It's my favorite spot for just catching my breath and feeling my Savior close by me."

"You have a spot where you feel more spiritual?"

"Yes, I believe we all should. That way when you get there your mind stops racing a million miles an hour and you can relax and summon His peace to flow through you again."

"That sounds great."

"It is great. Do you know where your spiritual place may be?"

"Not yet," Amber said, sitting down in the white wicker chair opposite Sadie. "Do you have something special you have to see, a statue or cross or something like that, to get you centered?"

"No," Sadie chuckled. "There is nothing physical I need to see or touch. I have physical things that remind me of Henry and my parents, but I don't need that for Jesus. He put the Holy Spirit inside me and that's all I need."

"Okay, about the Holy Spirit," Amber said. "I just have to be baptized and the Holy Spirit is inside of me, guiding me, right?"

"Well, Jesus did promise the gift of the Holy Spirit when we accept Him as our Savior, and that usually is in Baptism, but I don't want you to think that the Holy Spirit instantly takes over your body or life. You have to first believe in Him and then let your questions, your needs, be known to the Holy Spirit before He can help you. Say, if you need help with having faith, well, the Holy Spirit will guide you to the answers you need in the Bible.

So, He doesn't actually impede your free will as though you are possessed or something, He just points you where you need to go to find what you are supposed to find. So, have you been baptized yet?"

"No, but my father is a pastor so I'm certain I will be when I'm ready."

"Good. Your grandmother told me about your circumstances when she called to set up our first meeting. I hope all is going well with your new family."

Amber shrugged one shoulder and then shook her head. "To be honest, no. Going well is not how I would exactly describe things."

"Well, I am certain that the bumps in your road will be smoothed out with time and prayer. So, what exactly can I help you with today?"

"Again, I don't really know what I expect you to tell me. I just felt like it would be good for me if you had the time to talk. Anything you say will help me to... work on finding faith."

"Ah yes, finding faith. Well, first be assured that it is okay to admit you do not have faith yet. It is only natural to have doubts. Actually, now that I think about it, faith actually requires doubt. Building your faith is the exercise of overcoming your doubt. Only when you ask the questions can you find the answers."

"That makes sense."

"Thank you, but I was not the first to discover that. People who actually witnessed Jesus performing miracles still harbored doubts. Why think of Peter and even John the Baptist. And then in Mark something or other the father of a possessed boy came to Jesus for help for his son. The father believed enough to bring Jesus to save his son, but he also had to admit that he was not certain. The father said 'I do believe. Help my unbelief.' Now, if you think about that, the man is like a lot of us. We believe, because we very much want to believe that we do have faith but, please God, if it isn't enough, please help me with my unbelief."

Amber smiled.

"A philosopher once said, 'I don't believe in God, but I fear him greatly.' How is that for a quandary?"

"I have to wonder about that philosopher's credentials."

"Yes, I agree. But my point is that it is human to have doubts about something as important as this. So, do your homework, ask the questions and I think you will find that, in the end, your doubts will be answered by the truths you will discover. Why C.S. Lewis struggled with doubt most of his younger years of life until he was finally won over with the inescapable truth of God. He then said, 'I believe in Christianity as I believe that the sun has risen: not only because I see it, but because by it I see everything else.'

"That is great."

"Yes, C.S. Lewis not only came to have strong faith, he went from talking against believing in God to becoming one of the greatest apologists ever born. Here is another of my favorites by him, 'A man can no more diminish God's glory by refusing to worship him than a lunatic can put out the sun by scribbling 'darkness' on the wall of his cell.'"

"Guess I will have to read more about C.S. Lewis."

"His story is interesting. I mean the stories he wrote were interesting but also his own personal story. He was living proof that God did not promise us a smooth flight without trials, but He is there to see that we will have a safe landing."

Amber sat back in her chair. "You are so good at knowing just what I needed to hear. What I need to think about. I came here worried because I didn't have the faith that I thought I was supposed to have and you have made me see that that is okay as long as I'm asking the questions and remain open to the answers."

Sadie looked pleased. "It's a rare privilege to be able to help someone work their way through such an important journey. I firmly believe that educating our faith is the best way to defeat our doubts. The more you embark on an honest search for the existence of God, the more you will be convinced."

"I think I will start with C.S. Lewis. Let him show me what my questions should even be."

"Fine then," Sadie said. "Shall we call it a day?"

"Yes, and thank you for your time and, well, everything."

"When the student is ready, the teacher will appear," Sadie said. "That was Buddha I believe but still true. You are ready now and looking for your teacher."

"Well, I'll try not to be a pest."

"Like I am so busy I can't be interrupted? Really, I spend so much of my time alone reinforcing my own faith that it is good to share it, to say it out loud. Maybe God's plan is about both of us."

Amber left Sadie's house with a few more C. S. Lewis quotes and a spider plant. She was anxious to get home and talk to Gram. After her visit with Rachel, Amber had felt selfishly disappointed that Rachel was, right or wrong, deeply and happily into her spiritual journey where Amber was still questioning if she was genuinely interested in religion or if Rachel had been right to accuse Amber of pursuing faith just to please her newly found father. Amber needed to find the answer. She hoped that her research would convince her that God was her ultimate goal and not John.

Amber sat at her window and stared out at the night sky. It was a clear night, the moon a crescent of white imperceptibly moving through the millions of stars that were spattered across the black vastness. Amber still couldn't imagine that God was out there somewhere, knowing everyone, knowing everything that had happened and was going to happen. It seemed too much to think about really. Rachel's focus on a statue she had invented didn't make any sense, but then how could one really make sense out of God? He was too big and too unreachable. How could anyone even believe that he was there?

Amber sighed and turned back to her laptop. She had run so many ideas through her search engine that she felt overwhelmed. There were so many sites for and against God. One site led to another and another until she didn't even know what she was looking for anymore.

Amber picked up her notebook and scanned over some things she had written down. Jesus was the king who led by making himself a servant. He was a teacher who taught by living out His own lessons. He was a savior who saved by making Himself the sacrifice. She would ask John to help her fully understand these things.

She had seen a site on miracles that had drawn her in. But it said that miracles were part of the Gospel of Jesus and if miracles cease its because faith has ceased. If one had faith, could they then expect miracles? How did you know when you had enough faith to qualify for miracles? What would a miracle be like? Amber smiled. Well, she knew her personal miracle would be to actually... to intentionally, forgive Miriam. That would have to be a real God-assisted miracle.

Amber closed her laptop and lay down on her bed. She felt like a scavenger, ragged and gaunt as she scurried from place to place, gathering bits of information here and there. Filling her filthy sack with the snippets and remnants that were tossed to her from those who were comfortable and content in their faith. She pictured herself as a frightened little orphan peeking in the windows of the homes of believers, pressing her ear to the closed doors of the church so she could hear something that was valuable and then silently slip away unnoticed with it. She would find a safe corner to hide in and then dump out her bag of bits and pieces and try to fit them together to make sense of it all. And in her fantasy, the answer would appear. The truth would be spelled out clearly and she would suddenly stand straight, brush the dust from her tattered clothes, and just close her eyes and... believe.

Amber smiled. That was exactly how she and Rachel used to pretend. If they were playing the same game now she would call Rachel, no matter the late hour, and they would laugh at the silliness of their imaginations. But she and Rachel were not playing the same games any longer. They were exploring things that the other couldn't, and probably didn't even want to understand. As much as she and Rachel had always argued, were totally exasperated with each other, and had even gone days without speaking, Amber missed her friend.

Amber remembered how in one of her literary classes the teacher had warned them that when they understood literature, when they learned to read books of substance, they would then and forever lose their appetite for the fluff and triteness of poor writing. "For everything gained, something is lost." Was Amber trading her fantasies for the truth of the real world and would she then never be able to go back? Would she and Rachel never lie in the grass on their backs again and imagine their amazing futures with extravagance and silliness and hope? Growing up was proving to be very disappointing.

Sunday Amber sat in church between Gram and Grampa. James had to work but had assured her that any Sunday he was off he would be more than happy to go to church with her.

Gram was so cute in her soft flowered dress and matching hat. Grampa had told her that he hadn't seen one other woman in church with a hat, but Gram had just pooh-poohed him and said that was shame on all of them and not her. When she was young and had ever gone to church with her family for weddings, or any reason truthfully, but especially funerals, the women always showed respect by wearing hats and the men wore suits.

"Times have changed," Grampa said.

"And not for the better. Foul language is commonplace now. Underwear sticking out of dragging pants on boys and near nakedness is flaunted on girls! And what used to be people's private business behind closed doors now seems to be the only thing people find entertainment in on TV! And has all this rot made the world a better place? Do people appear happier now that they can cheapen themselves without censor? They are not! Everywhere you look people are unhappy. Drugs and suicide and gangs. Enough is never enough of anything for them so they better not judge me because I want to show respect for myself and wear a hat in the house of the Lord."

"Whoa," Grampa had said. "Have I mentioned how pretty you look in that hat?"

"John called me last night," Gram whispered to Amber as they waited for the church to fill. "And we talked about when I thought you may be ready to… well, be introduced to his congregation. I told him that, well, we obviously can't wait for Amber and Miriam to mend their differences, so maybe next Sunday. Would that be okay, do you think?"

"I guess it may be getting awkward for him. I mean, he can't hide me forever, especially if I want to find a place in his and Grace's life."

"That's what we were thinking," Gram said, patting Amber's hand. "So maybe next Sunday he can tell his people during the service and we can, as a family, kind of linger after the last service in case anyone wants to make your acquaintance."

"I'd really rather not," Amber said. "But I guess it is unavoidable. I just wonder how he can find a way to present me that makes sense to anyone else when I can't, at times, make sense of it myself and I'm living it."

"Isn't that the truth," Gram said. "I guess he may have to turn to higher help in figuring that out."

"Do you think Miriam will be well enough to come next Sunday or will she just, as usual, let all of us do the heavy lifting?" Amber asked.

Gram gave Amber's hand a quick tap. "Now be nice. You're in church. Didn't you have any proper up bringing?"

Amber smiled. "I was raised by old people and they let me run amuck."

Gram heard Grampa chuckle and she scowled around Amber until he felt her disapproval and got a hold of himself.

The pews filled and the doors were closed. The service started with John's prayer and then the congregation joined in a hymn and then sang "Hope In Front Of Me". Amber had never heard Gram sing before, Gram was more one to hum when she was busy or contented, but today her little voice trembled with the earnestness of her effort. How their lives had changed.

After the announcements and the offering John thanked everyone and went up the few steps to the pulpit.

"Today's scripture is Matthew 7:1-3 – Judging Others. Hear the Word of the Lord. 'Judge not, that you be not judged. For with the judgment you pronounce you will be judged, and with the measure you use it will be measured you. Why do you see the speck that is in your brother's eye, but do not notice the log that is in your own eye?"

Amber felt Grampa lean forward and raise an eyebrow to Gram. Gram ignored him and continued to listen.

"I read you this," John continued, "because there is so much misconception about judgment of others in the Bible. We have come to believe that it is wrong to have an opinion about anything. We hear people say, 'Stop judging and love.' And 'Jesus said, Do not judge'. They say this as though Jesus was telling us that all negative assessment is unacceptable to God. That we should not see or mention what we know is wrong. Jesus never told us that all actions are equally moral or that truth is relative. He did not say that we should not identify sin for what it is. The Bible never tells us to ignore what God has so clearly defined as sin. Lying, adultery, murder, stealing, obvious wrongs that we should not look away from because we believe Jesus told us not to judge. In Matthew 7 he is telling us to not judge hypocritically. If we have a splinter in our own eye, then we should not judge someone else with a splinter in their eye."

Gram leaned forward and looked at Grampa, her eyebrow raised. Grampa shrugged and nodded. He had to concede that his wife had not judged hypocritically. She had not abused him with profanity or wore her bra on the outside of her clothes or took mind altering drugs for the thrill of it. She hadn't worn her hat to the grocery store, but she had also not worn her pajamas to the grocery store. Grampa guessed that his wife was not, in God's eyes, hypocritical.

"In John 7:24 Jesus tells us, however, to stop judging by mere appearances, and instead judge correctly. We cannot know the full circumstances of everyone's actions. Those that we meet, and judge immediately, may be fighting a battle we know nothing about. Their actions may be influenced by forces that would not have ordinarily guided them. But still, if their actions are obvious sins, then no matter their battle, they may be judged as their actions dictate. However, in our hearts, it is necessary to consider their circumstances. If someone stole food because they are starving we can give them grace, but if they stole because someone had something nicer than they had, then we have every right to judge that on its merits. And if we had ever stolen anything just because we wanted it, then we are as guilty as they are in God's eyes, especially if we then chose to judge them with pious indignation.'

'Jesus was bothered more by the sins of the spirit than sins of the flesh. He preached against self-righteousness. Jesus's great concern for us is do we show compassion to one another. Jesus believed that there are no hopeless people. He believed everyone could be healed, saved and forgiven. He took care of our sins on the cross so we, and everyone else, can always start over. So, understand that we are free to judge the action but not the person. We can all be forgiven and the proof is that if God didn't forgive sinners then heaven would be empty. So, my point is, that when we are told that we should not judge the choices and the actions of anyone, know that that did not come from the Bible. Someone saying that simply because they do not want to be accountable for their own wrong actions is equal to someone hypocritically seeing past his own splinter to judge the splinter in his neighbor's eye."

Amber nodded. John had so much Amber wanted to think about packed in those few sentences. She wished she could get the transcript of his sermon so she could pour over it and list questions he would be able to clarify for her. Amber sat focused on his words, the inflections of his voice, the humor he would slip in to lighten the heaviness of his message. He was truly gifted in communicating what she hoped God was really like.

"The fact is," John said, concluding his sermon, "God loves us, and his love means he cares. He cares enough to judge us and not be indifferent to our sin. His love will not allow sin to win without a fight. God wants you to be in Heaven, not Hell, and he will do anything to get you there. Therefore, he will judge you, and he will want those who love you to judge you. He knows that people who let you hurt yourself with all types of immorality without telling you it is wrong, and not encouraging you to do better, are not showing their love for you. Love does judge but it does so with truth and fairness and grace."

After the service Gram asked Amber if she would like to go with them to Miriam and John's for lunch. Gram was pleased to let Amber know that Miriam had invited them herself and she had even said that Amber was welcome if she wanted to come.

Amber thought about that. Miriam's invitation felt like it was more of a challenge put to Amber rather than a well-intentioned offer, so she shrugged and shook her head. "Probably not this time," Amber replied.

"Oh, sweetie," Gram pleaded. "You have to start somewhere. And we will be there. And John and Grace will be there, so it shouldn't get into a power struggle with you and Miriam."

"Gram, it's not a power struggle. At least not for me. I don't want power over her or anyone. Well, especially her. All I want… I want…"

"What, dear?" Gram asked, leaning in for the answer.

"I want to forgive her from a distance."

Gram's face fell, disappointed in Amber's answer.

"Well, at least I'm trying with one part of it," Amber said.

"Now," Grampa offered, "how about if we keep you apart at lunch? You sit at one end of the table and Miriam at the other."

Amber smiled at him. Grampa was never comfortable with participating in this type of conversation, so she knew he was making an effort to help Gram convince Amber to just come to lunch and try to be civil to Miriam.

"Look," Amber offered, "you two go today and maybe next Sunday, after our family coming-out, we can all go somewhere together and have lunch. Maybe I'll be ready then."

"You can leave right after we eat," Gram offered. "You don't have to stay and visit."

"Yes," John said, coming up behind Amber. "You may escape at any moment you choose."

Amber felt her face flush and turned to see John's smile.

"I don't know," Amber said. "I just don't feel like it would be a good idea right now. I'm still working on the forgiving, and judging with love, stuff."

John nodded his head. "Okay, but you and I do need to talk before next Sunday service."

"I know, Gram told me."

"Are you okay with that?"

"I'll try to be," Amber said and then she felt her cell phone vibrating in the bottom of her purse. Amber pulled it out and looked at it. "It's Rachel's mom," Amber said, frowning up at them. "She never calls me."

Amber stepped away from everyone and called Rachel's mom back. Amber stood still and listened and then nodded and said that she would be right there. Amber closed her phone and continued to look at it.

"What is it," Gram asked.

"Rachel is having a meltdown apparently," Amber said.

"Oh my," Gram said.

"I'm going there now."

"Of course, you are," Gram said.

Amber swallowed her worry and looked at them all. "Rachel can be a drama queen, but her mom never overreacts and if you had just heard her now…"

"Go. Just go now and drive safely," Gram said.

"I don't know the circumstances, but if I can help in anyway," John offered.

Amber nodded and headed for her car.

Rachel's mother was standing on the front stoop when Amber drove up into the driveway. She hurried down the steps and met Amber as soon as she got out of her car.

"Thank you. Thank you. I don't think she will talk to anyone else."

"What is she doing?"

"She has smashed her altar, thank goodness, but then she just curled up on her bed and refuses to talk."

Amber went straight into the house and ran upstairs to Rachel's room. She turned the doorknob and went in. Cybele was shattered into a hundred tiny pieces on the floor. The holy water vile was lying in a small puddle on the wood floor. Crystals and stones and flowers were scattered everywhere.

"Wow," Amber said, walking carefully around Rachel's religious debris. "What happened?"

Rachel didn't answer.

"I only want to help you," Amber said, sitting on the side of the bed.

Rachel didn't respond.

Amber sat there for a few moments. "Can I clean this up for you?"

No answer.

"Okay then, would it be okay with you if I cleaned this up?"

No answer.

"Look, Rachel, if you don't tell me what happened then I can't help you."

Amber sat in the silence a few more minutes and then she lay down next to Rachel and wrapped her arms around her. "You're my best friend. You've been my best friend nearly all my life."

Amber could feel Rachel's body convulse with a smothered sob.

"Please tell me," Amber said softly.

"I just want to be by myself," Rachel said.

"Tough," Amber said, scooting her legs up next to Rachel's. "I'm going to stay here with you until you feel like talking even if we die of starvation and they have to burn the house down to get our stench out."

Normally, Rachel would have had to laugh at that but today she just lay still, not pushing Amber away but not responding to her in any way.

After half an hour Amber whispered that she may have spoken too hastily. "I have to pee," she said and then waited. Finally, she had to add that she didn't want to stink until after they had died so she had better get up.

Rachel reached up when Amber started to move and tightened Amber's arms back around her.

"Well," Amber said, "it's not an emergency. I guess I can wait."

So, they lay together until Amber could feel Rachel begin to relax.

"It's kind of scary how deeply you are hurt," Amber said.

Tears slid out of Rachel's eyes.

"You know," Amber said, "I was thinking about us last night. I was sad that you and I were going in different directions and that maybe we would never be able to be like we were again. I started to make up this silly scenario like we used to do where I was a poor ragged orphan looking for something I needed to know. Remember how we would do that? How you always had to be a princess and I was always the wench?"

Rachel sighed.

"I don't want us to not be best friends any more. Call me selfish, but I don't want to be just a wench without a princess."

"Oh Amber," Rachel said through her sobs.

Amber hugged tighter and just waited for Rachel's sobs to subside. Amber loosened one arm and reached around for the box of tissues on the bed stand. She handed a wad to Rachel and then returned to hugging her.

Rachel wiped her face and her nose and hiccupped. "This is the worst thing that has ever happened to me on so many levels."

"Wow," Amber said. "On many levels?"

Rachel nodded.

"Do you want me to guess or just wait until you feel like talking about it?"

"I'm never going to feel like talking about it because it is so humiliating and devastating and totally horrid."

"Okay," Amber said.

Rachel lay still for a few more minutes and then she released Amber's arms and sat up. "More tissues," she said.

Amber sat up and handed the box to Rachel.

Rachel blew her nose loudly and then looked around her room and sighed. "I really wanted to believe," she said.

"I know," Amber said.

"I mean Paganism was just so easy. So happy really. I mean, I could make it whatever I wanted and everyone was so encouraging. Telling me I was getting all the right things. I even," Rachel paused and sobbed. "I even bought matching amulets for me and… Cybele."

Now Amber was silent.

"Paganism fit in with all the things we used to play with. It was grown-up fantasy in a way. I mean I really did take it seriously. I really wanted to reach back in time and follow the ancient ways. The ways of worshipping the Greek gods and goddesses. Honoring the earth. I mean everything we are and have and ever will have is thanks to the earth."

"Or whoever made the earth," Amber said.

"Amber, really? My world is destroyed and you want to preach to me now?"

"No. Sorry."

That satisfied Rachel and she returned to her suffering. "So, you can just imagine how I felt when I got to the coffee shop this morning and found out that Alfred was leaving our coven."

Amber nodded. "Continue."

"So, today I was going to share how much I had been studying and practicing, and I even wrote a new chant for Cybele, but instead Alfred comes in smiling with his hair combed out of his eyes and he was with…" Rachel paused and held her breath at the memory of the shock she had felt. "He came in with Amy."

"Amy?"

"You know, that girl on his Facebook page that said studying the Occult had brought her to God!"

"Oh, Amy."

"Yes, AMY!"

"That is horrible."

"No. Well, yes, it is horrible but what was worse was why he was with Amy."

"She had convinced him to turn to the Bible?"

"Yes. Remember I never did trust her. I didn't understand what she meant by saying that but I guess I know now."

"But, Rachel, Alfred's leaving the coven doesn't mean you have to."

"I know but what I did next does."

"I can't even guess."

Rachel flopped back against the bed and flung her arm over her eyes. "I stood up and begged him to reconsider. I blurted that I thought I loved him and then the whole world stopped. Stopped. Everyone in the coffee shop stopped and stared at me. And I was left there alone and looking like a fool and so I ran past them and knocked into Amy on my way by her. She actually fell over. It was an accident. Okay, maybe not a real accident but I didn't intend to hurt her. Well, not too much anyway. But it was horrible. Horrible. All of it."

Amber sighed. "I see."

"I hate myself and Alfred and everyone in the coven who saw that I was a fraud."

"Fraud?"

"Yes, Amber, how could I be a real Pagan and then only care if Alfred was one or not? The moment he said he was leaving it was like suddenly nothing I believed or did was worth anything. It was like I felt empty. I mean, if I really believed in Paganism then wouldn't I have tried to persuade him to stay because I felt that was what was best for him and not to just stay because… I loved him?"

"It is probably hard to think clearly when you are blindsided like that. I mean, you didn't have a clue he was starting to doubt what he was teaching you?"

"No, no. If I wanted to learn and believe then he would have helped me no matter the turmoil he was going through. I know that about him," Rachel paused. "He was so wonderful."

"Can't you find another coven?" Amber asked, trying to direct Rachel away from thinking about Alfred.

"Don't you understand? I have lost my faith. If I ever really had it. How horrible is that on top of losing the man I thought I loved?"

"You've only been at this a few weeks. Maybe it will come back to you if you find another coven. There must be more."

Rachel turned her face away from Amber. She sighed mournfully and then after a few moments of thought she sat back up. "I simply do not have the heart to start over. I have lost everything. Everything."

"Hey, don't say that. If it weren't for the darkness we would never see the stars. Something good is just waiting to happen for you."

"No. No. I'm alone and a fraud. The earth will never accept me again."

"Well, you can always look for something else then. There are plenty of other options. Plenty of other faiths. Maybe this one just wasn't right for you and the universe is correcting that before you got too deep."

Rachel looked shocked. "Seriously, Amber, if I had a favorite cat that had gotten run over by a garbage truck would you immediately bring me a new kitten and think that would fix everything?"

Amber smiled. Rachel was feeling a little better.

"Don't smirk like that. My life is ruined. For once in our lives, please have some compassion for me."

"Sorry."

"No, you are not."

"Yeah, I really am. That was not sensitive of me and you certainly deserve to be treated respectfully after all that you have just been through."

Rachel slumped. She ran her fingers through her ragged hair and sighed deeply. "I'll never see Alfred again."

Amber reached over and patted Rachel's hand. "What are you going to do now?"

"That's the problem. That's why I have been lying here suffering for hours. I don't know what I am going to do. How do I fill all of these empty places inside me? Who am I?"

Amber stood up and went to start cleaning up the mess. "You are the indestructible princess Rachel. You always have been and always will be. You will rise up out of the ashes even stronger and more confident than before. God help us all. You have explored Paganism and you are now ready to move on." Amber straightened and held up one of the amulets. "Do you want to keep this? I mean just in case you ever decide…"

Rachel reached out for it. "Yes. It still has meaning even if Alfred doesn't believe it."

"Well, pooh-pooh on Alfred anyway."

"Easy for you to say," Rachel said. "Now go to the bathroom and I'll get the rest of this." Rachel stood up and let the tears flow again as she bent down to collect the precious pieces of Cybele.

Amber sent a text to Gram that she would be spending the night with Rachel and would be home after her day shift at the store tomorrow. Amber had gone home just long enough to collect her toiletries, pajamas and work clothes.

Rachel's father knew nothing of all that had transpired in Rachel's life except that she was out of high school and he thankfully had not seen Eddie around for a while. Rachel's father had come home from his golf game and watched a little TV while dinner was being prepared. He now sat at the head of the table and asked that the breadbasket be passed to him.

Amber passed it to him and he thanked her.

"Did you win today?" his wife asked.

"It was not a tournament so technically I just play against myself."

"I see. What happened to the other guys in your group?"

"Of course," Rachel's father said, mopping the gravy on his plate with half the roll, "there is always a best score, but it is mostly about being there trying to better your personal last game."

"I see," Rachel's mother said.

"Do you?" Rachel asked, her voice cutting.

Everyone looked at her. They were not surprised that she could be so insolent but tonight her mother and Amber had expected her to keep a lower profile.

"Well, Mom, tell us, do you understand what Dad meant?"

"As much as I need to, yes."

"So, what did he mean?"

"Hey, hey, hey," Her father said. "What kind of way is that to talk to your mother?"

"I just think that if she cares enough to ask a question then she should at least care if she understood the answer."

"Rachel," her mother said, "if I need more clarification then I am not too timid to ask for it."

"You better watch your attitude, young lady," her father growled.

"Fine," Rachel grumbled and pushed her chair back. "I think I have had enough. I'm going to my room."

Everyone watched her stride out of the dining room and head for the stairs.

"Is she on her cycle?" her father asked.

"No, she just had a great disappointment today and is still upset. She will be fine."

"Well, she has never been *fine,* but I do expect a little more control out of her than this." her father said. He looked from his wife to Amber. "Do you two even know what is wrong with her this time?"

"It has to do with a group she was trying to join that didn't work out for her," her mother said.

"What group?"

"Just some young people that meet at the coffee shop," Rachel's mother said.

"Well, good, that spending spree is over. Her credit card looked like she was buying a partnership in the place, to say nothing of the bookstore charges and all kinds of other crazy purchases. I was going to talk to her about it but I guess I don't have to now."

"No, her expenses should be curtailed for a while."

"She is going to college soon. She does realize that?" her father asked.

"Of course."

"Good, because I don't think she has a clue how much that is costing us, and she should be thinking about saving a little money for us instead of buying all kinds of crap she doesn't even need."

"That's true," Rachel's mother said.

Rachel's father left the other half of his roll on his plate and pushed his chair back. He paused and looked at Amber and then his wife. He grinned and nodded his head toward Amber. "I know I've asked this before, but is this one up for adoption? Or better yet, for trade?"

"I heard that!" Rachel shrieked.

"Good," her father yelled back. "Maybe you should think about it."

"Please, you two!" Rachel's mother said, sliding her own chair back. "Why does Sunday dinner always have to end like this?"

"Because," Rachel yelled from the stairs, "he never shows up for dinner any other day."

Rachel's father shook his head and headed back to his TV chair. Amber and Rachel's mother just sighed and looked at each other.

"I used to think all families were like the Waltons when I was little," Amber said.

"You used to watch the Waltons?"

"Well, Gram did, so I'd watch reruns with her sometimes. So, I used to think all families were that kind and thoughtful of each other."

Rachel's mother nodded. "Yeah, me too."

"Was your family like that growing up?"

"Oh no. No. But I blamed my parents. I thought that if I just had the right parents then our family would be like that. Now I know better. Only scriptwriters get to visit that fantasy."

"Yeah, guess the grass isn't really greener."

"With anything, Amber. It is hard to find anything that really lives up to our expectations. I think inside we all want things to be perfect, we intend to be prefect ourselves, even Rachel and her father. But," Rachel's mother paused and sighed, "life wears at us and we get sharp edges that we didn't ask for. And still we keep stubbornly pressing on until we eventually slip off our pedestal and show our ugly underwear."

Amber and Rachel's mother laughed at that together.

"Are you ever coming back up?" Rachel yelled to Amber over the banister.

"Yes, as soon as I finish helping your mom in the kitchen."

"Fine!" Rachel snapped, and they heard her bedroom door slam.

"You go on, Amber, I think I have the easier job taking care of this by myself."

"Ahh, she can wait a few minutes. I think the old Rachel is almost revived and back to her feisty self."

"I hope so," Rachel's mom said, stacking the plates. "I haven't seen her that hurt since she didn't get picked for Juliet in the school play."

"I know. Rachel soars so high on her own current that she crashes hard when it's interrupted."

"But we wouldn't trade her for the world," Rachel's mother reminded herself for the thousandth time.

Amber gathered the silverware and followed Rachel's mother into the kitchen. "Yeah, I guess we should all be faced with the truth that everything can't always be the way we hope it will be. Maybe it's a good thing to be stopped, and scared a little like this, once in a while so we can realize how lucky we are with what we do have."

"Isn't that the truth?"

Amber drove by the welding shop where James was working. He still had a few more hours to work but he could stop for a short break. He came out when he saw her and was wiping his hands on a ragged stained cloth.

"Is ice coffee okay?" Amber asked.

"Perfect, let's sit over there under the tree."

Amber followed James to a weathered picnic table set in the shade of a maple tree. Amber sat their drinks down and slid onto the bench opposite James.

"You off work already?" he asked, removing the lid and straw and drinking down a couple long swallows of ice coffee.

"I went in early."

James nodded.

"I stayed with Rachel last night," Amber said.

James pulled his chin back. "What did Miriam do now?"

"It wasn't Miriam. It was Rachel."

"Ah, my second guess."

"I told you about her following Alfred on Facebook and then joining his coven of Pagans?"

James nodded.

"Well, it seems Alfred has abandoned the coven for God, like real God not Thor god, and he is leaving the coven. But apparently Rachel was being drawn in to Alfred's charm as much as her interest in the Occult."

"So, his leaving broke her heart?"

"It actually devastated her. Rachel said she not only lost the hope of being important to Alfred she has lost her faith. She had actually had dreams of going off to Stonehenge with Alfred and then maybe on some pilgrimage all over... I don't know where."

"Do you think she is on something? I mean even for Rachel this is crazy."

"Well, it was real to her. So, to her the loss is real."

James finished his ice coffee and set the cup down. "Thank you for not being Rachel," he said.

"James, I need you to talk to Eddie. Maybe we could go out with them, like we used to."

"Ohhh Nooo! I am not getting involved with this. If Eddie wants to go out with Rachel, he will ask her."

"Well, he doesn't know Rachel may be interested in him again."

"Is she?"

"I don't know. I didn't ask her, but we have to help get her back to doing something besides moping in her room and waiting for college."

"Hey, she can always get a job. It's keeping us out of our rooms."

Amber looked away as James crunched the ice left in his cup. "I never thought about faith before," she said, looking back at him. "About how it would feel to be without it once you believed that you had it. I mean, before you know you want it, you're just going about your life, being happy enough, but you aren't even aware of the emptiness you are living with. When I'm with Sadie or John or even Grace, their certainty fills them and you are aware of it by the way they are. How they are content and positive in this harsh and sad world. I want to be like them."

"I know what you mean."

"I think Rachel was feeling like that."

"Really, Rachel was content?"

Amber smiled. "Yes, I know, God adjusted her a little too tight, but despite Rachel being Rachel, I could see she thought for a while that she had found something that she had been looking for. And now, without it, she is alternating between being her old bratty self and true, sincere sadness. We talked a lot last night and it wasn't just the loss of Alfred. I think when she was alone in her room chanting to a statue that she chose from some goddess line up, well, then she probably had to admit that at times she felt like a fraud. But she still didn't want to give up. Rachel was probably on the verge of admitting that Paganism wasn't her answer, but it took Alfred admitting the same thing that finally made her crumble. We know that Rachel never wants to be wrong, or have anyone think she is wrong, and she suddenly realized that without Alfred she would have to admit that she was wrong." Amber sighed at the thought of Rachel. "If she just wasn't so arrogant every time she threw herself into something then it would be easier for her to back out."

"Good luck with curing her of that."

"So, okay, my Eddie plan is still off the table?"

"If I have to be involved in it, yes. Guys just don't get involved in other guys business like girls do."

"So, as a guy, how would you rescue your buddy from this pit he was about to fall into?"

James tilted the cup straight up and shook the last shards of ice into his mouth. Amber slid her half full cup over to him. He smiled and sipped through her straw.

"Finish it," Amber said. "And answer my question. Would you, just because you are a guy, leave your buddy hanging all alone on the edge of the cliff or would you help him?"

"Well," James said, pulling the straw and top off the cup. "I guess if my friend was in trouble I would maybe ask him to help me with what I was looking for and, I don't know, maybe he would find something for himself along the way."

Amber thought about that. That was brilliant. She would ask Rachel to help her research Christianity and find out if they could believe it, or if it was just wishful thinking and then, maybe, Rachel would believe in it herself. But, of course, Amber would have to ask as though Rachel was strictly helping Amber.

"Anyway," James said, draining the last bit of coffee from the bottom of the cup, "are you babysitting Rachel tonight or do you want to do something with me?"

"I think I would like to get back to Rachel. I mean, of course, being with you is better than anything, but right now I have to help her get out of her pit."

James shrugged. "Sure."

"What are you going to do tonight?"

"The guys here are going to shoot a few hoops and then go somewhere to eat."

"Okay, but before you go back to work, I need a new saying," Amber said.

James shook his blonde head, thinking. "I don't know. How about, 'the repetition of it felt like evidence.'"

Amber frowned.

"You know, if someone repeats something often enough then people accept it as evidence of the truth."

"Okay."

"I read it in an article and it stuck out. Made me think."

"That's always a good thing," Amber said, and James grinned and leaned across the picnic table to give her a kiss before he was up and heading back to the welding shop.

Rachel parked in front of the church. She felt good. Prepared. Since Amber's challenge, Rachel not only felt ready to move on from Paganism but was enthusiastically motivated to convince Amber that her choice was also built on superstition by control freaks. And the very best part of Rachel's plan, the crowning glory, was that she was going to get John to help her prove his religion was built on sinking sand.

John was walking across the church lawn toward Rachel. A handsome smile on his face. Rachel almost felt a pang of guilt over her plan. Rachel got out of her car and met John at the church door. They exchanged pleasantries and went into the sanctuary.

"This isn't exactly what I expected," Rachel said, looking around at the sparse alter and walls. "Where are your statues? And is that tiny window all you have for stained glass?"

John laughed softly and nodded. "We are simply about God in here. No frills needed," he said. "Let's go back to my office. There is more for you to look at there."

John sat behind his desk as Rachel wandered around until she was satisfied she had seen enough then she sat in the chair opposite him.

"I know you think I am here about Amber. And you would be right to a certain extent," Rachel began, bending over to take a notebook from her large purse. "I am actually here for myself as well. Amber has given me a challenge. Now that I have," Rachel paused, it was still a little difficult to talk about, "I have abandoned my Paganism."

John waited.

"Did you even know that I was a practicing Pagan?"

John said that he did not.

"Well, I was. And I was happy worshiping Cybele. I truly loved her. But something tragic happened that shattered," Rachel blinked her eyes and sighed hard. "I mean she actually shattered. And then so did my heart. Can you imagine wanting to believe something with all your being and then having it ripped from you?"

"I believe I can imagine that," John said.

"Of course, you can. You have empathy for everyone don't you? I mean, any suffering by others is your suffering because you are a man of God."

"I do what I can," John said.

"Now," Rachel said, opening her notebook, "this may seem strange, but what I need you to help me with is to convince Amber that there is no God. I mean, your God. The God that is believed by some to have created everything…" Rachel flourished her hands in the air. "Everything like life and flowers and even the air."

John was silent.

"When Cybele shattered, I'm afraid my faith in everything was also shattered, so Amber came up with this challenge. She wants to debate Christianity. Her for Christianity and me debating against it. So, I figured whom better to help me than you? I mean I realize you believe in God, duh, but surely people have come to you with doubts and you have had to convince them to abandon their doubts and follow your beliefs. So, I thought that you would know what kind of doubts they came with. That's what I really need. Why did they doubt? Was it because of scientific proof or even the lack of proof? I mean how can you possibly prove anything two thousand years after it happened?"

"Two thousand years?" John said. "Why not start at the beginning and work our way up to two thousand years ago."

"Beginning? You mean The Big Bang theory? Sure, that sounds great."

"First, what does theory mean?" John asked.

"A theory is a, well, an educated idea of how something works."

"Did you say idea or proof?"

"I suppose the word theory suggests that it has not actually been proven. Just that there is strong evidence that it may be true."

"Please explain to me what caused the Big Bang?"

Rachel thumbed through her pages. She had taken notes so she would appear worthy of this debate. "The Big Bang was an explosion of an infinitely dense and hot mass. A microscopic cosmic egg."

"And where did this cosmic egg originate?"

"Well, I don't think anyone could really know. It was just there. And the most amazing part was that I read that the egg was many billion times smaller than a single proton. Smaller than an atom."

"That is amazing. And you can believe that?"

"If there is scientific evidence, yes, I would have to."

"So, are you telling me that there is scientific evidence, not just a theory, that our universe could have started from a cosmic egg?"

"They are still working on the actual evidence, but science is growing in leaps and bounds so it shouldn't be long before there is absolute proof."

"How long ago did this egg explode?"

Rachel smiled. She was so prepared. "I have read anywhere from six to thirty billion years ago. Billion. It started small and then expanded into the universe we know today."

"And from the chaos of the big bang of a microscopic egg exploding, we now have an intricately ordered universe that operates purposefully?"

"Yes."

"Tell me, have you ever witnessed an explosion? In person or on TV even?"

"Sure. Of course. I guess."

"And when the pieces landed did they create anything other than bits of junk? Was a new life created from the debris, or perhaps even a new building appeared from the explosion of a building?"

"No, of course not."

"But this gigantic explosion that came from nothing had some secret mechanism that allowed the universe to be created, and then to evolve into the intricately efficient universe we know today? Our planet started as a, what did you say, a piece of a speck billions of times smaller than an atom, and with no form of life on it, and now Earth is thriving with life that is scientifically so perfectly balanced that if there were the slightest deviation in any of our natural laws, life on Earth would cease to exist? Can you help me understand how that could be from just a simple explosion from an egg that no one has yet been able to explain its origin?"

Rachel frowned. This had all sounded so plausible in her research.

"Another thought to grapple with," John continued, "is that an explosion would propel everything out radially from the center of the explosion. Think of it. Would you be safer on one side of an explosion than you would be on the other side if it just went bang and spewed out debris? Also, why is our universe clumpy rather than circular? Our universe is composed of galaxies and voids and orbiting revolutions such as our Earth around the sun."

Rachel squirmed in her chair. Her head was beginning to ache.

"Rachel, a few years ago the scientists were pushing the steady-state theory. Then the big bang theory and now a new idea called the plasma theory is being touted. I am happy to spend time explaining all of these to you if that will help you convince Amber, but I believe Amber will read Genesis and conclude that a great creator is the only explanation that cannot be disproved. As an article I read, and often quote, said, 'Cosmology is unique in science in that it is a very large intellectual edifice based on very few facts.' I like this quote because it was the conclusion of several evolutionists. I can direct you to the article if you would like to read it for yourself."

Rachel just looked at him.

"The odds are astronomical against life coming from non-life naturally by way of an unintelligent mistake. Being a former Pagan, you believed that the universe is ordered by natural laws. These natural laws, these morals and the intricate biological miracle of our very existence, could not be the result of a random explosion of nothingness."

Rachel nodded. She felt scolded. John had not spoken to her in a harsh or condescending manner and yet her own failure was heavy to bear.

"Hey, don't look dejected. There are still many other doubts that you can research and debate Amber on. And I am always happy to help you."

Rachel thanked him and gathered her notes. "I think I have to regroup and get back to you."

John stood and came around his desk. "I'm sorry to hear that your faith has been shattered. I can barely think of anything worse. So, please, promise me that you won't stop looking. Your soul will connect to what it is searching for when you stay open to the possibility of finding the right fit. Look behind every door with high expectations."

"Oh, no, this isn't about me. I'm not looking for anything. I'm over that. I'm just going to get on with gettin' on. No, this is all about Amber. Just Amber. If she is getting into religion, then I want to be certain she knows exactly what it is about."

"I see," John said. "Well, I hope she is doing her own homework to keep up with you."

Rachel slipped the strap of her big bag over her shoulder and headed for the door. "Yeah, I think we will forget about the Big Bang though and just start with evolution. Who cares how the earth even got here. It is here, and we are on it. Bam. Done! Besides I have great notes on evolution."

"What are you thinking about?" Miriam asked John because the whole evening he seemed to be preoccupied. Which wasn't unusual, John was always thinking and worrying about everyone else. But still, Miriam could tell that whatever was on his mind was something he didn't want to talk about so, of course, he needed to. It wasn't healthy to keep worries in… and Miriam definitely was the poster child of that.

John slid his glasses back up to the bridge of his nose and said, "Just reading."

"Really? Usually when you read in bed you actually look at the book."

John smiled and nodded. "Usually that is true, yes."

"So, who is it? Me? Grace? Someone at church? Maybe even Amber?"

"Miriam, do you know that Paganism is on the rise all over the world? More and more people are looking for a faith to trust their eternal souls to and they are choosing one that they can make up out of whatever they want. I mean, certainly there are customs and probably rituals that are common to all individual covens, but how are people trusting that to be real?"

"Who knows?" Miriam said, a little surprised and disappointed that John was thinking about Paganism. Whatever that was exactly.

"How are we failing these people?" John said. "How are we Christians losing our message?"

"Oh, you are not, dear. You work very hard to bring people into the church and to give them what they need to stay there."

John sighed. "Just look at the world. Look at our own country that was built on religious freedoms. Pilgrims came from around the world to practice their faith here without fear of persecution. Now it seems that every religion, and non-religion for that matter, is protected except for the Christian faith. How can this be happening in this day and age? What more can our churches do?"

"Oh, John, this is way too heavy for late night thinking. Seriously, it's time to switch off the light and your worry-wart brain and get some rest."

"You're right. I'm not concentrating," John said, closing his book. "Maybe I will just go down to the office and work on my sermon and let you get some rest. Don't you see the doctor tomorrow?"

"Yes. I'm anxious to get this surgery healed so I can start treatments. This waiting makes me feel like new cancer cells are multiplying every minute. I can feel them just running amuck, just gleefully spreading here and there all over me! I'm so ready to poison and zap them all and… and not lose all my hair doing it."

John laid his book aside and drew her close to him. "I'm sorry, I should be thinking about you. I trust that you will be fine, but I can't forget what you are going to have to go through to get there."

"It's scary. I won't lie," Miriam said, snuggling into his embrace.

"I'll deal with the Pagans when you are all better and back to nagging me about painting the back fence."

"I don't nag. I've told you that repeatedly," Miriam said, happy now that John's attention was on her.

"Is Grace helping you out now that she is out of school?"

"Yes, you know Grace. Contrary to how rebellious and self-centered our first born is, Grace is a sweetheart."

"Our first born," John repeated. "We have missed so much of Amber's life."

Miriam drew away and sat back up. "Mom was here, and she mentioned that you are going to introduce Amber to your congregation this Sunday."

"I am. I asked Amber and she agreed."

"Really, well, why wouldn't she agree? It isn't innocent little Amber that will look bad in front of the whole congregation. I bet she is just giddy that I will finally be exposed as a liar in front of everyone I know."

John frowned and shook his head. "Seriously, you can think like that, you can say hateful things like that about your own daughter?"

"I can't think of her as my daughter when she doesn't even want me to be her mother."

"I am hoping that you really don't mean the things you are saying."

"Look, John, I can't expect you to understand. You are never around when she attacks me. When she accuses me of being a horrible person because I made the wrong decision when I was so young. I wonder if she would be any different if she had to make the heartbreaking choices I had to make at eighteen."

"Before we start worrying about what choices you or Amber may have made, I see that we first have to deal with your decisions now. Today, as an adult."

Miriam covered her face with her hands. "Please. I can't talk about her. I'm just not up to it."

"Hey, hey, I'm not judging you. I just want to help you. Nothing good can come from this standoff between the two of you. So, tell me, what were your hopes when you knew it was finally time to tell us all the truth?"

Miriam removed her hands and stared into the air. "I wanted to open Mom's door and find Amber waiting for me with her arms reaching out to me and being as anxious as I was to make up for our lost time."

"Okay, that is what you wanted. What did you expect?"

"That she would be a little standoffish maybe. A little shy. Maybe wanting to know me but not certain how to approach me. That would have been fair."

"Fair to her or fair to you?"

"To me. I'm not a bad person, John. I didn't expect her to instantly love me and understand why I had to leave her, but I did hope that she would at least be fair enough to give me the opportunity to explain it to her. I was ready to do all the work. I was ready to be sorry and work to bring her into our family. All I was asking of her was just the chance to fix things."

"You do realize that eighteen years is a long time? Especially to someone who is only eighteen."

"Time just got away from me. I swear I wanted to tell you from the first day I knew I was pregnant, but I had to measure all our futures. I made my decision for us all."

"And if it hadn't worked out for us, if we had never gotten married, would you have ever told me about Amber?"

"Yes, of course."

"Then the real reason you never told me was to protect the life you wanted with me?"

Miriam pulled back. "What do you mean?"

"Granted it was easier to get through seminary school with you working and with no children yet. And then when we were being sent to different locations to get my ministry started it was easier for just the two of us. But you wouldn't have worried about any of that if we had separated and the future I was trying to build did not include you."

"What is your point? I made the decision for us. There was an us, and there still is an us, and our life is better for my decision. The problem is just that once I made that decision I could never find the right time to change it. I kept planning on how and when to do it and then something would always come up to stop me. Until now, until I got cancer and had to face the reality that I may not have enough time to fix it." A sob escaped Miriam and she turned her anguished face to John.

John drew her into his arms. "This is fixable. We just have to stop worrying about who is to blame or who isn't reacting the way we want them to. First let's acknowledge that Amber is justified in her feelings…"

Miriam squirmed to pull away.

"Miriam, it's time for us to make a plan to bring our family together no matter the cost to ourselves."

Miriam stopped struggling and waited for John's plan.

"I've been thinking about the best way to deal with this Sunday and I really believe that the right way to handle it is for you to introduce Amber to everyone. Explain only as much as necessary and then invite Amber up front and ask Amber for forgiveness."

"That's your plan? For me to get up in front of the whole congregation and say that I abandoned Amber eighteen years ago and then, in front of everyone we know, ask Amber to forgive me? That's ridiculous. She would never do it. In fact, she would probably spew hate at me in front of everyone and then it would make matters even worse than they already are."

"Maybe, if you were sincere, Amber would forgive you. And if she could forgive you then who else is there in the church to deny you forgiveness?"

"I'm telling you that she would never do that. She has no intention of letting me off that easy."

"A genuine plea for forgiveness is not an easy thing."

"Are you suggesting that I don't genuinely want to be forgiven?"

"Oh, I believe that you want to be forgiven." John said.

"But?"

"Well, to genuinely ask for forgiveness suggests that you believe that what you have done has caused harm to another. Do you believe that your choices have harmed Amber?"

"Harmed? No. Not really. I left her where she would be well taken care of and loved. I did not abort her or give her to some mystery abusive adoptive parents."

"So, you are saying that death or abuse are the only forms of harm someone can cause a child."

"Well, when I said abusive I meant emotionally as well as physically. I knew Amber would never be abused in any way with my parents."

"Conscience clear?"

"No. Of course not. I'm not stupid. I know there are other things that Amber feels cheated about."

"Like a mother who regrets her choice because of the sadness it has caused to the soul of a little girl more than the complications it may have caused the mother?"

"Well, if I'm just all so self-consuming selfish then why are you even bothering with me? Why don't you just turn against me, too?"

"My point is that I can't tell your story. I can't ask Amber for forgiveness for you. You are going to have to do that yourself. But only if you genuinely regret what you are asking forgiveness for."

"Well, of course I regret it now. At the time I thought I was making the best decision but now I see how much trouble it has caused, and I wish I had just kept her with us and let your ministry go down the tubes. I guess that would have made us all happier."

"What ever happened to our future because of the circumstances of Amber's birth was only our loss to bear. The weight of it should never have been carried by an innocent child. If there was a cost to be paid, it was for us to pay. You and me. Never Amber."

"I keep telling all of you that I had always intended to go back for Amber. And I know now that if I had gotten her then everything would have turned out fine. So, yes, yes, I do regret leaving her and not going back for her. I genuinely do regret that."

"Because of the cost to Amber or because of the cost to yourself?"

"Both. I wish I could undo it for both our sakes."

"Good. So, Sunday you will have to make that case to Amber. You will have to convince her and let God guide her heart."

Miriam lay back against her pillow. "Oh, John, why couldn't you have just been a... a, well, just anything else and then no one would care how horrible your wife was?"

John reached over and turned the lamp off. "Well, I would always care what kind of a wife I had so you better step up to the plate. Your good looks and great cooking can only carry you so far with me."

Miriam snuggled into John's shoulder. "I love you. My problem has always been how much I love you."

"Touché," John said. "Touché."

Rachel was beside herself with anticipation. This was going to be a great day of debate. Rachel had invited a couple from her dissolving Pagan coven to go with her to Sadie's house to meet Amber there. Rachel had desperately wanted to invite Alfred because she missed him and because he was the most intelligent person she had ever met, but his sudden defection to the Christian God side would definitely stack the deck against Rachel. Oh, how she wished that she and Alfred could be on the same side again. Anyway, here she was with Brandy and Chip, the three of them sitting here in Sadie's ancient old house waiting for Amber and Sadie to retrieve beverages from the kitchen.

"This would be an awesome place for Pagans," Brandy said, cradling a baby spider plant that dangled by its long shoot from the overflowing Momma spider plant. "I hear Mother Earth singing all around us."

"Who knows," Chip said. "Maybe we can convert Sadie today and then we can meet here. It's much nicer than the noisy coffee shop. To say nothing of being cheaper."

"I really appreciate you coming," Rachel said. "I know you don't usually talk about the stuff I've asked you to research but I think it will be fun. Sadie and Amber are on one side, you two on the other and I'm flapping around in the middle trying to choose a winner."

"Yeah," Brandy said, "we really miss you being on our side. You didn't have to quit you know. We all have a major crush on Alfred. He's so smart and a natural leader. We can't help ourselves. So, don't be embarrassed about what you blurted out. It's all good. We are not judgers. So maybe after today, maybe after we prove our stuff, we can convince you to come back."

"We'll see," Rachel said, feeling pretty much healed from her Cybele devastation but still not ready to pick sides. Just as long as everyone goes away a little bruised and battered then Rachel can still be content to be flapping around in the middle somewhere without commitment. Today, unlike her meeting with John, Rachel couldn't lose because she wasn't really in the fight.

"Just remember," Rachel reminded the Pagans again, "we are not here to convince them to be Pagans necessarily, we are just here to challenge them to intelligently defend Christianity."

Brandy and Chip nodded agreement.

"This is so nice," Sadie said, carrying in a small tray of sweeteners and a plate of homemade cookies. Amber followed with a tray of beverages. "I'm afraid," Sadie continued, "that I just don't spend enough time with young people any more. It's such a shame for us old folks to miss out on the fresh perspective of budding wisdom."

Chip rolled his eyes and Rachel and Brandy tried not to snicker. Oh, this was going to be so easy.

Amber set the tray down and then sank back into one of Sadie's cushiony chairs. Amber took out her notebook and opened it. "You are our guests," Amber said, "so please, start where you would like."

"Well," Rachel jumped in right away, "we have decided to start with Evolution vs. Creationism."

"Oh goodie," Sadie said, stirring raw sugar syrup into her cold tea. "But first let us just agree on one thing. All great discoveries have been made from our willingness and ability to admit that we may not be right. We must enter all discourse with an open mind."

"Done," Rachel cried. "Now, let us just start with where life began. I know that Chip has researched Darwin for us. Chip, what have you got for us?"

Chip opened his folder and frowned. "Well, actually I don't have anything on where life began, just where it evolved since it first appeared. The only thing on where it could have originated was at scientificamerican. com and that said that the origin of life remains a mystery, but biochemists have learned about… and I'm quoting here… 'how primitive nucleic acids, amino acids and other building blocks of life could have formed and organized themselves into self-replicating, self-sustaining units, laying the foundation for cellular biochemistry'. And I'm still quoting, 'Astrochemical analyses hint that quantities of these compounds might have originated in space and fallen to earth in comets, a scenario that may solve the problem of how those constituents arose under the conditions that prevailed when our planet was young.' End quote."

Chip looked up at the confused faces. "There is more," Chip said, reading again from his quoted material. "Creationists sometimes try to invalidate all of evolution by pointing to science's current inability to explain the origin of life. But even if life on earth turned out to have a nonevolutionary origin (for instance, if aliens introduced the first cells billions of years ago), evolution since then would be robustly confirmed by countless microevolutionary and macroevolutionary studies. End quote."

"Well, thank you, Chip," Rachel said. "That certainly was a strong start. Any rebuttal from the Creationist side?"

Sadie reached for a sugar cookie. "I guess our rebuttal to all of that is just that our side believes life was created by intelligent design. Perhaps the other side would be willing to concede that if the first life form came from outer space then perhaps it was God and not a literal alien?"

"Wait a minute," Brandy said. "I have a theory on the origin of life. My reading said that a new science called abiogenesis has a theory called self-replicating RNA which stands for ribonucleic acid. I believe that is how it is pronounced. Anyway, that actual process has not been recreated in labs yet but hopefully it will be soon. Also, another theory is that life was first formed from non-living chemicals near hydrothermal vents in the deep sea."

"Interesting," Sadie said. "Very interesting."

"So," Amber asked, "all life forms began as a single cell and evolved from there?"

"Yes," Chip said. "And there are 8.7 million known species that evolved over billions of years."

"Whoa," Amber said. "That is staggering."

Sadie finished her cookie and brushed the dusting of crumbs from the front of her blouse. "Before we leave this area and move on to other interesting things, I have to wonder if we all appreciate how precise the elements have to be to allow anything to live? No matter how any living thing got on earth we have to stop and ponder the wonder of it. How did an astronomical mistake somehow end up as just perfect? Perfect enough to survive and thrive in a perfectly balanced atmosphere? To say nothing of there being 8.7 million perfect things. I am in awe, that's all I can say."

Everyone nodded.

"Okay," Rachel said. "We know for sure that there is life so now let's talk about how it evolved."

"Or was just created by intelligent design," Sadie interjected.

"There are several diagrams of the Tree of Life," Chip said. "They all begin from one point and evolve from there."

"Yes," Amber said sarcastically, "that is true because all of them were drawn like that. Hand drawings are not proof."

"Well, fossils and other evidence like bones and biology were used to figure the drawings out," Brandy said.

"Still," Amber said, "I don't think a drawing of a tree should be submitted as evidence."

"Well," Brandy continued, "there are a lot of trees drawn by different people so there has to be some truth to that."

"Do you believe in angels?" Sadie asked, sipping at her ice tea.

"What?"

"There are a lot of drawings of angels. That is all I'm pointing out," Sadie said.

"People. People," Rachel said. "Let's focus here. As of now there will be no further discussions of trees or angels."

"Okay," Amber said. "I just want to point out that through the billions of years of evolution I saw a few...well, diagrams of something that looked like a tree that had several, six I believe I counted in one diagram, periods titled 'mass extinction'. So, my question is, are you suggesting that after each tree ring of mass extinction the whole process of alien droppings or deep-sea bacteria had to start all over again? That's all I'm asking, it's really not debating the whole tree thing. Just wondering how the whole evolution thing got restarted if there were so many mass extinctions. That's all. Just wondering. Just trying to ask a real question."

Rachel looked at the confused faces of Chip and Brandy. "Look none of us profess to be scientists here."

"Or theologians," Sadie added.

"Exactly," Rachel said, "so let's cut right to it, is it so hard to concede that evolution is a real answer to how we have all… evolved from apes?"

"Yes," Sadie said. "That is hard to believe."

"But, but, but." Chip flipped through his pages of notes. "The evolutionists don't actually claim that we evolved from apes. That's where you people like to get all snooty and ask, 'then why are there still apes?' Well, I'll explain it. It isn't so much that we evolved from the apes that are here today, it's just that if we trace our ancestral branch back far enough we will see where we were the same and then humans and apes branched off in different directions and became different creatures from the same beginning."

"What?" Amber cut in. "I didn't see that drawing. Why would that even happen? Why split off into something different? Why wasn't the man/ape creature happy to remain itself?"

"Because of mutation," Chip said, so pleased with himself that he actually closed his notes. "The first process of evolution is mutation. Nature's imperfect reproduction methods have always produced mutations."

"And wouldn't that weaken and not strengthen the species?" Amber asked. "I mean if a frog was born with six legs then wouldn't he have to find another six-legged frog to breed with? Besides, I thought, and you nature worshipers would know this better than me, but don't the weakest, the deformed babies get abandoned in nature? I don't think there is a dating site for six legged frogs?"

"Hey," Rachel scolded. "Let's not get flippant here. We all agreed to be open minded to discovering the truth."

"That's right," Sadie reminded Amber.

"Sorry. I was just getting a little confused. I'll try harder. Explain mutation to us, Chip. And from the beginning, please."

"Okay, so the first single cell became the basis for all future life forms," Chip continued, not as certain now as he had appeared a moment ago.

"So, it split itself to create more?" Amber asked.

"One would have to assume that," Chip said. "So, it goes on and on until it finally mutates and then from that it splits off into two different things. The original and the new."

"So, a bed bug and an elephant are from the exact same single cell?"

"Eventually through billions of years of evolution of course."

Amber nodded.

"So anyway," Chip went on, explaining it as well as he could. He was a Pagan after all. He wasn't certain what he even believed as a Pagan about the beginning of life. "Mutation is how we get totally different creatures from the same beginning. Then step two is natural selection. Where mutation is not a choice, natural selection is nature choosing the strongest mutations to survive. After evolution gets going along for billions of years you have bigger and more complex creatures to dissect and actually see the progression of evolution."

"Like," Amber said, "like we all have bones so some of our bones may be like another creature's bones? And dolphin embryos have heads and bodies, and so do human embryos have a head and a body. So, having heads and bodies and bones proves that we all started from the same single cell?"

"Yeah, like that," Chip agreed.

"Well, now," Sadie said, leaning forward in her chair to pick up another cookie. "have we reached a consensus about what we believe?"

"Well, actually," Rachel said, pleased that she had noticed this. "I don't think you and Amber have even made any argument for your side."

"Tell you what," Sadie said. "I will give a thousand dollars to anyone here who can make me a flower seed."

"What?" Rachel asked.

"Yes, it's obvious that I love plants and I'd love to be the first to have a new flower. So, if any of you can make me a flower seed right now, I'll hand over a thousand dollars."

"That's impossible," Chip muttered.

"Now," Sadie went on, "I have a warm, freshwater stream in my back yard. There is probably a little algae and maybe some bacteria out there. You can use that if you need to."

Brandy grunted in disgust.

"Okay, I guess you are telling me that you can't make something out of nothing," Sadie said.

"Well, rejecting someone else's theory doesn't prove your own," Rachel said.

"I'm content with living on faith," Sadie said. "God created everything. I believe that. So, for me, there is nothing to debate on our side."

"Fine!" Rachel grumbled. "Great debate."

Everyone sat back in their chairs and thought about their afternoon. The Pagans were happy enough to put away their notes and ask for a few plant clippings, Amber was pleased with her new-found insights and Sadie had had a lovely time hosting these interesting young people. Rachel was the only one who looked troubled.

"If you have time, I'd like to show you a couple framed quotes my father kept in this office," Sadie offered.

Everyone glanced at the others and then nodded that they would be happy to see whatever Sadie thought would be of interest to them.

Sadie looked pleased and walked them through her home. "You all know that my father was a doctor?" she asked the kids.

Only Amber knew, but the others looked interested in this new information.

"Yes, he was a man of science. He studied the science of our human body and the science of everything else he had time to read. He was, like yourselves, very interested in the universe. He has several books on the subject if any of you would be interested in borrowing them."

Sadie opened the french doors to her father's office and the parade of gawkers trailed in behind her. It was as impressive as a serious doctor's office should be. Orderly and yet jumbled here and there with books and posters and even a small plastic skeleton hanging from a swag in the corner.

"Here," Sadie said, leading them to the far wall covered with framed diplomas and a breathtaking colored photo of the universe, "this was his small montage of famous quotes he was proud of showing everyone."

Everyone clustered around the frame and read. "It would be very difficult to explain why the universe should have begun in just this way, except as the act of a God who intended to create beings like us."

There were a couple puzzled looks exchanged when they read that the author of those words was the famed theoretical physicist Stephen Hawking in his bestselling science book *A Brief History of Time*.

The next quote was by physicist Freeman Dyson. "The more I examine the universe and study the details of its architecture, the more evidence I find that the universe in some sense must have known that we were coming."

"And this one," Sadie pointed to the last, "was Daddy's favorite. Albert Einstein said, 'The most incomprehensible thing about the universe is that it is comprehensible.'"

Sadie laughed again as though she had just discovered the humor in this herself. "You see," she said, "even though some believe that we all evolved from the same single cell as mosquitoes and dinosaurs and fiddle ferns, humans are the only animal species who yearns to understand our purpose. We want to know what our place is in this universe. Why are we here and why are we made the way we are? If all things are equal among life on earth, if we are merely just a mutation away from something totally different than us, then why is it that only man was given the yearning to find the answers to these big questions?"

Everyone was silent now. They had all come for answers and here Sadie had, instead, filled them with even more questions.

"I'd like to borrow the Stephen Hawking book if you really don't mind," Chip said.

Brandy jabbed him in the ribs with her elbow.

"What?" Chip hissed at her. "Sadie offered."

"Really, you are welcome to borrow anything," Sadie assured Chip. "What a waste to keep all these wonderful books to myself. Besides, maybe when you return the books we can engage in more intellectual pondering. I have to admit that I have thoroughly enjoyed today."

The young people had piled into their respective cars and were pulling out of her long driveway onto the main street as Sadie stood in her doorway waving good-by.

"Maybe God's plan for me is bigger than I had thought," Sadie whispered to the air. "Wouldn't that just be grand?"

"I have barely seen you lately," Gram said as Amber rinsed the dinner dishes and handed them to Gram to load into the dishwasher.

"Yeah, crazy right? Here I thought I'd be lounging around all summer looking for ways to entertain myself and instead it has been nuts."

"I'm glad Rachel is better. She is, right?"

"As better as Rachel can ever be. I thought James's idea was perfect. If

Rachel thought she was helping me sort out what I could and should not believe in, then she may find what was right for her. But, to be honest, I don't think she is getting anything from this. She was pretty moody today when we left Sadie's. I asked her if she wanted to do something fun tonight, but she just said that she had to get home." Amber paused and shook her head. "Tell me, Gram, when has Rachel ever wanted to go home instead of going out?"

"Oh dear, I'm sorry to hear that. But don't worry too much. I'm certain Rachel will work this out. It's just that this is a difficult time in all our lives. And especially yours and Rachel's."

"What is so difficult for Rachel? I mean really, so her three week old religion is over. To be honest, we both know that she is too superficial to suffer over that for very long."

"Well," Gram said, "Rachel is going away to school in a few weeks and even if she thinks she is going to be happy to leave home, she may be having second thoughts. I mean she has never had to think about taking care of herself before. She's never had to do her own laundry or be sure her gas tank isn't empty. I doubt she knows what to do for herself if she gets the stomach flu or even realizes too late that she is on her last couple squares of toilet paper."

Amber laughed and hugged Gram. "Whoa, I guess I'm glad I will still be in the nest for a couple more years."

"Plus," Gram said, "I think Rachel is a lot of huff and puff. She presents a bold front, but I think she is really insecure about a lot of things."

Amber nodded. "Yeah, that's Rachel, though she may not even admit that to herself. I know she must be a little worried. Six hundred miles from home isn't the other side of the world but it is far when you find yourself alone and feeling a little vulnerable. She is a big spoiled baby and there isn't anyone in college that will volunteer to take on the job of babysitting her."

Gram dropped the dishwasher tablet into the cup and closed the door over it. "Are you really okay with going to community college? I mean John talked to me and he is offering to help you go to a four year college or university if you would prefer that."

Amber lifted her chin and thought about that and then she shrugged. "Well, maybe if you had told me that before you scared me to death about going away on my own I would have said yes. But now, no, no, I'm still your spoiled baby for two more years. Besides, it's probably too late to get into another school."

"It's never too late to try if it is something you really want," Gram said.

"I'm fine," Amber said. "But I wonder if Miriam knows that John offered that."

"I believe she does. Miriam and I had a great visit today and I could see that she is ready to start over with you. She asked me to help her find a way to reach you."

"Okay," Amber said, waiting for the real shoe to drop.

"She said that she is going to present you to the congregation this coming Sunday and then ask you to forgive her in front of everyone."

"That worries me," Amber confessed.

"Why, dear? Forgiving Miriam shouldn't be a thing you need to dread doing. I would think you would be relieved to just let it go and get on with the positive things in your life. It isn't a win/lose thing. You don't lose anything if you forgive her. Except maybe a little of your stubbornness."

"Have you forgiven her, Gram? I mean really?"

Gram sat in the chair at the table. "I don't think I ever looked at it as forgiving as much as just feeling gratitude that it was over. I finally know where Miriam is and now, for the first time in eighteen years, I am able to help my daughter. Did you know that she has agreed to let me take her to her cancer treatments?"

"Humph," Amber said.

"I would want to do the same for you, Amber. I would want to be the one taking you to where you could get healed. I'd want to be there in case you were thirsty or feeling nauseous and needed a cool cloth on your forehead. I'd want to be there to give you a little comfort. Just small things really but things that would allow me to not feel so... helpless."

Amber sank down in the chair beside Gram. "I guess that I can't hate Miriam totally. Her abandonment did leave me with you to take care of me all these years."

"See. See," Gram said, brightening up. "That's the way to think about it."

"Yeah, I've seen what a shrew she is with Grace and I couldn't have survived in that environment."

"Amber, why do you always have to slip into that kind of stuff? Why can't you be sweet?"

"Because I'm afraid that God gave me too much of her and not enough of you."

"Well, you will be nice in church, right? I mean, remember what Mother Theresa said about being kind anyway."

"I'll try, Gram, I'll try."

"Good," Gram said, patting Amber's hand. "I just love helping my girls."

Gram and Amber sat for a few minutes thinking about chemo treatments and forgiveness and family when they suddenly heard the screen door scrape open and Rachel breezed in.

"Hi all," Rachel said, walking over to the table and sitting down with them.

"Well, you look better than when I last saw you leaving Sadie's," Amber said. "What a grump."

"Yes, yes, all that. Well, anyway I didn't have a plan then but now I do. So, yes, I am better."

"Hold on, Gram," Amber warned, "the earth is about to tremble, and beloved things will be forever lost in the quake."

"Grow up, Amber, this is a real plan," Rachel said. "And one, I might add, that will totally surprise you."

"Bring it on. I am steeled and ready," Amber said.

"I think that you and I should be baptized. And… and here is the best part, we should do it this Sunday in your father's church!"

Amber nodded. "Okay, I admit that this is totally surprising to me. First, that you would ever want to be baptized and second, you specifically told me that your Paganism could not so quickly be replaced with a new kitten. What changed your mind?"

Rachel drew in a deep breath for dramatic affect and then proceeded. "Well, all this God stuff you have forced me to read and think about has started to crack my skepticism for one thing. And for another, I read that when you are baptized the Holy Spirit enters you and, hey, if that is true then we will know it and then we will be convinced beyond a shadow of a doubt. And if the Holy Spirit does not enter us, then we will know that all the rest of it is also false."

"So, this is a test?" Amber asked.

"Yes, and isn't that a quicker way to prove your God than researching all this outer space and bacteria stuff? Really, I don't want to work that hard to find the answer."

"Oh my," Gram said. "I don't think that is how baptism works. I mean,

I don't think you can just expect it to ... *take* if you are only doing it to test God."

"Look," Rachel continued, "babies get baptized. What can they know about what is happening to them? I mean, if God sends the Holy Spirit to babies then why wouldn't he send it to me? I would at least be asking for it."

"What do you know about the Holy Spirit?" Amber asked her. "I mean, I don't think it is what you think it is."

"So, what is it?"

"Well, I don't know exactly. Maybe we better check it out before you make such a big decision for the wrong reasons," Amber said.

"No. I am sick and tired of reading. I say, let's just do it and see if it is true."

"Okay, aside from getting the Holy Spirit, what do you think baptism is? What is your commitment?" Amber asked.

Rachel shrugged. "Commitment? I don't know."

"Rachel, dear, I don't think this is anything you should just do on the spur of the moment," Gram said. "I think it is something you should be certain of for the right reasons."

"Hey," Rachel shot back. "Why all this negativity? Right reason this and that. Have either of you been baptized? No, you have not, so what do you know about what the right and wrong reasons are for doing it?"

"Well," Amber said, "I'm not getting baptized until I understand what it means and what I'm expected to bring to the table."

"And how are you going to find that out? Reading more books?" Rachel snapped.

"I don't know. I don't know how you determine when you are ready to be baptized."

"Exactly!" Rachel exclaimed. "So why not Sunday? Better too soon than too late."

"You're crazy. Do you know that?" Amber said.

"Okay, okay, I see that you have questions, so I will give you until tomorrow to figure it out and then we need to go visit your father to see how we go about doing this thing."

"Tomorrow? How generous," Amber said.

"Hey, Gram, you want to do it, too?" Rachel asked.

"I've been thinking about it to tell you the truth. I'm not getting any younger and I don't want to wait too late and get stuck in an uncomfortable place for all eternity."

"There you go," Rachel said, beaming. "I have saved a soul already and haven't even been baptized yet."

Amber glanced at the clock over the sink. "Oh hey, it's seven-thirty. I'm supposed to meet James." Amber slid her chair back and asked Rachel if she wanted to come along.

"Sure, why not? One more wild night of debauchery and intoxication before I have to clean up my act for the Holy Spirit."

"Baptism may be like a proposal, Rachel," Amber said. "Your asking doesn't guarantee His acceptance."

Rachel got up from her chair. "Okay, I'll forgo the debauchery part just in case. But you are definitely the designated driver tonight."

Police lights were flashing, and an ambulance was just loading a stretcher into the back, when John and his friend pulled into the Blue Lounge parking lot.

"Thanks for coming with me," John said to Andrew. "Hopefully, no one will need a lawyer, but it doesn't hurt to have one close by."

John walked toward the center of the cluster of young people and police officers. Amber saw him and came pushing through the crowd. She reached John, her chin trembling, and then she broke down crying. John wrapped his arms around her and just held her until she had stopped sobbing.

"How did you know to come?" Amber asked, accepting the handkerchief John had extracted from his back pocket.

"Your grandmother called me as soon as Rachel's mother called her. Are you okay?"

Amber nodded. "But Rachel…"

"I know."

"And James…"

"Look, why don't we just go back to my car where we can talk, and you can fill us in. This is my friend Andrew Frost. He's an attorney if we need one."

Amber wiped at the stream of tears as she followed her father to his car. Amber and John got in the front seats.

"Now start from the beginning. Slow and easy," John said.

"Well, Rachel came to my house and we both left to meet James for dancing at the Blue Lounge. Weeknights it's a dance club, I guess you can call it. No alcohol is served. Just a cover fee and dancing. Anyway, everything was fine. We were just dancing and then Rachel met this guy who seemed to like her, so we sat at the same table and just hung out for a couple hours. The guy, he said his name was Everett, was dancing with Rachel and then the next thing we knew James and I saw them both coming back inside. James said they had probably just stepped outside to sneak a drink from a bottle Everett may have in his car. Rachel seemed fine though. We didn't smell any alcohol on them so we all just started dancing again and then Rachel said she was feeling a little tired and wanted to go home. Everett right away offered to take her but James said no. Everett got a little pushy, but James insisted that he was taking Rachel home. James said he couldn't allow Rachel to leave with a guy she knew nothing about. James left us to go pay our food and drink tab. It was so crowded we knew our waitress wouldn't be back around for a while so James went to the bar to pay. Anyway, I told Rachel that I had to go to the ladies' room before we left and I would be right back."

Amber stopped talking for a while and John waited. Finally, Amber closed her eyes for a moment and then opened them and continued. "When I came back to the table Rachel and Everett were gone. James came up just as I got there and we hurried outside. We saw Everett jump in his car and slam his door. We couldn't see Rachel. We called out to her, but she never answered. James ran over to Everett's car and yanked the front passenger door open. He saw Rachel laying on the backseat and so he jumped in the car and grabbed the steering wheel and yanked it so that Everett's car ran into the side of a parked car. I rushed over when the car stopped, and Everett started punching James. 'Get her out!' James kept yelling at me. 'Get her out!' I opened the door and Rachel had tape over her mouth…" Amber stopped talking.

"What happened next?" John asked, his voice gentle.

"Well, I dragged her out onto the ground. She was like a rag doll. And then Everett grabbed a knife and stabbed James. He… stabbed James." Amber stopped another moment then went on. "Then he pushed James out onto the ground and backed away from the car he had run into and, with both passenger doors open, he sped off down the street. Luckily a couple was just pulling into the parking lot and saw what happened. They followed the car and got close enough to copy down the license plate and called 911 for us."

"Where are Rachel and James?" John asked.

"The first ambulance took James and the one that just left was taking Rachel to the hospital. We have to let her parents know. And James's mother."

"They were notified as soon as you gave the police all of their information."

"Yeah, right."

"So, how about if Andrew goes and talks to the police for a minute and, if it is okay for you to leave, we will go to the hospital and check on them."

Amber nodded. "I can't believe it. I can't believe it."

"I know," John said. "I'm just going to call Miriam and your grandmother while we wait for Andrew and let them know that you are with us and you are not hurt."

Amber nodded and fought to keep her sobs inside.

Finally, Andrew was back, and they had been given permission to leave.

"Was James conscious when you last saw him?" John asked.

Amber nodded. "Yes. Rachel wasn't but James was. But he was in a lot of pain. I think he was stabbed in the side and his thigh. There was so much blood everywhere it was hard to tell really."

"Okay, just try to relax now and we will be there soon," John said, reaching over to pat her hand.

"How could this happen?" Amber said. "Things like this don't happen here."

"Oh, they happen everywhere," Andrew said. "It doesn't take many evil people to change the world for all of us."

"I'm so scared," Amber whispered. "I'm afraid for James and Rachel. They can't die. They are not bad people. Surely they won't die."

"Did the police say if they caught the guy?" John asked.

"No," Andrew answered. "They just said that the chances were pretty good that the car was stolen."

They were pulling into the hospital parking lot and Amber saw Rachel's parents going through the open emergency room door. Amber started to cry again despite herself.

Inside the bright lights of the waiting room Amber noticed the dark stains on the front of her dress. James's blood. James's blood where she had knelt to try and help him. Amber began to tremble.

"Take some deep breaths, Amber," John said, putting his arm around her and leading her to some chairs in the corner of the room. "Andrew is seeing if there is somewhere else we can wait. I think we are attracting too much attention here."

Andrew came back with a nurse. "Does she need to see a doctor?" the nurse asked.

"No," Amber said. "I just need to see James and Rachel."

"Well, I'm confident the young man is on his way to surgery, so you can wait in the surgical area. At this time of night that waiting room is pretty empty. Except for the other families of these unexpected emergencies."

When they reached the surgical waiting room James's mother and sister were already there talking to a police officer.

Amber went over to them. "I'm sorry. I'm so sorry," Amber said.

James's mother nodded but couldn't speak.

James's sister, Janet, looked away.

"Is there a chapel in this hospital?" John asked the lone nurse that was walking past the door. The nurse gave him hurried directions and then was on her way again.

"I'm going there," John said. "Any of you are welcome to join me."

James's mother hesitated and then nodded. Janet shook her head. "I'll wait here in case there is any word on him."

John, Andrew, Amber and James's mother went to the chapel and Janet went to stand by the window and stare out at the night.

The sun was just beginning to crest the horizon when John pulled into Amber's driveway. Gram and Grampa were waiting by the door when John and Amber walked up the front steps.

"Oh, my dear girl," Gram said, pulling Amber into her arms. "What a dreadful night."

"Andrew and I are heading home but I will be back this afternoon," John said.

"Can I get you some coffee to go? I just made it," Grampa offered.

"No," John chuckled. "No more coffee. I'm afraid I have already had too much. And hospital coffee at that. Guess I should have prayed about that, too." John turned to Amber, "Everything is in God's hands," he said. "Take a long warm shower and then get some rest."

Amber nodded and headed up the stairs. She turned halfway up. "Thank you for coming."

"See you in a few hours," John said.

"So," Gram said as soon as Amber had gone into the house. "How are they? James and Rachel?"

"Rachel will be fine," John said. "The guy had slipped something into her drink apparently, but the doctors pumped her stomach and gave her some antidote for whatever it was. James will recover. The wound in his thigh was deep but not life threatening. The knife that went into his side was at such an angle that it broke two ribs but, fortunately, did not puncture the lung. He did lose a lot of blood, but the doctors felt pretty good about his recovery."

Gram sucked in her breath. "Oh my."

John sighed a tired sigh. "Yeah, it was a long night but the bottom line is that it looks like everyone will recover. The bad news is that there is still a dangerous guy out there preying on young girls. He knew what he intended to do, and he almost got away with it. If Amber and James had not stopped him, I very much doubt that Rachel would be alive right now."

Everyone was silent, thinking about that. It was nearly inconceivable to imagine.

"Well, I'm going home," John finally said. "I'll call Amber on my way back so she can know when to expect me."

Gram checked on Amber when she heard her get into bed. "Do you need anything?" Gram asked as an excuse to check on her girl. Things like this could happen to anyone in this run-amuck world. In half a wink everything could change, and that reality was frightening. How much more worry could her old heart take?

"Gram, will you just sit here beside me until I go to sleep?"

"Of course, sweetie," Gram said, pleased to be invited to sit on the side of Amber's bed... just like old times. "I know there must be scary thoughts running through your head right now, but you have to put them aside and get some rest." Amber had curled up on her side and Gram gently rubbed her back.

"I learned some things tonight," Amber said, her eyes closed.

"You did?"

"Yes, aside from the safety aspect, I learned that I love James. I couldn't bear to see him hurt and bleeding and I would have done anything to help him."

"I see," Gram said.

"And when I felt so desperate at the thought of losing him, I understood a little of what Miriam meant when she asked me if there wasn't someone I would do anything for. Of course, I would never give up a child to have James, but nearly anything else. I wanted to, somehow, take some of his pain on myself. I would have. He was so brave to do what he did to rescue Rachel. And then when he lay bleeding on the ground he was worried about Rachel and me. I think he would have died to save us."

"Yes, he seems like a nice young man."

"He is, Gram. I can't wait to see him."

"Well, just get some rest and you will be back to the hospital in no time."

"John was so wonderful. Like a real father. He came running when I needed him and took care of me all night. I'm glad he is my father."

"We all are," Gram said.

"I love you, Gram."

"Oh sweetie, I love you. And everything is going to be all right."

Amber was sitting beside James's bed when Rachel came in. Rachel was still in her hospital gown and orange nubby-soled socks. Rachel rushed over and wrapped her arms around Amber. They held each other tightly, accepting that the unthinkable had nearly happened and grateful to be here together. Then Rachel released Amber and turned to James.

"You will always, always, always be my hero," Rachel said.

James grinned. "At last my life is complete," he mumbled.

Rachel stuck her tongue out at him.

"I was just coming down to visit you," Amber said.

"Well, they are releasing me today. Mom is doing all the paperwork for me, so I thought I'd sneak out and find James before I leave. I'm sure when I get home Mom will keep me on house arrest for the rest of the summer."

"Probably for the rest of your life," Amber said.

Rachel grew grim. "It's kind of weird to think that I could be dead in some ditch right now. I mean it happens and this guy wasn't playing around."

"Have they found him?" Amber asked.

"No, he ditched the car. It was stolen anyway so there is no way to find out who he is. I told the police that I could identify him if he was in a line up, but I don't think they have brought anyone in."

"It's creepy that he is still out there," Amber said.

"I know. I'm glad I didn't give him any of my personal information. I may still sleep with my parents for a while though."

"Yeah, I can actually see that. Your Mom would put your Dad in the spare room if you asked her to," Amber said.

"Hey, this is traumatic," Rachel said. "We all need special care right now."

"Amen," John said coming into the room.

"Oh yea, you're here," Rachel said.

"Now that's how I like to be greeted," John said coming up beside James's bed. "How are you feeling, champ?"

James whispered that he had never been better.

"Seriously," Rachel persisted, drawing John's attention back to her, "my mind has been bouncing off the wall with all kinds of horrible and frightening and worrisome things all morning. I need to find some answers."

John opened up his hands, palms up, inviting her to ask.

"First, do you think that God, if he really exists, was punishing me last night because I was... you know, being so flippant and doubtful about him?"

"No. God doesn't punish."

"Of course, he does. Everyone knows that."

"No. Everyone does not know that. Why would a loving God want to punish you?"

"Because He didn't like the way I was angry about Cybele and that I was sort of targeting Him with that anger. He may consider that a sin or something."

"The good news is, Rachel, that Jesus paid for all our sins, past and present and future. Our sin was nailed to the cross and now we are flawless in God's eyes."

"I don't mean to be rude, but I don't want a sermon. I want real answers."

"I see," John said. "How about God gave us free will and delights in our journey of learning and not simply our blind compliance to His will. So, admittedly, you are a little out of the box but that is how He made you and He understands better than you why you do what you do and say what you say. He does not want to judge His own creation and label you bad. He wants to watch your journey and welcome you home when you realize He is real and interested in you personally. His greatest desire is for you to love Him back."

"Well, I'm not sure about that. There is hell you know. He must judge and send some people there."

"Hell is probably not what you think it is," John said.

"I think it is pretty horrible and hot and nightmarish. And I hope that creep that caused all of this goes there soon."

"That is understandable because you are human. But God does not deal with us as we deal with each other. Revenge and punishment for failing Him is not His style. He knows evil. But you are not evil. There is no reason for you to think that God is punishing you to make you afraid to not do His will."

"Still, I'm sure there is a score card somewhere and I am on the losing end right now."

"So," John asked, "you think that God sent that guy to try and kill you? Or maybe, could it be possible that God sent James to save you? Which do you think?"

"I don't know," Rachel admitted. "That's why I came to you for answers."

"Let's just look at it this way," John offered. "All of our decisions and actions have consequences. Some good and some not so good. You meeting a guy you knew nothing about and then stepping out of the building with him so he could slip you a drug was your decision and what happened was a consequence of that decision. James coming out when he did to save you was not a consequence of his decisions. So maybe he appeared exactly when he needed to be there because God sent James and not the evil guy."

Rachel pursed her lips and thought about that.

"Why is it so easy to believe that God wants to punish you but hard for you to believe that He may have just been the link that saved you?" Then John smiled and added, "saved you through James's noble act of self-sacrifice, of course."

"I don't know," Rachel said. "But it is easier to think He would punish rather than save. So much bad goes on that He doesn't save people from. Why me? Why would He want to save me?"

"I am not privileged enough to know God's plans, I'm afraid. I certainly wish I was though."

"It's just such a burden to have to worry about sin all the time," Rachel said.

"Relax. As I often remind everyone, God certainly must love and forgive sinners or else Heaven would be empty."

Rachel smiled at that. "Yeah, I'm probably no worse than anyone else."

"So?" John asked. "What else?"

"I don't know. This is a lot to think about."

"Glad to assist you. And please, call me if you need any help these next few weeks. I'm afraid that it will take a little time but, eventually the reality of what you have just escaped from will trouble you. I will be here to help you in any way I can."

"Well, I was thinking about getting baptized this Sunday. Would that work or not?"

"I think we can definitely talk more about it before you decide," John said.

"Yeah, that's what I thought," Rachel conceded and turned to James. "Well, thanks again, James. You are my hero for ever and ever and I will never forget that you took a knife for me."

James smiled and waved the hand on his good side.

Rachel hugged Amber and turned to leave the room but then she hesitated and turned back at the door. She looked at John. "So, you do, swear to God, believe that God does not sit in pious judgment of our every thought and action? You are telling me, straight up, that I can wander about without fear of him causing anything bad to happen to me?"

John smiled. "I swear to God that I believe that God did not cause what happened to you. In fact, I believe that it was His will that you be rescued. God may see us stumble but He doesn't love us any less. He will always be there to help us get back up. So, wander about without fear of God. But be ever fearful of man. Our actions do have consequences that have nothing to do with God's will."

Rachel thought about that and then, as she was going out the door, she muttered that growing up was not as much fun as she had thought.

John and Amber settled into the chairs by James's bed to just visit and get to know each other better when Rachel rushed back into the room.

"Wow! Just wow! The news people are everywhere outside. My mom just went to the car for something and she saw them with their trucks and microphones and TV cameras. So, she just casually asked one of them what they were waiting for and they said they were waiting for me. They wanted to interview me! Can you believe it? I'm going to be on local TV. No, maybe real TV even."

"Well," Amber said, "I was going to ask you how you feel about that but I guess I don't have to."

"Hey, I didn't ask for this... Well, I mean yeah, I was stupid, but I never thought that I did anything that may get me murdered...murdered! Wow, that is crazy. Anyway, I think I should talk to them. Sound out a warning to other young girls that this sort of thing is real and can happen anywhere."

"That is a good message, I suppose," John said. "But maybe your parents should be the ones to be interviewed. You have been through enough for now."

Rachel looked disappointed, then nodded. "Okay," she said. And then she brightened again. "I know, it may be more of a dramatic affect if I just come out all withdrawn and traumatized and reluctant to talk about it. Yeah, that may be better if people just get a glimpse of me and then they will want to see me again, when I'm healed enough to talk. I could be invited to be on the local morning talk shows when I am better. Yeah, that's it. I will not speak now so they will want me to speak later. When the drama has heightened."

John and Amber glanced at each other and then at the door as Rachel's mother came in.

"Is everything ready for me to be discharged?" Rachel asked.

"Yes. You just need to get dressed. I brought you clean clothes. They are on your bed. Just get changed and I'll be right there."

Rachel waved good-by again and was gone.

"I've called her father," Rachel's mother said, "about the reporters and he is coming to deal with that. I am going to pick Rachel up at the side entrance. Hopefully, there are no reporters there."

"Anything I can do to help?" John offered.

"Thank you. Really, I appreciate you all," Rachel's mother said and then her chin trembled and she walked to James's bedside. "I will be indebted to you for the rest of my life. I can't even endure the horrible thoughts that I have about… everything. If you had not…" She had to stop talking.

James reached over and gently laid his hand over her hand on the bed railing. "We have to look forward," James said. "There is no good in dwelling on what could have been. Believe me, I learned that a long time ago."

Rachel's mother nodded. "We haven't had time to talk about it yet, but I am certain Rachel's father and I want to do something for you. Some sort of something to show…"

"Please, don't feel like that," James whispered. "I was partly to blame. I should have kept a better eye on her. We didn't know the guy and yet we let him into our lives."

"No. No, you can't feel at all responsible. You saved her life. That is the bottom line. We are grateful, James. Thank you for saving our daughter's life."

Suddenly the door swung open and a nurse came in. "Time to get the patient up and walking around a little," she said. "If you all will wait in the hall I'll take his vitals and get another robe on him, for a little privacy, and we will be right out."

Rachel's mother hugged Amber and thanked John again and then went back to Rachel's room to make sure Rachel had not escaped to the allure of bright lights and the exciting attention of the TV cameras.

"I'm impressed with James," John said. "And he is right, you know, there is nothing good that can come from dwelling on how things could have been."

Amber sighed. "I know. Last night opened my eyes to a lot of things."

"We can never change the past, Amber. We can just learn from it."

"I know, and I'm not saying that I am there yet," Amber began, "but I, for the first time in my life, I think I can almost understand Miriam's choice. I have to see her leaving me behind as not something against me, not as only a rejection of me, but rather what she may have thought was her best choice at that moment. I will always be disappointed in her, but I realize now that I'm not damaged. Not damaged like I would be if James had not lived or Rachel had suffered at the hands of that maniac. Those I would never have gotten over. But the bottom line is that I've had a good life. I love Gram and Grampa for all they have done for me. I wouldn't want to trade that part of my life for anything else."

John smiled at her. "Maybe someday you can explain why James said that he had learned to keep looking forward a long time ago."

"Yeah, no one would know the heavy basket James carries by just being around him. I'm afraid I'm guilty of not appreciating what a strong guy he is. I guess I have overlooked a lot lately in my angry, self-pitying state. But after last night I feel so… I don't know, selfish maybe. At least too self-absorbed. I need to just be grateful for what I have and get on with my life."

"You are not selfish or self-absorbed. You are entitled to being disappointed in your mother. I'm just pleased that now you have reached the point of downgrading your anger to disappointment. I believe that you are finding peace within yourself and that's where healing starts."

"Yes, that's it. I do feel at peace with my past. I am okay being me. Being me just as I am right now. I could have lost everything last night. Things I would never recover from. But my life is still good. James is going to heal and that's what I prayed for."

"It never hurts," John said, "to ask for a little help. God's will prevails, whether we understand it or not, so all we can do is ask."

"Here we are," the nurse announced as James's door opened and he appeared wounded but walking. "Now, with broken ribs, it hurts him to talk and, with an injured leg, it hurts him to walk, so if you want to follow us the few steps we are taking, please do not try to engage him in conversation."

John and Amber nodded. Amber's heart ached as she watched the slow painful steps James was taking. He was clearly not enjoying the pain or the imagined sight of himself in a hospital gown scuffling along with his walker like some pitiful old lady.

Poor baby, Amber thought, which was exactly what James would have hated to hear but she just couldn't escape the feeling that she wanted to protect him and take care of him. Her eyes filled with threatening tears as she stood by his door waiting for him to work his way back.

"Hey," John said, looking down at her, "he's going to be okay."

"He just looks so vulnerable. He would hate that."

"He's made of steel. He will work through this."

Amber brushed at her eyes. "Do I have to forgive the stinking creep that did that to James, too?"

"Forgiveness doesn't make the other person right, Amber, it just lets you leave their behavior behind where it doesn't sour your life."

Amber sighed. "I suppose. But it's just so unfair."

"I read a quote once that said that forgiveness is me giving up my right to hurt you for hurting me."

"I suddenly hate quotes and sayings. I don't want to be logical and nice when I feel like going out there and hunting that creep down myself and… and stabbing him!"

John smiled. "There, do you feel better now?"

Amber shrugged. "Maybe."

James and the nurse were almost back to the room. James tried to smile for Amber and that made her tear up again.

"We have to get him back into bed and put an ice pack on those ribs. He did get a plating on one of his ribs so that will help him recover a little quicker. But after the ice, I'm afraid he will need to get some rest," the nurse said, opening the door for James to scuffle through. The nurse then closed the door behind her.

"I have to get back," John said. "Are you going to be okay?"

"I'm made of steel," Amber said.

"Do you want to wait on your introduction to my congregation? Is Sunday too soon?"

"I repeat, I am made of steel. Bring it on."

When the nurse came out of James's room, Amber went in and walked up to his bed. She reached down and smoothed his blonde hair back into place.

"Is your mom coming by after work?" Amber asked.

James nodded.

"Is there anything I can get for you?"

"You could, if you want to, make sure my dad knows that I will be okay. I'm sure he has heard something by now."

Amber reached out and took his broad hand in hers. "Of course, I will. Because you are going to be okay. Promise me that you will be okay."

James nodded. "I promise."

"James, I'm pretty sure that I love you," she said, watching his face for a reaction.

James squeezed her hand and looked up at her. "I was counting on that," he said. "I think I love you, too."

Amber leaned down and kissed him. "Good," she said. "That's great."

"All righty then," the nurse said, bustling in again with a needle for the IV and a pill for James. "This will make him groggy, so I hope you have other entertainment for a while."

"Got it," Amber said. "I'll be back after I do what you asked me to do, James. Get some rest and heal super-fast."

"I will amaze you," he whispered.

Amber was at the front door when she saw James's mother coming across the parking lot. Laurel's head was down and she was, as usual, hurrying. Amber loved James and she wanted to love this woman, this thin frayed woman with the world on her shoulders. Maybe together, Amber and James could lift some of that weight.

Laurel looked up as the door swooshed sideways and she saw Amber.

She smiled and self-consciously tucked her blonde curly hair behind her ears.

"The nurse is with him now," Amber said. "Can I interest you in a cup of coffee or something before you go up?"

Laurel nodded and walked with Amber to the cafeteria where she got a bottle of water and Amber bought an iced tea. They sat in a booth away from the doorway.

"How was he?" Laurel asked, unscrewing the top of her water bottle.

"He is in some pain, of course, but otherwise he is doing great. He was walking in the halls before I left."

"James is my rock. I don't know what I would do without him," Laurel said, her hand trembling a little.

"He worries about you, too." Amber said.

"Yes, and isn't that sad? That a young man would have to share in the burdens of his parent's choices."

"Actually, I think he is a better man for it. You have taught him to care about more than just himself. Look around us, how rare is that in today's world?"

Laurel agreed.

"In that vein," Amber said, "James has asked me to get in touch with his father to make sure his dad knows that he will be all right."

"I contacted the prison and they let me talk to him. Jim is okay. I'll tell James that when I go up."

"Has anyone contacted his grandparents?" Amber asked. Amber knew bringing up Laurel's parents may be a painful thing, but she thought about Gram and Grampa and knew that she had to ask.

Laurel shook her head, her eyes glistening.

"Would it be wrong if I went to see them?" Amber asked. "To assure them and maybe invite them to come and see James?"

"They have a right," Laurel said. "They were very good to the kids when James and Janet were little."

"So, maybe this horrible thing that happened will be, after all, a good excuse to bring them back into James's life," Amber suggested.

"I would like them to know how great James has turned out. And Janet too," Laurel said. "I have always hated how my parent's disappointment with me has separated them from their grandchildren. I understood their choice. Tough love I guess. Only I couldn't turn my back on Jim. I had to give him as many chances as it took to get right with the world. I knew he would eventually get there and then, if we, Jim and I didn't work out, at least I would know I had done the right thing and I could be strong enough to survive the next tough decisions."

"You're a good woman," Amber said.

Laurel smiled. "Truth is, I'm a mess. I just have good people around me to help hold me together."

"So, should I go see them?" Amber asked.

"Thanks, really Amber, I appreciate it, but I think you and, well, everything that just happened, has convinced me to reach out to them myself. It is time. Isn't it? We have all grown and learned since the big blowup. I think it may be time to try again. I can show them that I have been able to make it on my own so my reaching out wouldn't be for help. Just for family. Just being a family again."

Amber looked away to the trickling of nurses and doctors entering the cafeteria with their trays.

"What about you, Amber?" Laurel asked. "Are you finding peace with your family?"

Amber sighed. "Most of them. I don't think peace is a word that will ever describe Miriam's and my relationship."

"Do you think the struggle is worth the cost?" Laurel asked.

"Is caving in worth the reward?" Amber replied. "Would it even work if I forgave her because I wanted to just get this battle over with and not because I would actually mean it? Would it matter if my heart was just pretending and not really wanting reconciliation with her?"

"Forgiveness is a place to start. In time you will know if your heart wants to catch up. I hate to see families divided. I know James and Janet, and my parents, and even Jim, have lost so much because of my decisions. My parents are good people, Jim is a good person, it was never about that. It was about me keeping my promise to Jim no matter the cost. Jim loves his children and I was determined to show them the value of staying true to your vows no matter how hard it gets."

"That's just the point, isn't it?" Amber said, looking back at Laurel's thin face. "My mother didn't stay. She didn't sacrifice anything the way you have. I keep trying to understand that but I can't. I can't. And seeing mothers like you, like Rachel's mother, it makes it all the harder to forgive her weakness."

"Did you ever think that maybe we have weakness you don't see? We are very human too no matter how hard we seem to be trying. Where I may have stood strong on one thing, I can tell you that I have failed at many others," Laurel said. "But none of that matters now. James could have been killed. Rachel could have been killed. How can anything we believe we may have suffered really matter when we think of how fortunate we are at this moment?"

"You're right," Amber said.

"And that's why we can't waste more time, you and I, waiting for some miracle that could change our past. You grew up without your mother. I allowed my family to be separated because I didn't know how else to handle it. Miriam was wrong. I was wrong. But all that matters at this moment is that James is going to live. We can't waste this opportunity to throw open the window and pitch out our smelly garbage. We have to let go of our past. If not now, Amber, at this moment when we are so grateful, then when will we ever do it?"

Amber nodded.

"I hope that if, well, when you ever find yourself in need of being forgiven, I hope you remember this moment when you and I were sitting here together, each considering how we are going to ever be able to forgive. In your case, your mother. In mine, I'm afraid, I need to figure out how to forgive myself."

Amber reached across the table and laid her hand over Laurel's. "James is so much like you."

"I'll try to live up to that," Laurel said, and then she smiled. "But, as his mother, I can assure you that I have tales about James that would definitely tarnish your image of him. Maybe someday we will get to laugh over them."

"I look forward to that," Amber said. Then Amber glanced at her watch and apologized for leaving but she had to be to work in twenty minutes.

Laurel nodded and stood up. "Good talk. Thank you," she said. "Seems all sorts of good decisions can come out of the darkness when I let down the gate guarding my ego. First, I'm going to call my parents and apologize, and then I'm going to invite them to come and visit James. Then I'm going to go see James and let him know how his bravery, and the fear of losing him, has finally forced me into taking action. It's so easy to just let things go on and on until something horrible forces you to fix them."

Like Miriam's cancer, Amber thought as she followed Laurel out of the cafeteria. Without Miriam's cancer then Miriam would still be letting her smelly garbage go on and on building up in the darkness.

Why couldn't you have found less painful ways to wake us up? Amber asked God, in case He had been eavesdropping. *Really, cancer and stab wounds? Not subtle. Not subtle at all.* Then she smiled at the thought of scolding God, or even thinking of talking to Him in the first place.

"Seriously, dear," Grampa said, following Gram around the kitchen as she scurried back and forth clearing away the breakfast mess. "This isn't a royal coronation."

"I know it's not. It's even bigger than that," Gram said, moving around the annoyance of having that man in the middle of her kitchen when she was trying to finish up.

"Yeah," Grampa conceded. "In our little world this is pretty significant."

"Who would have dreamed? I mean really, I was so afraid that this day would never come," Gram said, shaking the toast crumbs out of the toaster and into the trash.

"Do you think Amber will accept Miriam's apology? Have you thought what will happen if she doesn't?" Grampa asked, setting a couple glasses in the sink instead of the open dishwasher.

Gram scooped them up and put them where they belonged. "Really, go read your paper for a few minutes. I need to get this finished and go change for church."

"Just trying to help," Grampa said, putting down the syrup bottle he had almost put back into the refrigerator.

"Thank you, but most of the time your help is just more work," Gram grumbled as she picked up the syrup bottle.

"Well, lucky for me that I have you," Grampa said, chuckling and giving Gram a gentle pat on the backside.

Gram stopped in mid stride and whirled to scowl at him. "Really? Really?"

Grampa grinned like a monkey and said, "Get back to work woman. We have a big day ahead of us."

Grampa met Amber on his way out of the kitchen. "Better hurry. She kept a plate warm in the oven for you, but, I must warn you, it would be to our detriment to slow her down."

Amber nodded and went on past him. "So sorry," she said to Gram. "But I stayed to help close up the store and didn't get home until…"

"I am well aware of when you got in," Gram said. "I can't rest anymore with all the trouble that's been going on around us."

"They found that guy."

"I heard," Gram said.

"Yeah, he had helped himself to one of the empty camps on the pond. The other campers had seen him but thought he was renting. In fact, the car he stole belonged to Beverly Graham. I guess he knew she never went anywhere after dark, so he could use it and return it and no one would ever be the wiser."

"It's just so creepy. Poor Beverly realizing now what kind of maniac was just steps away from her door." Gram shuddered and then revived herself and went to get the warm plate of pancakes and bacon from the oven.

"How is James," Gram asked, setting the plate in front of Amber.

"It hurts to laugh or sneeze with broken ribs I understand, but other than that he is getting stronger every minute."

"I wish he could come with us today," Gram said pouring Amber a cup of coffee.

"Ugh, today!" Amber said, buttering her pancakes.

"It can be whatever you decide to make it," Gram said, standing by Amber's chair with her hands on her hips. "Besides, all the stress should be on Miriam. This is her mistake we are trying to correct, not yours."

"I reread Mother Teresa's words before I went to sleep. Forgive anyway. Forgive anyway. I shall chant that all the way to church."

"But she means it," Gram protested. "Miriam genuinely wants to be forgiven. Your forgiveness will free her and then she can work on just getting well and then everything can finally be right."

"Okay then," Amber said. "I will try to pretend that I didn't just hear that Miriam wants my forgiveness so she can then move on and concentrate on herself again instead of maybe just because she wants to be forgiven for abandoning her daughter."

"Oh, Amber, please don't take it like that. I'm sure I didn't say it right."

"Actually, Gram, I chose the wrong mantra. I should keep reminding myself that in the end it is not about Miriam and me. It's about God and me. Yeah, that is the winner."

Gram poured some milk into Amber's coffee. "What ever works to get you over the hump," Gram said. "Then, I promise, it will be all down hill from there. If you get through today, then we can all look forward instead of backwards."

"Then I shall not disappoint. I will set this family free."

Gram shook her head. "Sometimes I wish I could spank you."

"Too late," Amber said, smiling up at her grandmother. "I am not fixable. You have spoiled me and now you have to live with that."

"Eat before your breakfast gets cold," Gram said. "I'm going up to dress for the best day of my life."

"You can go on and get some seats," Amber said to her grandparents. "I just saw Rachel and her parents, and I want to talk to them before I come in."

Gram and Grampa nodded and went on into the sanctuary. Amber waited for Rachel to get closer. Amber frowned. Rachel looked glum. Her shoulders were slouched and she walked looking at the ground. Amber would have bet the house that Rachel would have arrived at the church as her usual perky self and thrilled to be witness to Amber's drama.

"Thanks for driving over," Amber said to Rachel's parents. "You have always been important in my life. Your being here makes this easier for me."

"You know we love you," Rachel's mother said.

Amber nodded. "How about you, Rachel, any last-minute advice for me?" Amber asked.

Rachel looked up. "They caught Everett."

"I know," Amber said.

"It feels worse now. I had hoped that he had run off to some other place and I would never have to see him again."

"He needed to be caught. You know that."

Rachel nodded.

"The reporters are swarming back since they caught him," Rachel's mother said. "I've warned James to be ready when he gets out of the hospital. They have interviewed our neighbors like that means anything. What does our neighbors high or low opinion of us have to do with what that low life scum tried to do?"

"Hey," Rachel's father said, "we aren't here about that. We are here to support Amber."

Amber looked at this man she had been around most of her life and apparently had never really known. She would never had expected him to give up his own plans and come to church today, to take a silly girl's feelings about reconciling with her long lost mother, seriously. Amber almost felt like hugging him. Apparently, Amber had value she had not ever realized.

"Come on," Amber said, looping her arm through Rachel's. "How can we worry when we are surrounded by so much love?"

When they walked into the church Amber saw her grandmother motion for them all to come down to the front. Amber groaned.

"What did you just say about not worrying when surrounded by so much love?" Rachel's mother reminded her.

There was an empty space left for John next to Miriam, then Grace and Gram and Grampa. Amber sat beside Grampa and Rachel sat next to her. Rachel's parents sat next to Rachel. By the looks on everyone's faces this could have been a funeral instead of a regular church service. Grace leaned out and smiled at Amber. Amber winked back. There, that felt better.

Amber sat still with her hands folded in her lap. She turned only once to see the church filling up behind her then she looked back at the basket of pink and white assorted flowers sitting on the table in front of her. Just a regular Sunday. No biggie. Nothing different except the pastor and his family getting up in front of the congregation and laying their dirty laundry out for all to see.

Amber saw a small figure approaching and looked over to see Sadie coming toward her. Amber stood up and hugged her. "What a surprise," Amber said.

"God is on the move," Sadie said. "He will do amazing things."

"You do help me believe that," Amber said.

"He has gotten you this far. Trust Him and He will get you through anything."

"I see Brandy and Chip have not converted you to Paganism yet," Amber said.

"Actually, Chip drove me over today. He's a nice young man. I don't know if it is my cookies or my faith that keeps him coming over, but we have had some lovely conversations."

"Chip is with you today?" Rachel asked, standing up now, memories of Paganism pulling her from her sullenness.

"Yes. When I told him I was coming for Amber's baptism he asked to come. To see what that was about."

"I'm not being baptized today," Amber said, confused where that could have come from.

Sadie frowned. "Really? Now where could I have gotten that idea?"

"Maybe," Rachel said, "you could have misunderstood when I left your house and told you that I'd have Amber baptized by Sunday. That's when I first got my idea about the Holy Spirit test."

"Oh," Sadie said.

"I'm sorry you came all the way over here for nothing," Amber said.

"Going to church is never for nothing," Sadie said brightly. "I'm certain I will hear exactly what I need to hear today. Or Chip will. God is on the move for one of us."

"Oh yes," Amber said. "I'm certain everyone will hear something of interest today."

Sadie smiled sweetly and turned around, touching Gram's arm as she passed her, on her way back to her seat next to Chip.

Amber glanced back at Sadie. Somehow her presence suddenly made Amber feel more... more, charitable? Is that the word? Did Amber feel a greater need to not disappoint Sadie than anyone else? Did withholding forgiveness in front of Sadie feel more selfish than withholding it in front of all the rest of the people here? Amber frowned and started to turn around when she saw Laurel. What?

Laurel smiled and waved a tiny wave.

Amber shrugged and looked confused.

Laurel left her seat and scurried down to explain that James had asked her to come - for moral support for Amber.

Amber thanked her, and Laurel went back to her seat. Good grief! Who else would God stack the deck with?

The service finally started without more surprises. Worship songs were sung, the pastor's prayer was given, announcements made, the offering collected and finally John stood to present his sermon.

"Our scripture today is from The Sermon on the Mount, Matthew 5:38-42. 'You have heard that it was said, 'An eye for an eye and a tooth for a tooth,' But I say to you, do not resist the one who is evil. But if anyone slaps you on the right cheek, turn to him the other also. And if any one would sue you and take your tunic, let him have your cloak as well. And if anyone forces you to go one mile, go with him two miles. Give to the one who begs from you and do not refuse the one who would borrow from you.' Hear the word of the Lord."

The congregation replied, "Praise be to God," and Amber settled in.

She knew better than to judge John's sermons on her first impulse. Her first impulse here, of course, would have been to get her feelings ruffled because she was afraid John would start lecturing her on being good in God's eyes and giving Miriam another cheek to strike. But instead she relaxed and let John lead.

"This presents us with a challenge," John conceded. "Our basic impulse is to succumb to the natural instinct of survival to protect ourselves. What Jesus is asking of us here isn't easy. It isn't anything we would, as protective parents, advise our children to do. Yes, Benjamin, let the bully blacken your eye, take your favorite team jacket, then I want you to carry his book bag two miles and then lend him your allowance. Come on, that doesn't seem like anything that even God could expect. But the bottom line is that it is. God knows that turning the other cheek requires courage. Showing kindness when you are angry takes fortitude. To do what He asks is to ignore your fear of pain, and your aversion to being rejected and humiliated. You must be willing to risk being taken advantage of and looking weak. Where is the justice and reward in that you ask?"

The congregation glanced at the ones next to them. How could the pastor explain this one?

"And we all want justice. But whose justice? Certainly, God does not want us in this tit-for-tat struggle all our lives. We can't want that for ourselves, either. So, how do we break free of that mentality? How do we turn the other cheek because we care more about who lives inside of us then who lives in the world? When we accept Jesus as our savior, the Holy Spirit dwells inside of us and we are no longer without guidance. The righteousness that Jesus lived with, that Jesus died with, can never be matched. Jesus lived through being spit on and persecuted. He suffered all that he speaks of in his sermon and still he asks us to follow his example and be righteous. Looking through the heart of God we can see that striving to live righteously is a gift for ourselves as well as others. When we can let go of the urge for revenge, we are freeing ourselves to trust the Lord and find peace through our faith. Who wouldn't want that over the gut wrenching agony of always worrying about what is equal and fair, and who we must reek havoc on to make ourselves feel better? If we spend our time consumed with retaliation because we feel we have been treated unfairly, then we miss the joy and grace that the freedom of letting go gives us.'

'Our Christian culture tells us to love and serve others. This calling is in no way bound to the character and motives of those we are asked to serve. It is up to God to determine their worthiness not us. And let's be honest, just loving and forgiving those who love and forgive us is no great accomplishment. In Matthew 5:43 – 48 it is written, 'You have heard that it was said, 'You shall love your neighbor and hate your enemy.' But I say to you, 'Love your enemies and pray for those who persecute you.' So that you may be sons of your Father in heaven. For he makes his sun rise on the evil and the good, and sends rain on the just and the unjust. For if you love those who love you, what reward do you have? Do not even the tax collectors do the same? And if you greet only your brothers, what more are you doing than others? Do not even the Gentiles do the same? You therefore must be perfect as your heavenly Father is perfect.'

'Of course, we cannot be perfect, but Jesus has given us the perfect standard for a Christian life. How much good ever comes from revenge? Revenge escalates the struggle until we are consumed with unhappiness instead of peace. Jesus wants his followers to be set apart. He wants us to be judged by the love we show not the battles we have waged and the enemies we have crushed. The law of the land in biblical times was written as an eye for an eye to restrain unlimited blood vengeance. The law limited the retaliation to exactly what was lost. But Jesus asked his followers to live differently. To realize they are the sons and daughters of God, and though legally we are entitled to justice in equal measure to the crime, we are instructed to measure our options carefully for revenge can be a two-edged sword.'

'I give you the example of the old west horse thief. We all know stealing a horse in the old west was a serious offense. A horse thief could be hanged. Well, it happened that this particular man whose horse had been stolen made it a point to always get the best of any person he dealt with. Consequently, this man had not a single friend in town. But, still this man had a right to have his case for justice tried and presented to a jury.'

'After thirty minutes of deliberating the strong evidence against the horse thief, the jury returned to the courtroom. The judge asked for the verdict. The jury chairman read the verdict. 'We find the defendant not guilty if he will return the horse.'

'The judge silenced the laughter that ensued and sent the jury back until they reached a better verdict. After an hour the jury was back. 'What is your verdict?' the judge asked.

'We find the defendant,' the jury chairman read, 'not guilty, and he can keep the horse!"

The congregation chuckled, and John returned to the meat of his sermon. Amber tried to listen, but she felt a knot in her stomach for the verdict to come after John's sermon. Miriam was guilty. No one could morally deny that. And yet what was to be gained by forcing her to stand in front of her jury with a scarlet letter on her chest? Amber glanced down the pew at Miriam, sitting straight, waiting for the moment she must explain herself and grovel for forgiveness. Suddenly, Amber felt drained of the burning need for justice that she had carried all her life. She glanced at Grace sitting beside her mother, probably briefed and prepared for the coming of Amber's justice, but certainly not deserving of the emotional toll it would cause her. And Gram and Grampa? When was enough heartache enough for them to suffer? Amber wrestled with a need to suddenly bolt the church, to leave all this drama, and just be… free. She wanted to just slip off the heavy cape of victimhood she had worn for so long and get on with her life. John was right. How much easier it is to forgive then to continue to struggle and constantly measure and adjust the scales of justice.

John ended his sermon and asked that those in the congregation to that could do so, to stay in their seats a little longer. He said he and his family had a personal announcement to make that he was very pleased about. He waited for those who wished to leave to do so and then everyone settled back in quiet expectation. John extended his hand to Miriam and she stood to join him in the front. Amber hesitated, half wanting to hear what Miriam may have to say to justify herself and then again, why? Why?

Amber stood up and walked up to stand beside Miriam. "Some of you may have noticed that I am new to your church," Amber began. "So, I want to introduce myself and ask for acceptance into your church and, finally, into my family. You see, I am John and Miriam's daughter, Amber. For reasons that have no need to be explained, and can't be undone, I have grown up in my grandparent's home. I have been loved and cared for by these sweet people everyday of my eighteen years. I honestly could not have asked for more. God knew his plan and it was good. I am grateful that we are all exactly where we need to be and, as a member of Pastor Davis's family, I would like to meet you all and hope that you will accept me even though I am… well, late arriving at the party."

The congregation was quiet and then suddenly Sadie stood and walked stiff-backed down between the pews. She turned when she was in front of Amber and addressed the congregation. "Why are you in church today if you do not even have the heart to accept this brave young woman into your fold? Come on, come on everyone, let's welcome this family with open arms!" Then Sadie whirled around and tried to hug in John and Miriam and Amber with one stretch of her arms.

Rachel and her parents came forward. Then Laurel came down the aisle and soon the pews began to empty as everyone came forward to live God's will.

The congregation had finally trickled out of the sanctuary. Word would now spread, and the drama would eventually fade. Amber's family stood in the front of the church, a little shell shocked to be honest.

Gram sighed and sank down on the front pew to rest. "I wish I had come to an earlier service also," she said. "I'm afraid I was so busy stewing over what could happen after John stopped talking that I think I missed a great sermon."

"He told us that God thinks it is wrong," Grampa said, sitting down beside Gram, "to punish an old coot even if he may really deserve it. Right, John?"

"Something like that," John said, smiling. Then John turned to Amber. "I think you caught us all off guard. Why didn't you tell me that you wanted to handle it yourself?"

"I didn't know that I did until the time came to put us all on trial. Then I looked down the pew and saw all of you ready to bare your souls for my benefit. And then I thought, who needs that? What good will any of that do? Whose opinion of the details really matters to me anyway? It's old news and besides, whatever the truth was, we have lived through it and it is time to move on."

"Thank you," Miriam said.

"I don't think the way I have behaved deserves a thank you. But fine, I accept it," Amber said.

"I know I have been…difficult to deal with. I know now that I was wrong about it all. About leaving you behind, about being too cowardly and selfish to come back for you, and for not trusting that you may be more like your father than like me."

John slipped his arm around Miriam's waist. "How about that? You have finally lived through what you have been dreading to face for eighteen years."

"I know. I would never have dreamed that we would be standing here together like this," Miriam said, betraying herself with actual heart-wrung tears streaming down her face.

"Now, now," Gram said, getting up to gently touch her daughter's arm. "Let's get ourselves rounded up and go on to your house. I have a couple casseroles warming in the oven there and a pan of my famous bread pudding. I have the brandy sauce on the side…" Gram glanced at John. "If we can have it, that is."

John chuckled. "I may not be Catholic, but our church can be traced back to monks who have been rumored to have distilled spirits."

"Now, who can argue with monks?" Grampa said.

"Please," Grace said, "I want to say something before we go."

Everyone paused in their motion to give her their attention.

"I want to go away," Grace began.

Gram sucked in her breath and covered her mouth.

"The four of us," Grace continued, looking up at her parents and then to Amber. "I want us to go away from the church, the doctors, Amber's work and boyfriend. Away from everything. I don't care if it is just a day or two. I just want us to be together as a family. To wake up together and eat together and talk. There is so much to know. I want to know it all. I want us to cover our wounds with the same color bandages."

"Yellow bandages?" Amber asked.

Grace nodded because…who could be sad when their broken places were patched with yellow?